G000055247

The FEATHER REPORT

The
FEATHER
REPORT

Mark Illis

BLOOMSBURY

FOR SALLY

First published in Great Britain 1992

Bloomsbury Publishing Limited, 2 Soho Square,
London W1V 5DE

Copyright © 1992 Mark Illis

The right of Mark Illis to be identified as the Author of
this work has been asserted in accordance with the
Copyright, Designs and Patents Act 1988.

A CIP catalogue record for this book is available from
the British Library.

ISBN 0 7475 1245 0

Typeset by Florencetype Ltd, Kewstoke, Avon
Printed by Clays Ltd, St Ives Plc, Bungay, Suffolk

'I was pushed,' he said. 'Did you see anyone?'

'No. It's a kind of egotism, you know, to think that there's an exterior cause involved in an accident like that. I bet you'd like to think someone's conspiring against you. Wouldn't it make it all worthwhile?'

'I'm not paranoid, Victoria. I'm just sensitive to situations.'

'You fell, that's all. There was no one even around, except students and lecturers and a chef from the refectory.'

But Paul Feather is right – he was pushed and circumstances do stand poised to engulf him. Paul has been preparing a report on the patterns of violent behaviour, but, as he tells his sister Hazel (herself a sufferer of mental imbalance), 'My research seems to embrace the whole world.' As Paul struggles to regain his fast-dwindling equilibrium, he realises unwelcome forces are spreading into his life, carried like a virus with the information he has gathered.

Meanwhile, the peculiar Mr Walsh, who has pressing motives of his own, can hardly wait to see what will become of the experiment he has designed, involving Paul, Hazel, and a certain Edmund Staples, a man who unfortunately killed his own father . . .

In *The Feather Report* Mark Illis skilfully knits wit and a rare vision into a dark and complex psychological drama – it's a *tour de force* that fulfils admirably the promise already shown by his highly acclaimed novels, *A Chinese Summer* and *The Alchemist*.

Acknowledgments

The first chapters of this novel were written at Hawthornden Castle, probably a perfect place to write, and I would like to thank the Hawthornden Trust for giving me the opportunity to stay there. Acknowledgments are also due to *The Printer's Devil*, where *Just Before the End of the World* was first published. I would also like to thank Louise Doughty and Matthew Hamilton for their valuable suggestions and advice on the manuscript.

One

The first indication that Paul's world is going to be changed comes on his answer-machine. A series of separate messages, like the delicate, restrained dabs of a dentist's drill. He tilts his head slowly back and breathes through his mouth, as if floating. There is in this intrusive voice a smug background which remains consistent while other notes vary. Alone, but no longer absolutely alone, he listens.

. . . Thou.
. . . Still unravished.
. . . Bride of quietness.
. . . Thou.
. . . Foster-child of silence.
. . . And slow time.
. . . Sorry, slow day at the office. Learnt it at school you know. Funny how we remember these things. You might like to put that down in your notes – how we remember these things. Do get in touch, Paul. People are getting anxious.
. . . I worry about your machine, I think it may be ill. Do you know it's buzzing now, not beeping? And the pauses are getting longer. I would put it down to over-use if I were you. Yes, it's me, Boyd again. Are you on the move? I'm

1

impressed by your diligence, but it's becoming frustrating. It would be helpful if you would return my calls. It's been a little while now, hasn't it? I'm not saying anything, I'm just saying it would be *help*ful.

. . . You see, we do feel we have a right to be updated on the progress of your research. I don't think you can deny that we have a right. Those were, you will remember, the terms of the contract.

. . . 'Buzz' Boyd, my friends are beginning to call me.

. . . Boyd here. I have a theory I would like to share with you: it's my theory that you are sitting beside your machine listening to me even now, even as I speak. If that is the case I advise you to pick up the phone, Paul, I really do. It's in your best interests. Mr Walsh himself has become cognisant. Hmm? No? Are you sure?

. . . Well, I shall be along to see you on the thirteenth. Fortunately, I'm not superstitious. You, I see from your extensive file, are. Can't be helped. Don't trouble about refreshments. Tea and biscuits, you know the sort of thing. You would be well advised to be there. I'm looking forward tremendously to meeting you, I really am.

Paul was anxious not to move too much. Any sudden motion and the quivering pile of documents and folders on the right arm of his chair was likely to fall to the floor. This would be a major irritation: the documents were extracted from several folders and were only separated by slips of paper. If they fell they would become confused, perhaps form new, arbitrary groupings. All Paul's research was inter-related, and the result might possibly produce something interesting, but it wasn't an experiment he wished to try. Experiments, hopeful ventures into the unknown, were inappropriate for his project, bordering on the unprofessional. A careful and logical approach was what he favoured, and what he felt his work demanded. He tried to transfer this approach to his present problem: the best tactic would have been to shift the papers a few at a time from the unstable pile to the floor, but a heavy volume of the *Oxford English Dictionary* open on his lap was making the delicacy of movement that this required awkward, if not impossible. What's more, it was a much-used volume, its spine was decaying and it had quite a few loose pages. To move might damage it irreparably, and to damage the cool, omniscient world of the *Oxford English Dictionary*, Paul felt, would be vandalism of the worst kind. He didn't move.

Although he tried for a few moments to reconstruct the events, Paul couldn't remember how he had arrived at this unlikely position. He looked around him, turning his head slowly, without moving his body, surveying the whole room like a remote-controlled camera. No solution to his problem presented itself. As far as he could see, there was only one logical response. (Paul is a great believer in the logical response.) An inch at a time, as if wary of pain, he settled more deeply into his armchair, leaning back in slow-motion luxuriance, and closing his eyes with a sigh that sounded like surrender.

What he had seen in his scan of the room had reminded him of something. It was only the usual mess, but it produced a brief, unexpected visual echo, a sense of *déjà vu*. Odd, since he usually scorned such things. (Nor was he superstitious – he was quite comforted by the fallibility of Boyd's extensive file.) His eyes were closed, but the room's image lingered.

Shelves all around, sagging paunchily in the middle. Paul prefers his books heavy, thick with information, with illuminating example and cogent detail. To his right on the desk beneath the window is a pyramid of tins, a pyramid with several extensions. Tuna, baked beans and chopped tomatoes, the ingredients of his favourite meal. Beside them, folders in different colours, and loose sheafs of paper. A grey mug holds a variety of pens, a ruler and two combs. Paperclips are scattered on everything, many of them bent into unnatural shapes, like little creatures crawling over his work. Providing counter-balance to the cans, a word-processor sits at the other end of the desk, its printer on a chair beside it. Opposite the desk is a sofa draped in a blanket. An orange-and-brown ethnic print is just about visible beneath piles of newspapers and magazines. There is a vaguely orange-and-brown look to the plates, and the frying pan on the floor, too. (Visualising them, Paul became aware of the smell of tuna and tomato sauce that he usually didn't notice.) There is a chest-expander, a bar-bell, two dumb-bells and assorted weights. Clothes, books and more papers conceal the carpet. Directly in front of Paul, obscuring the fireplace, are a TV and video on a black metal trolley with cuttings stuck all over it. The telephone and answer-machine are on a similar trolley beside him.

Mentally, he tracked back: papers, plates, books, weights, clothes. Clothes. A few shirts, two pairs of trousers and a sweater. They provided the answer. Hazel. Paul's bungalow had somehow, insidiously, turned into a version of his sister's flat.

The last time he saw her they were on their way to the opera. It was a treat for Hazel, a special day out. They sat opposite each other on the crowded tube, and Paul watched her cautiously. Beside her there was a small man, his feet just touching the floor. His grey-and-blue anorak was too long for him. Over the top of his *Evening Standard*, all that was visible was his cap. Hazel glanced at him, and picked up her own paper. Paul felt himself relaxing. It would be a good evening, he had a right to feel pleased with himself. Not everyone would have made the effort. The small man folded his newspaper and took out a letter, Hazel leaned over and looked at it unselfconsciously, and then she began to laugh.

Hazel laughing was never something to be ignored. The sound she made was high pitched and staccato, not immediately distinct from a stuttering cry of pain. Faces turned.

'What is it?' said the man. 'Are you laughing at me? Are you laughing at *me*?'

Hazel, like a retuned radio, at once returned his anger. 'What are you doing with that newspaper? Let me look at it.'

She snatched it from his lap and pulled it open with her fists, as if it was offering resistance. Within the narrow confines of his seat, the man began to move away from her. 'What are you? What are you doing? What are you, crazy?'

'I thought so,' she said. 'This is the exact same one, this newspaper is *iden*tical to mine. How do you explain that? How do you explain that, my friend?'

Paul wanted to shrink smaller than the small man. His objectivity, he knew, was fragile. He knew it was only a matter of time before her rage pulled him into its orbit. Perhaps she would calm down. 'Don't you back away from me, I know what you're trying to do.' Perhaps she wouldn't. Another station, another surge of passengers. Paul stood up, while Hazel's face was still turned, and walked off the train as, behind him, the argument escalated. Paul had a talent, finely tuned and much exercised, for avoiding confrontations. He watched the train disappear into the tunnel, and dropped the opera tickets without regret into a bin on the platform.

Later, he found that the heading of the letter Hazel had read had been 'Brain of Enfield 1989'. He could forgive the laughter perhaps, but not the rest. 'What are you, crazy?' He couldn't forgive the fear in the man's eyes. Objectively, Paul knew that he had probably over-reacted, but by his own standards his action had been both justified and responsible. His own standards were the only ones he cared for.

It was darker when he woke, and the first thing he noticed was the flashing light on the answer-machine beside his chair. A series of flashes, a pause, another series of flashes. 'Dot, dot, dot,' he said. 'Dash, dash, dash.' But quietly, as if afraid of being overheard. The machine was just about close enough to reach safely. He had heard all the messages as they were left, he didn't want to hear them again, he just wanted to turn it off.

He reached out carefully, slow motion, to his left, delicately extending his middle finger. Its tip, his fingerprint, rested on the 'Rewind' button. Nothing stirred. 'What a *superb* performance,' he whispered. He leant a fraction further in order to press the button and felt simultaneously the sudden, incontinent slide of his documents in the other direction. Taking a stab at the button, he lunged back towards the tower of papers too late to stop them, but just in time to see them crash on to a similar pile below, and scatter in reckless miscegenation. As he slumped in despair there was a further slippage as Volume Thirteen, Quemadero to Roaver, of the *OED* fell on to his foot. A large section slid from between its covers and spread over the floor like a puddle, its separate pages sliding neatly between the other

5

papers already lying there.

'Thou,' said his answer-machine, abruptly coming to life, '. . . still unravished . . . bride of quietness . . .'

Two

Pacing up and down, drinking coffee and gathering items for the latest instalment of his report, Paul was interrupted by a knock on the door.

'Another bloody back-breaker.'

The postman, with his welcome deliveries and his perpetual hostility, was always a complicated element in Paul's morning. His black moustache and long, curling black hair might have been sinister if his face hadn't been fat and florid. Red-and-black face, red-and-blue coat; even his colours were a loud intrusion. But he brought the journals and the books, the daily load that was the excuse for his temper.

'What's that?' Always something accusing in his manner, as if he spent his time imagining what Paul might get up to in his isolated house.

Paul was carrying a cutting from a morning paper. He glanced at it as if he needed reminding. 'Thing about the death-race.'

'Eh?'

'Two men, racing each other off the lights, killed half a bus queue and a girl in one of the cars.'

'Animals.' He shifted his sack and looked at Paul suspiciously. 'What do you want with it?'

'It goes in my report.' The man was still glaring at him, and hadn't yet handed over his packages. 'My road safety report.'

The postman leaned into his face. 'Surprised you get a chance to write it with all this lot to keep you busy.' He dropped the packages into Paul's arms. 'It's my taxes, is it?' He bared his teeth on the word 'taxes'.

'No, no,' said Paul. 'Private foundation. Not a penny of yours involved.'

'Private? Bloody typical. Fine if you can afford it. Waste of money, anyway. There's too much information in the world already. If we didn't tell people so much, they'd have less to get upset about. Am I right?'

'I'm hoping my report will be widely circulated.'

'Well, it won't. It'll be shelved, it'll gather dust and grow mould. You wait.'

'Thank you very much,' said Paul. 'Good-bye.'

Awkwardly clutching his post to his body with one arm, he closed the door. He sighed with relief and, like an inflatable leaking air, he slid slowly down the jamb as he sat down on the mat. He had the odd feeling that the postman was still there, just on the other side, listening, hoping for clues. He looked up, half expecting to see a hand come questing through the letter box above him. Why was the postman so inquisitive? Perhaps a complaint to the sorting office would fix him. Probably it would just make him angrier. It seemed to Paul that he quite often inspired aggression in people. It was a mystery to him.

He opened his parcels. One was a free gift, a mail-order catalogue for a bookshop; the other was a video he had ordered. Next, the large envelopes: a literary magazine, one about films, a medical journal, a soft-porn magazine, two newsy weeklies. Then the colourful junk mail, always proliferating because of the many different subscription lists his name appeared on. 'Dear Mr Feather, Congratulations! You have been chosen . . .' One letter. He looked at the postcode and then, leaving a bill lying on the mat, he took the rest into the sitting room. He took two wire baskets from under the desk and dropped his magazines in one, and his junk mail and gifts in the other, before sitting down with his letter.

Dear Paul,

We've acquired some things that you might want to look at. In any case, it would be good, as ever, to see you. The wheel keeps turning here, old faces are going, new ones will be arriving. I need a dose of stability, someone who is not going anywhere. That's you, Paul, my love. (I can't think of anyone else who would take it as a compliment.) Please come. I promise no scenes, just fun, as well as possibly some useful materials.

                                                    Victoria

He stared at the letter for a while, particularly at the signature, then folded it and put it in his pocket. It was the only place where it was unlikely to get lost. 'Road safety,' he said quietly, unhurriedly, as if testing the words. 'Road safety?' He went to his desk, opened his window slightly, and began typing on to his word-processor, glancing now and then at a newspaper. He typed: 'A man, picking his nose while driving, hit the car in front and drove his right index finger into his brain, killing himself instantly.' He looked at this for a moment and then added: 'A cautionary tale for kids?'

He remained at the word-processor for the rest of the morning, typing efficiently, referring constantly to papers, documents and magazines littered around the room. Once he spent several minutes staring at a wall covered with clippings, before picking out the one he wanted, taking it off the wall and returning to his desk. Once he paused, when it began to rain. He likes to watch the rain. To sit indoors with the window open, smelling its fresh, enlivening smell, watching it spray dots and commas on to the glass. The trees opposite change colour beneath the grey sky, the wind shows the pale undersides of the leaves. He likes to sit indoors, sheltered, watching it falling and smelling its fresh, clean smell.

After four hours of work, he printed out what he had written, added it to a pile on his desk, picked up one or two items from the floor, and put the whole lot into an envelope, which he sealed immediately. Then he switched on the television and watched a quiz programme. Four middle-aged people stood behind brightly-coloured stripy lecterns, with their fists hovering over swollen red buzzers, while the compère paced up and down in front of them, shuffling question cards. 'Of which country,' he asked, pausing slyly, 'is Paris the capital?' Hysterical, two-handed slamming of buzzers all round, which for some reason struck the question-master as hilarious, so that he laughed helplessly for some time, holding his sides as if in pain. His guests watched with tight-lipped smiles, one even managed a tight-lipped grin, as they waited for his judgement on who had buzzed first. Paul couldn't make out whether the compère was the same age as the contestants or a good deal younger, and he noted this down, along with several other observations.

The afternoon was similar, but less productive. Less typing, more TV. Some exercises. Some browsing, meandering without any clearly defined purpose through text books and reference books. Paul had to watch himself: without self-discipline he could do this all day, losing himself gladly in the unrolling paths and their byways. Everything is connected, everything has its place. That is the beauty of the work. There are no anomalies, no surprises. Or rather, there is a prepared category, into which anomalies and surprises fall. They are expected, they do not distress the system.

After a three-hour shift, Paul left the house carrying his envelope, limping slightly. His big toe was painfully swollen where the dictionary had fallen on it. His package was addressed to the Walsh Foundation. Enough, he thought, to placate them for a while. It had occurred to him to enclose a letter, questioning the need for Boyd's visit, but he had decided against it. Better to face the man. There were questions to be asked on both sides, and there was nothing to feel guilty about.

It was bright now, but windy, and thick dark-grey banks of cloud rushed from the background into the foreground, before being pushed away again to the edge of the sky. Dramatic light, giving the trees a harsh clarity. The pressure was changing rapidly, something which Paul knew from his day's reading would lead to more road accidents than usual, as well as bad behaviour in classrooms. He decided to move his research towards weather. Ozone depletion, world warming, the avalanche effect, the weatherman as secular prophet, the psychological benefits of sunlight, fear of flooding, stress in weathermen, fear of skin cancer . . . it was fertile ground. It might lead on neatly to statistical overkill, the buzz-word effect and compassion fatigue, areas he had already had reason to explore. He smiled comfortably. Everything, of course, was fertile ground, if looked at properly. Every effect was also a cause, leading to another effect which, at its best, might have global, social and personal ramifications. There were innumerable paths to follow. That was what Boyd evidently didn't understand: Paul might be sitting by the answerphone, not leaving the house, but he was still intrepidly exploring dense forests of consequences.

A half-mile walk brought him to Aldesham. The village was a triangular patch of grass with a few houses clustered around it, a small pub and an equally small shop which sold general provisions and served as a Post Office. Greater Aldesham, four miles away, was similar, but included a church and a school. Unusually, there was a car parked outside the pub and, as Paul entered the shop, he thought he caught the eye of its driver.

'Howdy.'

Paul sighed as he saw who was behind the counter. The boy was wearing a check shirt, a red handkerchief round his neck, and a stetson. 'How are you, Tod?'

'Guess I'm fine, Mr Feather, how are y'all?'

'And your mother?'

'Yep, she's jest fine too. Now what might this be?'

'I want to send it to London, please, first-class.' As Tod weighed it, Paul turned to the shelves, to discourage conversation. The shop sold just about everything. His kitchen was well stocked with tins, but he could perhaps try some variation. Maybe he ought to have some fresh vegetables? Moving to the front of the shop, he glanced out of the window, and again had the impression that the driver of the car was looking in his direction. Staring. There was a thin whistling behind him. 'Do Not Forsake Me'. Tod, nineteen, worked for his mother in order to earn enough money to go to Arizona, or Colorado, one of those places. He intended to start a dude ranch there, on those fabulously wide plains. So far, he had spent most of his savings on clothes and equipment. He had a Western saddle which he used when he went riding every weekend, and a replica pistol, which he liked to wear at work. He spent his days practising draws and twirling it on his index finger. His mother wouldn't let him get a real gun.

Paul turned back, and paid for a pint of milk and his stamps. 'Who's that then?' he said, nodding at the parked car across the road.

'Reckon he's just passing through. Stranger in these parts.' Tod's Norfolk vowels battled it out with his Texan drawl. 'Don't fret though, if he causes any trouble,' he dropped Paul's change as his hand whipped to his holster and drew out his gun, 'I'll run him out of town for you.'

The gun was polished, and gleaming. The hand holding it was steady. Paul had an urge to put up his hands. Instead, as Tod disappeared beneath the counter, looking for the fallen coins, he asked, 'What is it about cowboys? Can you explain the attraction for me?'

There was a long pause, accompanied by the sound of Tod's fingernails scratching on the floor, and then the hat reappeared, followed by dreamy eyes, followed by a broadly smiling, slightly open mouth. He looked like a converted sinner, with his mind on the Kingdom of Heaven. He held out Paul's change, not saying a word, just shaking his head and smiling, as if the question baffled him too.

The driver of the car had gone when Paul came out. Giving it a moment's thought, he could not even remember what the man had looked like. The pub was closed, and the inside of the red car, when he peered through the window, told him nothing – an AA road-map sat beside a half-eaten sandwich on the passenger seat. A tall policeman was ambling away in the direction of Greater Aldesham. Paul, feeling foolish, turned towards home, nodding at Tod, who was standing in the doorway of the shop, watching him. He looked, as he often did, across lawns and into the windows of the houses that he passed. Catching the glimmer of televisions, sometimes some movement. He began to hurry, deciding as he pulled his coat closer around him that it was indeed time for a brief connection to the world outside.

Three

The campus was a collection of concrete blocks tumbled into green landscaped grounds. Victoria was walking around the lake, as she did on most mornings before she entered the library. Sitting on a bench, she would change into trainers and then set off on the circuit that soothed her. Grass and water, ducks. You could be sent down for killing a duck. You might get away with theft if there were mitigating circumstances, even cheating, but duck killing was unpardonable. She smiled, remembering that Paul had found this pleasing. He liked to have the limits of acceptable behaviour so clearly circumscribed. She stood and watched a black coot with a white face dive beneath the choppy surface of the water. There were no visible ripples. She waited. The bottom shelved quickly, apparently there was a whirlpool effect in the middle, where it was very deep. There were rumours of drownings, although some people said they were circulated by the authorities, to scare off students. She was still waiting. How big could a duck's lungs be? About as big as her fist, if that. She looked at her hand, rosy in the cold wind, and when she looked back the duck had reappeared, bobbing carelessly on the dark water.

Walking back to the campus, she was wondering if her letter might persuade Paul to come. Better, she thought, not to dwell on the possibility, and tempt disappointment. Not that her feelings were that strong, but some variation from routine would be welcome. She corrected herself: all right, her feelings *were* strong, but they were limited. To lust and anger, she thought. Mainly. It was Victoria's wish to be honest with herself, but she was stalled by uncertainty. Her relationship with Paul was never less than awkward. It was unflattering after all, to think of oneself primarily as a research resource, and his feelings, like everything else about him, could sometimes seem so carefully measured.

She was walking past the supermarket and the launderette, heading towards the library and the faculty buildings. Almost everyone around her was wearing black. It wasn't like a funeral – there isn't much tasselled leather at funerals – it was more like hell. Black shades on grey walkways. Victoria shook her head, irritated with her mood. Why feel unhappy? She would be moving on soon. She reminded herself how she stood out, in her short-skirted red suit, with her wavy blonde hair and her wide-rimmed glasses. She should feel daring in this company, one of a kind.

Paul arrived at lunchtime. Not moving, she watched him, framed in the rectangle of the lift's open doors. A short man, smaller than her when she wore heels, in a grey cotton shirt, jeans and a tie. He wore his hair short. It was easier that way, he had once said, there was no need to comb it. He put his hand through it even as she watched, leaving it slightly more untidy than it was before. He seemed nervous. At the prospect of seeing her? Probably not. Probably just because he was off his territory, among unfamiliar people and in a tall, modern building. He hated, he had told her more than once, tall, modern buildings. She remained still, watching him without attracting his attention. He had always taken care to stay fit, but his face was his best feature. Imperfect oval, almost round, with a good chin and cheeks that she loved to touch, feeling the bones beneath. His eyes always on the move. Were they nervous, or observant? Were they avoiding hers shyly, or deceitfully?

The doors behind him closed, and he saw her. He came up to her and, after only a moment's hesitation, they kissed. Her arms were full of books. She had an urge to drop them all, which she

15

resisted. As it was, they were stared at. A girl in black jeans, white T-shirt and black coat looked disapproving.

'Hello,' said Paul. 'Victoria?'

'That's right. I must just finish this.'

'Don't let me get in the way.'

'Because I'm right in the middle of it. And then we can eat. Do you want to eat? Is it lunchtime?'

'Yes.'

'I'm so glad you came, Paul.'

'Ssssh!' This was the monochrome girl. Paul followed Victoria as she pushed the book trolley between the rows. He gained some pleasure from watching her, from her self-conscious movements, from the neatness of what she was doing. It made him think of his house, and resolve, the next morning, to tidy it. It wasn't as if he enjoyed working in virtual squalor. Hazel briefly entered his mind again, along with a familiar pang of guilt. He ignored her, suppressed the guilt, watched Victoria picking up each book, and putting it without hesitation where it belonged.

'I saw your man Walsh in the paper a few days ago,' she said, in front of the lift. 'Did you see it?'

'Of course.'

A small item saying that at fifty he was one of the richest men in Britain, and that he had connections, in some unspecified way, with the Government. It was one of those pieces which covers its ignorance by hinting that there are things which cannot be revealed.

'Is it true?'

He shrugged. 'Gossip.'

On the way down they talked about the weather, and he asked her how she was. She said she was all right. She asked if he was still working out, and he said that he was. She realised that she was appraising the shape of his body beneath his clothes. What was the phrase? He strips well. They were standing two feet apart. When the doors of the lift opened on the ground floor, they found that they were kissing in front of an audience of four students. There was some applause.

In the foyer he asked, 'So, what have you got for me? Have

16

you found something good for me?' and she turned and spoke coldly.

'What am I, Paul, your secretary? Is that it? A little chat, then down to business?'

No scenes, he thought. 'What do you mean?' he said.

'I've got some new theses for you. Two of them might interest you, as far as I can tell. On sociology and geography.'

'What do you mean?'

'Geography. Study of, you know, whatever geographers study. Maps and stuff.' Victoria discovered, with some surprise, that she was furious. Anger had sprung from nowhere, fully formed. Her eyes were on him as she gave him time to respond. There was a whole history in her eyes, but he didn't look as if he was aware of it. He was still speechless, so she continued, icy. 'They're both looking at how geography relates to sociological trends. That's what you like, isn't it? Interdisciplinary research.'

Paul nodded absently, still trying to adjust himself. Tactfulness was a habit he had lost. Unused to conversation, he felt like a raw recruit experiencing a surprise attack. Victoria was listening too carefully, more carefully than he was. She treated words seriously, was able to follow back a chain of implications to find a subtext. It was flattering, to have attention paid to him in this way, but also alarming. It meant he needed an unusual degree of engagement with what was being said, and even with what was being felt.

'What I mean, Paul, is I get the feeling I'm being used. But forget that, don't let that worry you at all, you know where the theses are kept.'

'I'll have a look at them this afternoon. Let's have lunch. I was only making conversation.'

'Well, you succeeded in that, didn't you?' She had a word with someone at the desk and they left the library.

Outside, it had become busy. A thick crowd of students was moving down the steps towards the coffee bar, which was in the centre of a kind of paved arena. Stairs led down towards it on three sides.

'I'm sorry to fly off the handle,' Victoria continued, 'but you have to be a little bit more sensitive when you just show up like

17

this, without warning. Living the way you do isn't good for you.'

The steps were steep. They seemed to have been built with small feet in mind. The wind, gusting up the street of shops, swirled around the refectory. Paul said, 'You're probably absolutely right,' but he wasn't sure Victoria had heard him, because the wind had begun to whistle. People were jostling and hurrying. One girl, parted from her friends, was running away, spinning as she ran, arms outstretched for balance, apparently set on escape. Most were looking into the sky admiringly, not used to audible weather, the elements making themselves felt so theatrically. Paul saw the girl, spinning like a compass needle, move away, and then, disorientated, he looked up, pausing on his way down the steps, and found that the clouds moving across the sky made him feel precarious. He began to sway. Then he felt a hand on his back, he thought it was Victoria steadying him, he felt the fingers and then the palm, and then a sudden, sharp push.

And now he was leaning far out over the steps below, on tip-toe at forty-five degrees, like a diver with desperate, last-moment second thoughts, his arms flailing as if to carry him back up to the vertical. Time stopped, leaving him in the lurch, impotent. His mouth was open but he couldn't close it, his lungs were full but he couldn't breath, he could see the rail but it was out of reach. He could see the rail, and he could see the ground some fifteen steps below. He had time to find it odd that he was able to estimate the number of steps at such a moment. He even had time to wonder if his estimate was accurate. His last words to Victoria were in his mind, specifically one word: absolutely. It seemed so appropriate as the wind blew around his face, suspended over the drop below. Ab-so-lutely. Did his lips move? He felt a hand, was it the first hand or was it Victoria's?, clutching at his back. It pushed him slightly, down and to one side, and time started again. He flung himself at the rail, taking off from his step with a sliding push of his feet and, his body stretched taut, streamlined, he flew. For the space of a few accelerated heartbeats, his whole being was reduced to one purpose. He flew like Superman, and the moment when his outstretched left hand caught the rail was one of almost pure ecstasy.

It was only when he caught the rail that he fell. His body, previously flat and hard, the embodiment of effort, crumpled like a rag, and he crashed and tumbled down five steps, battering shin, knee, hip and ribs on the sharp edges of the steps, a series of sharp pains interpolated into snatched glimpses of feet, steps and sky. Only his fist remained firm, arresting his fall with a muscle-twisting jolt.

In the Medical Centre, they strapped a soft cotton dressing on to the large friction burn on his chest, sprayed Deep Heat on to his bruises, and asked him to sign a form which made it clear that the University wasn't responsible for his accident. Victoria bought him a cup of sweet tea in the coffee bar, and then a whisky in the pub. She sat with her arm around him as he described what had happened, as if she hadn't been there. Other people hadn't been impressed by his acrobatics, they had brushed past as he clung to the rail, trembling, but Victoria had looked over his toppling back at the fall below and caught a glimpse of the terror on his face as he hung suspended. She had enough imagination to be impressed.

'I was pushed,' he said.

'That was just me trying to catch you. I couldn't get hold of your jacket.'

'But before that. I didn't slip or anything, I felt a hand on my back.' He shivered as if he could feel it there now, like a weighty spider clinging to his spine. He insisted, 'I was pushed.'

She hugged him. 'No. Who would push you? No, what you need is something to eat now. Could you handle something to eat?'

She was talking to him like a child. They both became aware of it at the same moment, and then normal life began reasserting itself. He had escaped death or injury, therefore he was Paul Feather again, an adult, in control of his destiny. He took a deep breath; it felt like the first breath he had taken since he was on the steps.

'Let's eat,' he said.

Suddenly very hungry, he had fish, chips, beans and an egg, with a side salad. She watched him stretching his lips around great forkfuls of it while she took occasional bites from a ham roll.

As if the food made things easier, he spoke with his mouth full. 'Look, I am grateful to you for keeping an eye open for me. You're right, those theses sound like just my kind of material. But that's not the only reason I'm here.' He heard himself talking, and was pleased with what he was saying. 'It's good to see you. It's always good to see you. You mustn't draw conclusions from the fact that I'm no good at keeping in touch. I never have been, with anyone, not even my own family.'

'Especially your own family.'

He conceded this with a nod. 'So you won't draw conclusions?'

'I think you like being the mystery man. You think it suits you. I still only have a vague idea of what you're up to.'

He leant forward, whispering. 'Look at that man's paper. You can win the kitchen of your dreams. Have you ever in your whole life dreamt about a kitchen?' He looked at her as if this was an important point, and then shook his head. 'Me neither. What's the point in having your dreams come true if all they involve is a particular arrangement of cupboards, cooker, sink and fridge?'

'Is that what your report is about?'

'No. Yes. Partly. Partly it's about what people dream of these days. Partly it isn't. I'm incorporating a lot, it's growing all the time.'

'I dream of accomplishing things. Bibliophilic acts of bravery. An admiring audience gasps as I scale the side of the library to rescue rare manuscripts from terrorists. It means I'm dissatisfied.'

'There always seem to be women in my dreams. If I dreamt of a kitchen Mona Lisa would be in it, and I'd be trying to find out what she was thinking. She never tells me anything, she never even smiles.'

'It's probably guilt about your sister.'

'What guilt?'

20

'When are you going to see her again?'

'Never.'

'Paul, how can you say never?'

'I admit it's a difficult concept. Nothing is certain.'

'Why won't you?'

'Don't want to. Why should I want to?'

'Tell me why you won't.'

It wasn't something Paul liked to talk about, but the confidence seemed a fair exchange for his earlier tactlessness. He pushed his plate to one side. 'I used to cry when I vomited,' he said. 'Not because there was any pain – I'm thinking of mild stomach upsets – but at the sheer shock of it. That my body should do such a thing, turn on me like that. You know? It bends you over, and then this stuff comes flying up out of your stomach, you feel it moving in your throat, liquid and solid, and in your mouth. This is your body, your private property, and this vile stuff has been living there. And then you *see* it, coming out of you, this soup, and as soon as you see it, you smell it. And taste it. It just never seemed right that it should be happening, it didn't fit in with anything else. It's the same as what I felt outside, that helplessness. There was nothing of me left when I was hanging there, nothing but horror, nothing but the expression on my face. That's what it is: whatever you think of as being you is made irrelevant, reduced to nothing. That's scary, isn't it?'

He looked as if he wanted an answer, but Victoria didn't speak.

'Hazel scares me in that same way,' he continued. 'It's scary that you can get mentally ill, isn't it? It frightens me. I want no part of it. It doesn't fit in. I'm not intending to be helpless if I can avoid it. And what I've found is that I *can* avoid it. It's sad, don't think I'm not sad about it, but Hazel at the moment isn't a part of my life. Did I ever tell you some of the things she wanted me to do? She had this thing about clothes . . .'

'I don't want to hear, Paul. Why don't we go and get you photocopies of the theses now.'

'What's the matter?'

'Nothing.'

'Are you going to take the afternoon off?'

'No.'

'Take it off. We could, you and I, I'd like to . . .'

'It's not going to happen.'

'What have I said now?'

'What have you said? You cry when you vomit. You're scared of death and mental illness. You have deliberately abandoned your sister. You live like a hermit until you feel like sex, when you show up here, pretending you're after more data.'

'I didn't say all that. Did I say I was scared of death?'

'Yes. And if you didn't say it you meant it.'

'I don't cry when I vomit any more. Nowadays I just feel unhappy, I just feel lonely. And you've left out things. I still pump iron. In a crisis I'll be strong, if I'm given the opportunity. Who knows, if I improve my body enough, maybe the rest will change too. You have to have a little faith in me.'

'Is that a blouse or a shirt?'

'A shirt. Why?'

'No reason. I'm cursed with an attention to detail.'

'Blouses are baggier, I think. What was it about Hazel and clothes?'

'She wanted to swap with me.'

'Kinky.' She kissed his chest. 'I've known women with less well-developed breasts than this.'

'I don't think that's a compliment.'

She shrugged. 'Why not?'

When he rolled on to his side, he cried out as pain shot up the strained muscle in his wrist, and blossomed in his thigh, wriggling up and down his leg. The novelty of these two exquisitely uncomfortable sensations almost paralysed him, and he dropped on to his back again. 'Your poor body,' said Victoria, 'and you've looked after it so beautifully.' She didn't so much climb on to him, as slide over him, contriving never to put her weight on him. Yet their skin seemed to be in total contact. 'Have a little faith,' she whispered, as he winced. The pain subsided to a bearable level as she sat astride him, avoiding grazes and bruises, and then it faded, and he surrendered to her absolutely.

Sleepy, she dozed. It was a talent she had, to drift off quickly, replenishing herself. He always wondered if it was in preference to talking to him. Her blonde hair, bunched beneath her head, would become knotted and creased. He touched it, and she stirred. Strange, how sensitive. Her peaceful face, turning blind eyes to him. The curve of her. We are more flexible than we know. Her back curves away from him, and small folds appear in her stomach. Flesh, hiding behind drawn up thighs. She is modest in sleep, concealing. Experimenting, he licked her thigh, tasted her, and she rolled over, more revealing, more vulnerable. Is she awake? She makes a sound. 'Nnagh.'

Paul rolled away from her, on to his back, arm across his forehead. In spite of anxious experiences, he felt good. There had been an unpleasant interlude, but that was to be expected, venturing out. Life isn't too bad, give or take a few scrapes and bruises which, like irrational midnight fears, will make it difficult to sleep comfortably.

When she drove him back to the university, he talked to take his mind off his aching muscles and the pain in his flayed chest.

'How long has it been, *Victoria*?'

'Not long. But it's permanent this time.'

'I'm still not clear what's wrong with Jane.'

'What's right with Jane? Janes are the wimps and victims of history. Lady Jane Grey is your archetypal Jane.'

'What about Jane Eyre?'

'Oh, literature. Bugger it. Bugger books.'

'You'll get the sack.'

'Unless I resign first. I'm looking for a job where I can be in charge of things. People management, projects, three-year plans. I'm wasted here. Victorias are people who make things happen. As in Queen. I'm an Empire builder. Victoria is the female form of "victor", and "victorious". You can't go wrong with a name like that.' She found a space to park. 'Come on, I'll show you your theses.'

She was back behind the issues desk when he emerged with his heavy pile of photocopied papers. 'I *was* pushed,' he said. 'I suppose someone was in a hurry to get past. Did you see anyone?'

'No. It's a kind of egotism, you know, to think that there's an exterior cause involved in an accident like that. I bet you'd like to think someone's conspiring against you. Wouldn't it make it all worthwhile?'

'I'm not paranoid, Victoria. I'm just sensitive to situations.'

'You fell, that's all. There was no one even around except students and lecturers and a chef from the refectory.'

'When are we going to meet again?'

She said, straight-faced, 'I think it's your turn to get in touch.'

There were hundreds of cars in the car park, so there was no reason to think that the red Cavalier he was looking at was the one that had been parked outside the pub in Aldesham. They were common enough. The road map was hardly conclusive. And even if it was the same car, why shouldn't its driver want to visit the University? Feeling slightly foolish, Paul looked around, turning 360 degrees, scanning the area. There was no one staring at him, no one who looked remotely threatening. He was trying to live a life in which no one could bear a grudge against him, but Victoria had already shown him that he had failed. He could still feel the hand on his back. He wondered how much evidence one needed to scientifically distinguish between paranoia and legitimate suspicion.

Four

Pausing for a minute, Paul lifted his chin up on to his chest and studied the flesh on his ribs. He had removed the dressing, to reveal a long, wide section of roughly-textured red-and-black scar tissue. He gazed at it, trying to spot any improvement since the day before, and then lowered his head again and, cautiously, lifted the dumb-bells. This was the exercise that Paul's doctor had sanctioned: he was to lift the weights directly upwards, thus strengthening his wrist without putting unusual strain on it. It was a compromise they had agreed on, and its only drawback was that lifting the dumb-bells tended to stretch the lake of thin scar tissue over his graze. This was a bad idea, because whenever it was stretched beyond the demands of calm, even breathing, it broke, either in a single wide fissure which made him feel that his chest was being cut in half, or in an agonising delta of cracks, which made him feel that a broken bottle was being ground into his flesh.

He lowered the dumb-bells, slowly, struggling to keep his breath steady, to keep his wrist straight, and not to become so breathless that he created serious ripples on his chest. He knew that it was time to stop, there was a tautness there that he had come, over the past few days, to recognise. His body was giving him fair warning. His breath emerged from marginally-parted lips in a long whistle through clenched teeth. One more. There was always this compulsion, he didn't feel it in any other area of

25

life, but when he was exercising there was always this compulsion to go that extra step, to prove beyond question his body's competence. Just one more. He lifted the weights, straightened his arms, stretching them up towards the ceiling triumphantly. What's a little pain? It's all a matter of confidence. It's all a matter of fitness. He grinned tightly.

Storm on the lake.

Fissures broke out across its entire surface like cracks on ice, and pain spiralled down in localised whirlpools deep into his chest. Desperate not to make it any worse, he tried to keep the weights in the air, swaying at the end of his rigid arms, while he waited for the commotion across and all over and inside his chest to subside. This was over-optimistic. He was managing to keep the weights in the air, but the pain was getting worse anyway, and still worse, until finally he realised that he had to drop them. He lowered his arms very slowly outwards, aiming for the minimum movement required to make the weights clear his body, and then he opened his fists, and instantly his injured wrist screamed its protest with a jagged lightning strike of pain down his arm which seemed to race the dumb-bells to the floor. The pain won.

Paul lay spread-eagled, eyes closed, unmoving. After a while he could hardly feel his body at all, although he sensed that it was trembling. He took this to be an improvement, and didn't try to stop it. He lay on his floor, shivering. It was surprisingly pleasant, to feel so utterly physically drained. He didn't know how much later it was, when he spoke to the empty room, his words distributed unevenly between ragged breaths: '*Am* I scared of death?' He opened his eyes, and they were speculative. He sat up, gingerly, found himself surrounded as usual by papers, picked up his pen with some difficulty, and began to write on the bottom of a typed sheet. He could still barely control his muscles, and his shaky handwriting looked like that of a six-year-old, but he wrote at length, going on to the other side of the paper, drawing up an alphabetical list (burglary, depression, illness, insanity, insects, poverty, scenes, strangers, tall modern buildings, violence), using long, zig-zagged arrows, drawing a complex Venn diagram. As he became engrossed his tongue emerged slightly from between his lips. He had forgotten his pain and fatigue. He didn't know it, but he was smiling.

Boyd was making notes too. He was slumped slightly in his seat, and his notebook, an old hard-backed diary, was propped on his thighs, leaning against the table. His stomach, a considerable obstacle, was slightly in the way, but he wasn't writing very much, so it didn't matter. His striped shirt was stretched so that it parted in between buttons, revealing his vest beneath. His attitude suggested comfort rather than industry. He had raised the arm of the seat to give himself more room, and put his jacket, coat and briefcase on the seat opposite him. He was reading from a file open on the table, and although his pen hovered over his notebook, he mostly just mused aloud.

'What shall we say about you? What do we know about you?'

As he considered, his tongue moved over his lips and then, inside his mouth, from one cheek to the other, as if he was relishing the last mouthful of a succulent meal. He was developing a picture of his man. This was how he liked to work, gathering facts in a casual way, getting to know the subject gradually, learning more as one learns from an acquaintance who imperceptibly becomes a friend. Walsh himself had initiated the project, but Boyd was never content to stand back and watch.

'One parent dead when young. A sense of abandonment resulting. You felt lost, didn't you? Your family, anyway, was strange to say the least. You never felt that you fitted in. School was a trial, and home was worse. Childhood was a state of nervous tension. Putting faith in routine, searching for an explanation of things. What things? Unhappiness. Holding yourself together with structures imposed on you, beliefs inherited by you. Death of the second parent, the dominant, shaping force. What promising territory that is. And you found, to your surprise, that this liberation was only another kind of abandonment. How you searched then, and what a pleasure, what boundless pleasure, when you found someone who offered control, and the lack of responsibility that goes with control. Clever, clever Mr Walsh. I have to admit it, he has an unerring eye for this type.'

A woman bringing tea and coffee was standing beside Boyd's

seat, staring at him. Becoming aware of her presence, he looked up, and met her eyes. Her amused smile became sheepish, she waited a second, awkward, and then pushed her trolley on down the aisle, only wondering a few moments later why she should be feeling embarrassed when it was him, the fat, balding businessman, who had been talking to himself. Beneath his notes, which constituted a couple of abbreviated phrases, Boyd wrote his subject's name: *Edmund Staples*. Beneath that, after a little more thought, this time in silence, he wrote:

Feather Report. Acceleration is indicated. Acceleration may be effected through exposure.

He underlined the last word twice, and then began to doodle. A long, gently-curving line, several short diagonal lines on either side of it. First it was an arrow, then a feather. With a few hard strokes, Boyd put it inside a box. Then he began to embellish the box.

After lunch Paul took his plates into the kitchen and put them in the sink. He moved like an invalid, aware of his body as he never had been before. He came back into his workroom and looked around. In two trips, he took his dumb-bells and the bar-bell into the bedroom. Then he gathered papers, sorting printed ones into a pile on his desk, written ones next to them, blank into a drawer, spoilt ones and draft copies into the bin, which soon needed emptying. He hesitated over the sheet he had just been working on, and then put it on top of the written pile. He took some tins and other shopping which had never made it much past the front door into the kitchen. Next, he began to gather newspapers and magazines, whistling tunelessly but jauntily as he did so. This was the normal cycle of things, accumulating mess, growing worse and worse over a period of weeks, and then a sudden burst of tidying. It was less a chore postponed, than a treat saved up. He found it rewarding to make order out of chaos, and enjoyed the mindless, gently physical activity of putting things in their places, of vacuuming up dust and debris, of making a small, limited space clean.

The memory he always returned to was of a woman washing her car. It was a sunny day, and he was on his way to the post office, looking at the houses he passed as usual. Something quite out of the ordinary happened. This woman said good morning to him. She wore a sleeveless, brightly-patterned shirt, and she was dipping a big yellow sponge into a bucket full of frothing water. The sun glinted off clean, dazzling white metal and almost, it seemed, off her bare, pink arms. Colour and mood combined in an energetic kind of harmony. He would have said good morning back, but he paused too long and he was past her, and anyway by then she was already at work on the roof of the car. On his way home, looking out for her, he saw her moving around in a front room of her house. Standing at the bottom of the garden, shiny green lawn, he had to resist an impulse to creep up to the net-curtained window. Only for the most innocent of motives. Only to watch her, to share a little of her contentment in her work. He envied her. The only people he ever envied were housewives.

Shortly afterwards he had done some research, hoping to prove that, by spending their time keeping home and family in order, housewives made themselves happy and fulfilled. Her smile, her greeting, the clean car – how could it be otherwise? His research took into account educational background, composition of family, occupation of husband, prosperity, achievements of offspring, aspirations, hobbies and credulity in relation to advertising. Already a little disillusioned by his preliminary findings, Paul cross-referenced to incorporate daytime TV and radio ratings, and information relating to frequency of orgasms, visits to GPs, debt defaulting, court appearances, divorce rate, tranquilliser use, alcoholism, domestic violence, child abuse and suicide rate. Sometimes he regretted his own thoroughness. His starting point, a woman washing her car on a sunny day, was drowned in detail, and came to seem as unrealistic as a scene from a Walt Disney cartoon. His ideal, a structured life spent maintaining a small world of order, was obscured by the mass of statistics he had gathered. All that remained was his own stubborn attraction. The essence of the appeal was predictability. In the evening, the spouse comes home, in the meantime one might go to the supermarket, on a sunny day one might wash the car, but the territory was limited, and perfectly mapped. Lack of surprise, and lack of mobility. To be a housewife, for Paul, was to be in complete control of one's environment. In a changing world, surely that remained desirable?

Reflecting on this, he continued his tidying. He collected books and put them on shelves, he collected pens and paperclips and put them in a mug on top of a pile of folders. He dusted surfaces and, when a space had been cleared, he vacuumed. The gentle exercise was like physiotherapy, tiring him, without straining anything. He adjusted his ruler so that it was parallel with the edge of his desk, and he wiped the screen of his word-processor and the top of the printer with a damp cloth. He had picked up clothes and dropped them on chairs and furniture. Only now did he begin to gather them up. They had multiplied since he had last noticed them. Trousers over the back of the sofa, shirts on the desk, the arms of a sweater hanging in front of the television screen. Semi-rolled-up socks everywhere, like mice. And he had only picked them up, not taken them anywhere, when he sat down on the sofa abruptly, almost dropped on to it, as if felled by the impact of his second memory, no less vivid than the last. Clothes and Hazel, the link was just the same as before.

She had said she would meet him in Laura Ashley. He had arrived five minutes late and, catching sight of her admiring a dress, had watched her. She looked well, and he found himself pleased to see her. Surely there was nothing wrong with her. She wore a denim jacket over a pale-blue dress. There was a red ribbon in her shoulder-length hair, which was the same dark brown as his own. She wore make-up, her face was a creamy pink and her lipstick was the colour of her ribbon. A silvery brooch, red moccasins. This was a young woman in control of her appearance, presenting a well-chosen image to the world. Paul resolved to make more effort to keep in touch. To have someone he had never heard of tell him he ought to visit his sister was, after all, slightly humiliating.

'She's unhappy. Apparently she's not seeing her old friends, avoiding them in fact. She's fairly edgy. I realise it must be a difficult time for you, too, in the circumstances, but I think perhaps you should come and visit her. She mentions you quite a lot. She has confidence in you, you know.'

Until the incident, they had met regularly at their mother's house, a ritual they had both enjoyed. After it, everything changed, and it was only when her tutor got in touch, that he heard she was unhappy.

He saw her in profile: his nose above a smaller chin, a more elegant line. She was studying the dress carefully, feeling the material. Her left hand was at the hem, fingering the security tag. Was she holding something? A deft movement, and the tag came away, and now she was touching the collar as she read the label. The skilful part was the way the dress seemed quite naturally to drift towards her bag. Then another twist of the left hand and in a second the whole thing had disappeared. A ghost crumpling into nothing. Hazel was examining the next dress on the rail. Paul could almost believe it was the same one.

He approached her, touched her shoulder and she turned, eyes wide with excitement. 'Good God, I thought you were the detective.'

'Hazel, what was that?'

'What?'

'Put it back.'

She put her arms round his waist and kissed him. The bag thumped against his thighs. 'Don't I even get a hello?'

'You have to put it back, Hazel.'

Her face was inches from his, long lashes at the level of his cheekbones. She pouted a little, joking, but he could feel her tension. 'You *are* the detective.'

'Look, I'll buy it for you if you want it. A present.'

Her arms were still round his waist. He could feel her heart, beating hard from the shock he had given her. She didn't kiss him this time, but she touched her cheek on his. Cold. 'Now you're Paul again. Why do we see so little of each other?' She brought a wallet out of her bag. In it there was only a five-pound note. 'I seem to have forgotten my credit card.'

'My treat, Hazel.'

'All right then, but hurry, we'll be late for the film.'

As they left the shop she took hold of his hand, and held it tightly. He followed her slowly, almost at arm's length, like a recalcitrant child.

A few hours later, the positions were reversed as she dragged her feet in the hall, pausing in front of the door to her flat.

'It's a horrible mess.'

They hadn't particularly enjoyed the film, it had been more of a pretext than anything else, and on the way back to her flat her tension had returned. 'I don't know why you're here, you know how you hate London. I know it, you know it. Why are you here?'

'I just thought it would be nice to see my sister. I'm having an evening with my sister.' Paul forced a smile, but she pushed in front of him, and opened the door.

It was as if a cyclone had hit a small boutique, swirling at its centre for a few minutes, picking up clothes, sheafs of dresses, nests of sweaters, whirling them around the room like water around a plughole, and then suddenly dropping them so that they fell at random, in carnal tangles, covering every available surface.

At first Paul didn't step inside.

She looked into his face, as if seeking her own reaction there. 'I've been having a bit of a spree, I suppose.'

'What's happening, Hazel? Are you selling these things, stealing them to sell them? Is that it? You don't even need the money.'

She shook her head. 'Don't be big brother, Paul. I just like them, they're just nice clothes, and I can never get rid of anything. Look,' she picked a grey cashmere sweater off the floor, and touched his cheek with it. 'It's lovely, isn't it? Have it if you like, it'll probably fit. It's your colour, isn't it?' She held it out to him with both hands. 'There's no sense leaving it in the shop you know, after the sales they just tear it all up to use for something else.' She was looking right into his eyes now. 'Don't ask me what's happening. What do I know about anything? Don't you know what's happening to me? Isn't that why you're here?'

'It's all right,' he said, 'we can sort everything out.'

'You think so? How do we start? It wasn't even supposed to happen, young men are only supposed to do that sort of thing to each other, and then only when they're drunk, or in packs, or excited about a football match.'

He didn't know how the subject had changed, or how to respond.

'Death comes suddenly, Paul. You should know, you weren't even with her when she died. It's only good sense to make the most of what you come across.' Hazel was still holding the sweater. She offered it to him, the soft material draped over her hands, and he took half a step away from her. Her voice became quieter, as if he had stepped nearer. 'It's a bit of a mess, I know, just at the moment. But it's soon tidied.' She moved her shoulders as if tired already, at the prospect of tidying, of making some space, of clearing it all up.

With his arms full of clothes, Paul thought he would find it awkward to stand. He didn't really want to, anyway. As he had when trapped by his dictionary and documents, he decided to keep still. This was something that was happening increasingly often. He found himself abruptly lacking any will to move, stopping in the middle of the most mundane activity, unable to continue. Instead, he would rehearse past events, mostly things he didn't do and should have done, places he could have been and wasn't. ('You weren't even with her when she died.') He would look at what might have happened, and what might not have happened, and how things could have been avoided. Sometimes when he woke up in the morning he would find that he couldn't get out of bed. Not because he was tired, usually he wasn't, but because he lacked any will to move. He would drift into a monologue, recriminations, or into vivid visual scenes, in which either his absence or his presence was crucial. When he finally made it to the bathroom and washed his face he would sometimes find that he had been crying.

Burdened by clothes, he sat back, deep in his comfortable sofa, tilted his head back, as if floating, as if holding his mouth out of the surrounding water which threatened to drown him.

He had talked to Hazel for most of that night, and had finally persuaded her that she must stop both stealing and buying clothes, and that she must give most of her collection to Oxfam. He had left the next morning, and over the following fortnight

33

had exchanged letters and phonecalls with his sister. ('I'm down to a few *rags*, Paul, and it's *won*derful. It's like a great re*lease*!') She was caught shoplifting at the end of that fortnight, and when the police visited her flat they found it exactly as Paul had.

The doorbell roused him. He got up in a fairly fluid movement, easy enough, after all, with a little incentive, and went straight to the door. He managed to open it by stretching a hand out from under the fat pile of shirts, trousers and sweaters he was still holding. He thought, with some pleasure, that Victoria had come to visit him.

Boyd filled the doorway. He was at least six inches taller than Paul, and much bigger, and he was smoking a large cigar. Dark-suited, grey-faced, he looked like an old-style East European politician.

He took the cigar from his mouth, exhaled and said, still puffing out smoke as he spoke, 'Laundry? I think you've forgotten about me, haven't you? I'm disappointed, Paul. I'll be frank with you, I'm disappointed.'

Five

Paul had read about victims of burglary, their reactions to the violation of their homes. Some added extra locks to their doors and windows, some redecorated, others moved. Paul already had an adequate number of locks, he had a burglar alarm, lights which turned themselves on and off while he was asleep, and a tape which he sometimes played of a dog barking. He had taken precautions. He hadn't anticipated the violator entering, smiling, by the front door.

Boyd's first move, as he strode in confidently and put his briefcase down by the armchair, was to the answer-machine. 'Here it is.' He touched it with fat fingers. 'I feel quite an affinity with this you know, I feel we're quite close.' He turned to Paul. 'Two sugars, please. Do you mind my smoking?'

Paul moved slowly in the kitchen, giving himself time to think. He was trying to plan a strategy when he heard Boyd entering behind him, filling the small area between the units. Paul's movements became self-conscious as cigar smoke crept around his face. Fussing with kettle and cups, teabags and teaspoons, he began to feel vulnerable. It was Boyd's proximity, his self-assurance, and something else: his pleasure.

'I have looked forward to this chat,' said Boyd, as if responding to these thoughts. 'Remind me to ask you later about violence. It's your great preoccupation, isn't it? I want to hear your opinion of the urbane killer. Not the pathetic type who kills fifteen strangers and then himself; I mean the one who's interested in people, develops a relationship with them, and a personal style of killing them. What do you think about the evil in individuals?' Paul turned finally, holding out a cup, but Boyd, reaching out, seemed to miss it. His fingers closed over Paul's forearm. 'I could take your hand,' he said, 'and pour boiling water over it. I'm bigger than you, stronger, I could stub my cigar out on it, or press it on to the red-hot hob.' He released Paul's arm and took the cup. 'If I chose to. Why don't I choose to? That's what I'm getting at.'

Boyd lounged in the armchair, and Paul sat on the edge of the sofa, the pile of clothes at his feet, trying to imitate composure. The tea lurched in his cup as he brought it to his lips.

'Why, actually, are you here?'

Boyd didn't answer immediately. Putting his hands together, palm to palm, he appeared to pray. His large face was impassive. Paul noticed a scar, a thin red valley in his cheek, just above the line of the jaw, beginning in front of his right ear and leading halfway to his mouth, as if pointing to it. He tapped his fingertips together and spoke about the attitude of the Foundation, and the welfare of its employees. He was civil but brisk, and there came a moment when he asked, abruptly, 'How would you, in your own words, describe your work?'

Paul stood up, for once feeling a need to be in motion. Trying to adopt a thoughtful air, he walked to his desk, and then back to the sofa.

'Prevailing conditions,' he said, without any thought, 'the climate . . .'

'A weather report?' Boyd raised his voice to interrupt. He sounded impatient. 'The Feather Weather Report. Well, by the look of all this material,' he gestured with his cigar towards the crowded desk, 'it's not going to be featherweight, is it?'

Paul paused for a moment beside the desk. 'Why are you here?' he insisted, addressing his papers. 'Am I going to be sacked?'

Boyd's face seemed to be naturally inexpressive. It barely creased when he spoke. Even his eyes moved slowly and unobtrusively. His voice however, was versatile. Listening to the voice

36

on the answer-machine, modulating with ease from jovial to sardonic, speeding up and slowing down, lingering before and even during certain words as if reluctant to release them, Paul had imagined a younger, livelier man.

'I have been working hard,' he said, feeling like a schoolboy in front of his headmaster. 'If I've been a bit slow to produce the copy, it's because I don't like to leave anything out. I believe in being thorough.'

Boyd nodded. 'Tell me, Paul, because I'd like to hear it from you, what exactly has happened to your expenses?'

'I've spent them.'

'Would you like to enlarge on that at all?'

'I've spent them almost entirely on subscriptions to periodicals, and on film and video material.'

'I imagine your postman doesn't like you.'

'As it happens, you're right. He doesn't by any chance work for you, does he?'

'Are you suggesting that *we* don't like you?'

'Do you have anyone watching me?'

'*Is* there anyone watching you?'

Paul stopped pacing and sat down, leaning back into the corner of the sofa. 'I don't know. It's possible.'

Boyd sighed, the headmaster disappointed in the schoolboy. 'Anything is possible, Paul, you know that. I wouldn't rule it out. On the other hand it does sound improbable. Staff monitoring . . .' he appeared to ponder '. . . it's hard for me to say anything with any certainty. My department doesn't much go in for certainty. That's the nub of it.' The question didn't seem to interest him. 'But your expenses,' he said, 'which we were discussing, are regarded as a travel allowance. And you haven't been travelling, Paul, have you? You never go anywhere. Don't I remember,' pausing, as if even now he was remembering, 'some brave words at your interview, about your willingness to travel? I'm quite sure I do.'

There was a pause, long enough for an answer, and then Boyd dropped the stub of his cigar into the remains of his tea, and it appeared that the subject had been discarded along with it. Paul wondered if he had made the right responses. He had been complacent, he hadn't considered before Boyd's arrival that his job might be at risk.

Boyd began again. Paul was distracted by the voice. It was the wrong sound to be emerging from the heavy, almost entirely still face. Paul found himself dwelling uncomfortably on the thick red line on Boyd's cheek. It wasn't entirely a valley, part of it was a ridge. At the mouth end, a little drop of skin hung loose, and wobbled from time to time. Somewhere perhaps, Paul thought, a younger, livelier man with a similar scar was using a dull, deep and toneless voice to tell a gruesome story that no one would believe. In his mouth a clumsy, too-large tongue flapped unresponsively, like an exhausted fish.

'Let me tell you what we *don't* want, Paul. We don't want you to sit here totting up the lies in the media. We have several people doing that. We don't want a thesis on the poverty of imagination, or the poverty of desire. We already have a few of those. We know all about the man who won the pools but wouldn't give up his job in the sock factory. We know what became of him. We don't want to hear about the everyday absurdity of the world, or the everyday ugliness. Even though you may justifiably feel yourself to be an expert. We already know about it, you see. We're not really looking for a demolition of popular myths, an anatomy of cultural decline or a stab at defining the *Zeitgeist*. They're just not what my department is looking for. Not from you, Paul. We're looking for something more exciting from you.'

'What you want has never been clear to me.'

'Oh, come. You've had your induction, that stage is over. You've just had a free clarification.'

Paul shook his head. It was like struggling over a translation, or trying to remember a date, knowing that the headmaster was becoming angrier. 'It's still not clear.'

'You could be a useful worker, Paul, in spite of your preference for secondary sources. Mr Walsh himself has noticed your infrequent copy. He read your last package with interest, particularly those pages of the dictionary you included. Unlike myself, he's an admirer of idiosyncrasy, the personal touch. His cryptographers have been at work. But we want something more specific from you.'

'If you want something more specific, please *be* more specific.'

Boyd paused, watchful, and Paul prepared to be told he was out of a job.

'Mr Walsh wants you to find your sister.'

Paul sat forward again. 'What?'

'He wants you to find your sister and then come to his office with her for a little chat.'

'Hazel?'

'Hazel.'

'I don't think so.'

'Oh yes.'

'It doesn't sound very likely.'

'You of all people, Paul, should know that that is hardly relevant. How often has the *likely* cropped up in your notes? How often does it ever crop up? Where would the bookies be if the favourite always won?'

'Why does he want to see her? Does he know that she has a criminal record? Does he know about the shoplifting? The credit-card fraud? The debts?'

'Yes, he does, of course he does. And he knows that the magistrate referred her for psychiatric assessment, and he knows the result of the assessment.'

'So why does he want to see her?'

'Ours not to reason why, Paul.' One corner of Boyd's mouth curled upwards. 'That's my favourite quotation. Somehow I knew I'd have a chance to use it.'

Paul wasn't listening. 'She's spent the last three years or so in institutions.'

'Only the first one in an institution in fact. Since then, what is termed, the community.' Boyd lifted his briefcase on to his lap, opened it slightly, and took out his notebook. 'But you know that, of course. You last saw her in fact,' he consulted the book, 'a little less than two years ago, shortly after the move to the halfway house. You visited her and took her out. There was some difficulty, I believe, an unfortunate scene on a train, and she returned to the house alone. Has she not been in touch with you since?'

'We've lost contact. She doesn't know where I am.'

'I see. Well, we haven't placed her precisely, either. Since leaving the house she has been somewhat peripatetic. It's going to require some detective work on your part, isn't it? I'm surprised at you, Paul. She is your sister, after all. Blood of your blood.'

'I have nothing in common with Hazel. Only a constellation of moles.'

Boyd consulted his notebook. 'Something like Orion.'

Paul, unamused, laughed, and Boyd raised his eyebrows mildly. 'Well, I have seen the photographs. You remember the induction procedure, the check-up.'

'I was pronounced fit. A-One. The doctor was impressed. Do you have access to medical records?'

Boyd looked at his book again. 'You were pronounced physically fit.' He looked up. 'May I ask, purely out of curiosity, why you take such trouble over your physique when you so seldom leave your home?'

'Just for that reason,' said Paul, surprised. 'I need the exercise.'

'But why do you need it? For what purpose?'

'I suppose vanity is involved. Is that what you want me to say?'

'Vanity.' For the first time, Boyd sat forward in his chair. He looked even bigger. He shook his head slowly. 'You don't strike me as a vain man. I would look elsewhere for the reason. Anyway,' he looked down at his notebook again, 'it was felt that you were slightly deficient in, in layman's terms, emotional responses. In particular, you had little to say about the recent death of your mother.'

'I had little to say about it, that much is true.'

'Unlike your sister.'

'Hazel was very upset about a number of things. I remember her doctor mentioning our parents.'

'Her doctor seemed to think that the death of your mother was crucial. After all, it was a traumatic series of events, wasn't it? The two strokes after the incident, the loss of speech after the second. And your sister present throughout, unlike yourself, witnessing. When her breakdown came, when she returned to college, she was considered a suicide risk. I presume you were aware?'

He looked up, eyebrows raised. 'No,' said Paul, 'but . . .'

Boyd returned to his notes. 'However, you did see her, shortly before that time. Visited her flat?' He looked up again.

Paul felt as if one of his internal dialogues was being brought into the light. He shook his head, not to answer Boyd's question, but in response to Boyd himself. No, I don't want to talk to you, I don't want you here. 'Why are you questioning me?'

'There's no need to be evasive, Paul. If there's anything you feel ashamed of, you may rest assured that it will remain confidential. *Is* there anything you feel ashamed of, Paul?'

Boyd had placed his tea on the table by the answer-machine, and was looking ready to leave. Paul had one more try with the question that was bothering him:

'Will you, just before you go, tell me why Mr Walsh wants to see her?'

Boyd sighed again. 'It's not your place. You must have faith. Mr Walsh's methods are sometimes a little antic, they can be hard to fathom, even for me, but his reports are unparalleled.'

'Mr Walsh writes reports?'

'We do not always agree, but I will admit that he is an artist of the report. He facilitates them, using researchers like yourself. He composes them. He extrapolates, studies precedents and long-range prospects, and makes predictions. He finds areas that the Walsh Foundation should become involved in. Where information is lacking, he obtains it, sometimes quite ingeniously. People often work on a report for him without even realising it.'

'And will you tell me the fundamental subject of mine? I suppose he's working on mental illness, is he?'

Boyd replaced his notebook in his briefcase, raising himself from the armchair. He looked down at Paul. 'Mr Walsh sometimes prefers researchers not to see the larger picture. It might prejudice your findings. Find your sister. That's all.'

Paul, feeling daring now the interview was almost over, addressed Boyd's back: 'Is it true how he's so rich? And is he anything to do with the Government?'

Boyd opened the door and turned around, speaking slowly. 'Imagine being sacked,' he said. 'What would you do? With no references, if it was generally known that your work was unsatisfactory?' He stared at Paul for a couple of seconds, and then softened his tone. 'A lot of nonsense is talked about Walsh. It's wiser not to add to it. Yours but to do or die. Good-bye, I've enjoyed meeting you, at last.'

Boyd drove away in a rented car, a big black Granada, which he made look cramped. It was quickly hidden behind the hedge and the bend in the road, on its trajectory towards Norwich, the station, London. Paul walked out to the end of his drive, not quite sure what he was expecting to see. A red Cavalier perhaps, containing an urbane killer. Nothing, only the trees and the lingering smell of the exhaust.

Inside, except for the pile of clothes on the floor, his work-room was now immaculate, his own micro-environment, arranged exactly as he wished.

But he no longer believed in it. Boyd had drifted irresistibly in like some huge polluted cloud. He had left something, some toxic deposit which weakened the integrity of the whole. Now Paul's house was no less frail than his body. Gingerbread. Straw. He locked the door, turning the key with his good wrist, and sat down at his newly-tidied desk. 'Why do you take such trouble over your physique?' Boyd's question jeered at him, Boyd's scornful face awaited an answer. Paul found the piece of paper he had been working on earlier, screwed it up into a ball, threw it away, and began to write again, drawing up a new, more extensive list of things that he was afraid of.

Six

Edmund had murder on his mind, but he wasn't as clear about it as he would have liked. Uncharacteristically, he hesitated on his way into the station. The drunk, his devious eyes catching this faltering, wheeled on him and began to address his rant to him. '*You* know better! You know what I'm speaking of!' Tracksuit bottoms of indeterminate colour, and one of those thick overcoats, which seem stiff with dead and rotting things. Pointing accusingly: 'You know better!' Edmund stopped, gazed up into the cathedral-like arches of the roof for several seconds – This isn't what I need right now – then retraced a few steps, back around the corner, and found a bench. His mood wasn't right, he needed to settle. The drunk forgot him as soon as he was out of sight, found a new victim.

Elbow on the back of the bench, hand on his forehead, Edmund covered his eyes, took a breath.

This isn't what I need right now.

His mood wasn't right, hadn't been right, in fact, for some time. He needed to think things through, study his steps again. The key to composure usually lay in the past, and the subject of murder led him naturally to think of his father. The drunk had given him the place to begin.

Hilary. Hilary towering on the table like the Statue of Liberty, dictating, playing the preacher. Sitting outside the station,

Edmund pictured him, unsteady idol, more devil than divinity. Overcoat, tennis shoes, pyjamas all lopsided. His prick hanging out, drooping below his hairy paunch. He should have been a rugby player, one of those not very skilful workhorses who end up covered in mud and blood. Muscular Christian gone to fat.

'He was humiliated and tortured foooor . . . *you*!' His big, stubby-nailed finger would shoot out and suddenly he had turned into the host of a crazy game show, standing up there, dribbling at both ends, the General Kitchener of the Kingdom of Heaven. 'Do you understand? He left Paradise, left His Father, for *this*!' All his sentences ended in italics. 'For the filthy, heavy human cloak of *flesh*!' And he would pinch himself viciously, making all watching wince, as they remembered those fat, pincer fingers. By this stage he would be swaying dangerously. Edmund, his brother and his sisters had no trouble with the concept of Jesus's omnipotent Father; the only puzzle was why it was such a sacrifice to leave Him.

Then what? Then he would crash to his knees, land on a plate and crack it into several pieces. He would be on all fours, like a dog, and whining like one too. 'He *loved* them,' trying new stresses, 'He *loved* them, the people who humiliated Him. That's what you have to live up to, that's all I want to say to you.' That pretty much was all, because he'd be near enough unconscious by now. The only one humiliating Hilary was Hilary. Snot and tears dripped into his beard, and at last he sank on to the tabletop, and started coughing, snorting, and finally snoring. Tamed giant. He was air-conditioning in reverse, cranking out waves of sour, vomity alcohol fumes.

Edmund briefly opened his eyes, and lowered his hand. 'Ugly,' he said. 'Ugly.' His father might have been in front of him. This was better, he was feeling some anger now.

It was as if Hilary felt it necessary to demonstrate the filth and squalor that he described. And the evening wouldn't yet be over. Out of silence, shots in the night.

One.

Two.

Three.

Accompanied by groans and whimpers, and the splintering of

plaster. Because by now he had taken himself off to bed. Hilary kept a gun beneath his pillow, but the only intruders he ever dealt with were the ones that barged into his dreams. And he never effectively dealt with them, because they always came back. Bullets wouldn't do the job. Michael and Edmund in their room, Dinah and Ruth in theirs, none of them slept very well. Not that they were afraid he was going to come staggering out after them, it was just the groaning that kept them awake.

Groaning. Edmund opened his eyes again and for a moment thought that his memories had conjured the ghost of his father. The drunk was slouching by, scratching himself, and making a sound that could be a groan, or could be a throaty gurgle intended to hack up phlegm. Things were clearer: there was a message to collect, a job to be done. Edmund watched the drunk disappear and then stood and straightened his uniform, navy-blue with red piping, and walked into the station. The left-luggage lockers were in a spacious room alongside Platform One. He entered the room, withdrew the key he had been sent, and found the appropriate locker.

He may visit Senate House library. It is the one he always visits when he is in London. You may wish to wait for him there. He will certainly visit the following address:

Edmund read the whole note, and put it in his pocket. On his way out he was accosted by an enquiring passenger who he directed at random, but with an air of unquestionable authority, to the nearest train. Then he made his way to his car, which stood out colourfully in the station car park.

Seven

It is necessary to get the image just right. Straight spine, one hand resting on the pommel, the reins held loosely in the other, in the crook of the fingers. Above all, it must be effortless. The face is impassive, although not humourless, the eyes move slowly from side to side. Speed in stillness, strength in silence.

Tod didn't see arching trees creating a green lane, the sun dappling through, he saw a horizon as wide as the sea. Monument Valley, high rugged red buttes, cigar stubs of rock, rising out of the sand and the stony ground. His horse was ambling, halfway between nowhere in particular and somewhere else, the movement was gentle, soporific . . . The breeze on his back roused him, cooling the sweat beneath his shirt, and he opened his eyes with a shiver. His horse, a tall chestnut, was munching grass at the side of the lane. He pulled her head up with indecorous irritation, took hold of the reins in both hands, and jabbed her with his heels. In moments he was galloping, lifting himself off the saddle, feeling the wind swarming over his face, glancing back over his shoulder at pursuing Indians.

Paul was at the stables when he returned. Surprised, but pleased to have an audience, Tod sat up again, ramrod straight, and came into the yard like a sheriff riding down his Main Street. He tipped his hat to Paul, as he might to a pretty lady sitting on a porch. 'Mr Feather.' With a creak of his leather chaps he swung off the horse. Paul joined him as he led her to the stable.

'Are you reckoning to take up riding, Mr Feather? I'd be mighty proud to teach you.'

'No, Tod, no thank you. I have a favour to ask, and your mother said I'd find you here. I'm going away for a little while. I want to cancel the papers, and I'd like you to look after the house for me. Just go up there every morning and make sure everything's all right. Would you do that for me, Tod? I don't want parcels piling up outside the door. I'll tidy up, and I'll take some things away with me.

'You're going away, Mr Feather? Where to?'

Paul sighed. 'London.'

'How come?'

'I'm going to see a man called Walsh.'

'That's who you work for, right? He's going to get a Lordship, or a knighthood or something? I saw that somewhere.'

'I'm not too sure how long I'll be. Of course I'll pay you whatever seems reasonable for helping me out.'

'Don't trouble about that.' They were in the stable now. Paul backed away, into the light, offended by the strong, unfamiliar smell of dust and straw and shit. Tod, not noticing, was stroking his horse's neck and feeding her a little hay by hand. 'I guess I envy you, Mr Feather, you jest gitting up and going like that. That's what I want most I guess, to be able to pack up my kit and move right on whenever I feel like it. No restrictions. But I reckon you know that already. How about a drink, Mr Feather, to see you on your way?'

Standing just outside the stable, Paul had not quite heard. 'Thank you. I've left the keys at the shop.' Now Tod was unbuckling a strap beneath the horse's belly. Indifferent, it was dropping fresh turds in a steaming pile. 'I'm very grateful. Good-bye Tod.'

Tod heaved the saddle from the horse's back and turned, to see Paul already walking away. He gazed at him for a moment, uncertainly. 'So long,' he said.

Paul, the man who damaged dictionaries, had the thirteenth volume of his *OED* open on the floor in front of him.

Quemadoro to Roaver. He had leafed through it and found that the missing pages included the word 'report'. He had no idea what significance that might have for a cryptographer. Now he was just browsing.

> **quemadoro** – In Spain and former Spanish territories, a place where convicted heretics were executed by burning.

> **roaver** – *obs.* Rover.

Intrigued, he took Volume Fourteen from its shelf and found the word. There were several definitions, but his eye was not caught by all of them.

> **rover** – 1. *Archery.* A mark selected at will or at random, and not of any fixed distance from the archer. 3. One who roves or wanders, *esp.* to a great distance. b. An inconstant lover; a male flirt.

He felt uneasy at the thought of Mr Walsh drawing conclusions or making plans on the basis of these entries. They seemed a little too prescient. He was now to become a wanderer. Victoria might well accuse him of being an inconstant lover and a flirt. Had he also become someone's target? Paranoia or legitimate suspicion? He picked up the phone, and dialled the number of the University library. It seemed the only reasonable response. His own standards, in which he had placed so much of his faith, now seemed less reliable. He needed an objective opinion.

'I've started to wonder if it could be a blackmail operation. I'm asking myself if my research indicates likely subjects. I don't trust big organisations, and hidden motives. I'm thinking that may be why they want Hazel, to blackmail her, or someone she knows, or me. I've always been willing to listen to conspiracy theory, it's always made perfect sense to me. Maybe it's British Intelligence, some lowly section where staff don't even know who they are, gathering information for some larger purpose. Didn't Boyd mention cryptographers? What was that supposed to mean? I know it sounds unreasonable, it's probably completely ridiculous, but could it be true anyway? Boyd reminded me himself that my research would be nowhere without the unreasonable and the ridiculous. In the last few days I've had a man killing his baby because it cried during his favourite TV programme, a judge hoping a rapist will treat his months in prison as a holiday, and an American senator introducing a bill for chopping the fingers off drug dealers. He wants repeat offenders to lose hands, and then limbs. These are the facts I'm dealing with, and they have nothing to do with laws of probability. According to Boyd, Walsh is making predictions based on these precedents, does that in itself sound likely? What can he be predicting? What can anyone predict? Let me tell you what I mean.'

He shifted a little, to make himself more comfortable, and glanced at her, to make sure she was still listening.

'About a year ago I ran myself a bath, climbed in and, the second I touched the water, felt an excruciating, bristling pain scorching all the way through me. I screamed. I thought I was having a heart-attack. I thought *This is what it's like*, I thought I was going to drown in the bath, I thought, *It's not fair, it shouldn't be happening to me*. But I had it wrong, it wasn't a heart-attack, because in the same instant, all this happening in one stretched moment, I was shooting out of the water like a missile, surface-to-air, I mean I don't think I touched the sides of the bath at all, I just rose straight up on this stunted trajectory, possibly somersaulting, guidance systems burnt out, and I crash-landed on my head on the bathmat. Because it was an electric shock. My bath-water was *live*. Somewhere a wire had lost its insulation, it was rubbing up against something else, that was the story. You see what I'm saying? You just run yourself a bath, and you're taking your life in your hands. The next minute you're a wreck, vibrating on the floor in a puddle of crackling water. I have no idea what was stopping it from being a lethal shock. I didn't understand a word the electrician said. He told me a lot of things I didn't understand.'

He paused again, got no response, and continued. 'I don't know what I'm saying. God is an electrician, that's what I'm saying. What's your feeling, Victoria? Is someone trying to kill me or what?'

For a long time she didn't move, and he began to wonder if she had fallen asleep. Could he repeat that speech? Finally, however, she raised herself on one elbow. 'Let's look at the facts, shall we? Facts are supposed to be your forte. You think someone is trying to kill you, because life is unpredictable and God is an electrician. You fell down the stairs, you've seen a red Vauxhall twice, there are some violent words in the *Oxford English Dictionary*, and your employers want you to leave your house and do your job. Well, on that basis, Paul, I don't think there can be any doubt: have you made a will at all?'

'So you're saying I'm paranoid?'

'Don't dignify it, Paul. Mildly neurotic, self-obsessed, eager to believe that you're the centre of somebody's attention. In other words, just like everybody else. But your big ego, and your attention to detail, which you pretend to regret but which you're actually so proud of, mean that you have to be different, find a place to file yourself. Self-aggrandisement is at the heart of it.'

'It's straightforward for you, isn't it?' Paul spoke without resentment. 'You systematise, you're in control. Empress of India. Will you come with me? I need your influence, to steady me. You could help me. It might not be easy to find Hazel, and it certainly won't be easy for me when I have found her.'

'Listen to yourself, Paul. "I need you." Was that a slip or did you mean it? Here I am, invited to your house for only about the third or fourth time ever, and now I'm needed. Whatever happened to the self-sufficiency you were so proud of? Don't tell me it was all an illusion. Life *is* full of surprises, isn't it? But I thought you knew, Paul, I thought I'd made it clear: Victorias don't play supporting roles.'

'You're not interested.'

'Yes, I am. I like you, you know that. You're an interesting man. Look at this body of yours, you're already losing all those nice colourful bruises, you're already getting back into good shape.' She pinched his bicep just beneath the mauve stain of a healing bruise. 'Look at this, it looks like someone's taken a bicycle pump to it. It's the body for a crisis.'

'So come with me, come with me if only for love of my body. It'll be my body and your brain.'

'You don't want me for my brain. All you want me for is this.' She held up her right hand, as if to display the palm, its propitious lines. 'You want me to hold your hand, squeeze it, and tell you everything's going to be all right.'

'I'll have my motives, and you'll have yours. I don't know what they are, but they'll be compatible. It doesn't matter what they are. You'll be surprised how easily we can get by. We don't have to know each other, in fact we don't even have to know ourselves. We can get around to that later, that kind of thing just happens, eventually. It's a big mistake to hurry it. Analyse yourself and you'll come up with a hundred and one disappointments and flaws. What's happening here exactly? Why are you saying no?'

'I hardly know where to start.'

'But I want what you used to want me to want. Don't laugh at me. Will you marry me?'

'Good God, no. I *already* know myself, Paul, I know what I want, and that's not it. I have an interview next week, the one I've been hoping for. I'm going to enter the business world, a whole new world. New values, new perceptions, new wardrobe, and quite possibly a whole new me. Seems to me you should try it.'

She got out of bed and went to the bathroom. He followed her, rinsed his face in the sink while she showered. He tried to think sensibly about the latest packages he ought to take away with him. They dressed and went downstairs. When she was leaving, they kissed and he held her right hand.

'Well,' he said, 'is it?'

'Is it what?'

'*Is* it going to be all right?'

She laughed, let go, and waved over her shoulder as she left.

Leaving the station with the message he had collected, Edmund pulled in abruptly, and parked at the kerb-side. Lately, his movements had been like this. Jerky, interrupted by inconvenient memories, by periods of reflection, speculation. Like Paul, he was subject to internal interrogations. He watched the people walking along the pavement towards him. Everyone has similar powers, he was thinking, but not everyone is aware of them. Everyone could kill. Edmund had been thinking about it a lot. For instance, if he saw someone now that he didn't like the look of – someone like that drunk – he could get out of the car, shoot them, and drive quickly away. He would stand a better than even chance of escaping. Once you become aware that it is an option, if you are a serious person, everything changes. This awareness was something that Edmund felt strongly, it was something tangible. Sometimes he felt that he was flattening his palms and the side of his face against it. It was as if he was outside a window, and a beat of his fist would shatter it. He had been there once, on the other side. He had killed one person. It was in his mind to kill another.

Paul, in the course of his research, had looked into this subject. He could tell you where it is most dangerous to live (the North-West, and East London), what age it is most dangerous to be (under one year old), and which room in the house is the most dangerous (the kitchen). Men should beware of strangers and friends; women are safer, but should beware of lovers and family members. Both should avoid staring at people, especially in pubs or clubs. Women get strangled, men get shot, both get stabbed.

More than ninety per cent of murders, Paul would have been quick to tell Edmund, are solved. Edmund might have had several replies. The first would have been that he didn't much care. On reflection, he might have added that most murders are committed by people in bouts of temper, who become troubled by conscience. Conscience, as far as Edmund could see, should not be a factor for him. And he always avoided temper. He drove away from the kerb, pulling back into the traffic. He also eschewed randomness. Everything depended on a purpose, even if that purpose wasn't his own.

Eight

Hazel liked the semi-circular drive so much that she walked all the way around it and back out on to the road before returning to the front door. She scuffed her feet in the pebbles as she went, and looked back to see if she could see where she had walked. There were no footprints, just a trail of unplanned valleys and mounds in the meticulously raked pattern.

The house was of reddish-brown brick, warm in the sunlight. Two wide windows on the ground floor, four smaller ones above. Hazel liked this regularity. It was what she expected, and she was very keen to have her expectations fulfilled. The door itself was a paler brown, panelled and well polished, gleaming. Bright brass figures above the spy-hole told her that it was number thirty-seven. Over it there was an arched, opaque window, with red and blue panes; on either side of it, utterly incongruous, white pillars set into the wall. Hazel touched each of these, arms outstretched, as if embracing the doorway. She couldn't flatten her palms against both at once, instead her fingertips played on the stone and she felt a sense of the size and solidity of the place. She was pleased, no one was going to demolish this house with a flex of over-developed biceps.

Behind her, beyond the gates of the drive, a bus passed noisily. She took out her keys, three of them, and inserted each into the appropriate lock. Unhurried, she walked straight in and punched the code which stopped the burglar alarm's shrill beeping. She closed the door and stood with her back to it. The sound of the traffic was cut off. There was a hint of mischief in her smile, as in a child who expects to meet with disapproval.

Shoulders pressed to the door, Hazel called out 'I'm ho-ome!'

Paul disliked the High Street intensely. The house he was looking for was at the end of a Victorian terrace. You turn off the High Street, head up Malory Street towards the technical college, and it's on your left. The instructions were clear enough, but he was dawdling. It wasn't just that he was nervous about the visit, it was London too, having its usual effect on him. The great sprawl of the city made him uneasy, the knowledge that he was completely surrounded by it unnerved him. If he wanted to escape from it, he would have a long way to go, and it would take a very long time. It didn't give you up easily, it held you in its streets of clogged traffic, or on its crowded platforms, waiting for delayed and defective trains. He could travel fifty miles on Suffolk roads in the time it would take him to get from here to the edge of the city. Seven miles to the suburbs. Which would be more bearable, the crush on the tube or the jam on the streets? These were the kind of calculations that went through his mind, along with his general, unspecified unease.

Make it specific, he thought, trying to distract himself. Defining it will take away its power.

The rubbish on the pavement.

The stink and noise of the traffic, especially a motorbike which makes an angry, ripping whine as if it is tearing up the air behind it.

A mother shouting at her child.

Three people walking abreast who seemed not to see me and nearly collided with me.

Two people arguing outside a grocer's.

The sudden blare of a radio behind me.

Overheard chatter, which may well be benign, in a foreign language.

People's faces which, although not all hostile, or even frowning, all seem purposeful, and quite exclusive, intent on a personal world without connections to any other.

Paul walked close to the shop-fronts, brushing windows with his shoulder, and then, finding that he was getting in the way of people using doorways, he walked at the edge of the pavement, trying to bypass the flow. It made no difference, either way he felt vulnerable. Every face a stranger, and now, the new element in his anxiety, the secret ingredient for added zest, every stranger a potential assassin.

This thought, coming as he tightroped along the curb and then stepped down to the gutter to avoid a bus queue, contained a surprising, redeeming touch of humour. Back on the pavement, he stepped out of the way of an old lady pulling a basket of shopping behind her. Assassin. The word was absurd. Politicians are assassinated, and pop stars. Paul had looked into it. People, by becoming larger than life, make themselves targets of those who wish to steal a little of their glamour. When it comes to motives for assassination, principles, these days, are less common than mental illness. There was comfort in this. By no definition could Paul be called larger than life. Glamorous wasn't the word that came to mind. Unobtrusiveness had always been his goal. How could a man who assiduously avoided confrontations, who winced at the sound of other people's arguments, possibly be the target of an assassin?

Hazel began to explore. She had been here before, and the layout downstairs was familiar, but she was interested in detail: the contents of cupboards and the fridge, the books on the shelves and the collections of records and videos. This was always her favourite time, exploring virgin territory, feeling the frisson of guilty pleasure as she looked in private places, adding crucial details to the picture in her mind. She spent more time upstairs, shedding her coat on the way up, leaving it on the landing. She inspected the bathroom cabinet, and noted the wallpaper in the toilet, cream with angular red flowers on green stalks. She looked only briefly in the first room. White walls and a pink bedspread. A tennis racquet in its press in the corner, a child's picture of a house and stick family framed on the wall. The bed made up with clean sheets, a little frill around the pillowcases. Everything uncreased, unsoiled, apparently untouched. She gave a short nod, expectations fulfilled again. She lingered longer in the two bedrooms that showed signs of use. She opened every drawer and cupboard, rummaged through their contents, looked through the wardrobes and under the beds. In each room she sat for a while, unmoving, her expression thoughtful.

'You won't forget the plants, will you?'

'Don't nag her, Emily.'

'And I've left you food to be going on with. You must raid the freezer, dear, to your heart's content. It all needs eating, anyway. But you'll be able to cope with the cooker, won't you? Was it all clear?'

'Of course it was clear, Em, leave the poor girl alone. I'm sorry, Hazel, my wife thinks you need a degree in astrophysics to deal with household appliances. Don't mind her.'

'Darling, don't *pat*ronise me! Oh, he does patronise me all the time, Hazel.' Mrs Standish looked delighted. Mr Standish gave her shoulder a fond squeeze and winked at Hazel. Adam yawned.

'Now is there anything else at all that you want to ask me, dear? Anything whatsoever?'

'I don't think so, Mrs Standish. I think everything is absolutely fine. I hope you all have a lovely time.'

'We've told them at St Matthew's that you might pop along.'

'They're a very nice congregation, you'd find them very welcoming.'

Mrs Standish leant out of the car window and shouted something about the alarm as they drove away. Hazel thought she looked like a poorly-trained Labrador.

There was little to look at in the spare room, where a bed had been made up and a note left for her, reiterating most of Mrs Standish's instructions and guidelines. Hazel returned to the second bedroom she had looked at, a small one with a view of the long garden. Adam's room. On the wall a black-and-white poster of James Dean, walking down a shiny wet, grey pavement. All in black, hunched in on himself, shielding half his face with the hand that held his cigarette. Over the street a cinema showing Fifties' science-fiction. Under the picture, in bold letters: Boulevard of Broken Dreams. Hazel took off all her clothes and put them under the bed. She lay on the bed for a minute, eyes closed, and then, with a little shiver, she got up, took socks and a pair of underpants from the top of the chest of drawers, a blue T-shirt from the middle, and began to dress. From the wardrobe she took a ragged pair of Adam's jeans and a black leather belt. She caught sight of herself in the mirror on the inside of the door, and ruffled her short hair a little. Finally she sat down at Adam's desk in front of the window. She had stuck a picture of him over the desk, and she looked at this for a moment, then she opened the drawer, took out his diary, and began to read.

The cul-de-sac was a short breathing space, but Malory House was disappointingly easy to find.

The door was opened by a slight, middle-aged man in a suit, who looked surprised. 'I thought you were Alan.'

Paul wasn't sure how to react to this. He spoke slowly, with clear emphasis. 'No, I'm afraid not. I'm looking for Mr East.'

The man shook his head and tutted. 'That's Alan,' he said, and went into a room off the hall, leaving Paul standing in a doorway, wondering if he had just spoken to a resident or a member of staff.

He came in. There was a room on either side, stairs straight ahead, and a passageway to what looked like a kitchen. He hesitated. The light in the hall was of a low wattage, giving little more than a yellowish glow to reveal the beige walls and worn rug. The smell was one Paul remembered from his visit to Hazel two years earlier: boiled vegetables and stale air, weak but pervasive. Hoping to avoid the difficulty of talking to the man again, he turned to the right, and found himself in an office. This was better. Fluorescent light and big windows, one of them open. A desk and typewriter, folders and loose papers, a couple of comfortable chairs and a filing cabinet with a kettle and mugs on it. The *Daily Mirror* poked out of a briefcase next to one of the chairs. Standing in the doorway, Paul heard himself breathe out, like a sigh of relief, and he wondered if he had been holding his breath since he entered the house. Eyeing the kettle, the paper and the chair, he felt like a benign intruder, like Goldilocks.

He hesitated again. He was beginning to realise that he was

unused to choosing a way forward, to making even the smallest decisions. He made an effort to think reasonably. Hazel was unlikely to be here, was most likely to be in a bedsit somewhere, living a fairly independent life. But to make himself comfortable with a cup of tea and the paper would be less than conscientious. He was working after all, and he had something to prove now to Boyd, as well as to himself. There was information to be gathered.

The man who had answered the door was reading the *Telegraph*. Paul found this confusing, still unsure of his status. He sat down, not next to him but within conversation distance. This room had large windows too, but thin curtains were drawn halfway across them. There was another weak lightbulb, doing nothing more than changing the colour of the darkness. Paul knew about workplace illnesses and environmental stress; he thought he might mention it to Mr East, if he ever turned up.

Fortified by this idea, he turned to the expanse of newspaper beside him. 'My name's Paul,' he said. 'I wonder if you'd mind if I asked you a couple of questions?'

The man lowered his paper and rested it in his lap, leaving his finger inside the page he had been reading. 'Vic,' he said. 'I don't really feel like answering questions.' He adjusted his tie slightly. 'Alan didn't say anything about anyone coming. He usually does.'

Assuming he was being taken for a socialworker, Paul continued, feeling on surer ground. 'Well, it was Alan I wanted to see, really, but I wondered if you could help me at all. I'm looking for Hazel Feather. Did you know her at all?'

'Alan didn't say anything about you. Two weeks ago, someone came with a whole list of questions, he went on for an hour and a half, and I missed my tea.'

'Well, it was really only Hazel I wanted to ask about. I'm her brother.'

'Well, you'll know it all then, won't you? Or you'll learn soon enough.' He had a thin face, with clusters of wrinkles around the mouth and eyes. It was easy to see why, because while he was talking he would now and then screw both up a little, as if monitoring what he was saying, or what he was about to say. He

58

never looked at Paul, he looked above him and slightly to one side, speaking querulously, clearly not pleased at being prodded into conversation. 'I don't know what to tell you,' he said. 'Things go all right here, and I'm almost out of it. Do you want to hear?'

Paul nodded, solicitous.

'I've been here ten years and I'm ready to leave next year. They said to me I should have left before, but I've been going on in my own time, and I've been right, haven't I, because I'm all right now and I'm ready to leave next year. I just find it difficult to get out of bed some mornings, but that's normal, isn't it?' He darted a glance at Paul, who was thinking about some of his own mornings. 'I have these lines, you have them too, on my forehead, because of worry. Can you see them?'

Paul nodded, involuntarily drawing his fingers across his own forehead. Maybe Vic had taken him, appropriately enough, for some kind of researcher. A researcher of a kind that Paul tended to feel contempt for, working on some small, specific project, not relating it to any larger picture. This was fine: once Vic had got past his own story, he could steer him towards Hazel. He said, 'I'm familiar with what you're talking about.'

'I know you are. I get restless, I pace up and down, you know what I mean. But I went at my own pace, that's what I recommend to you. Next year is my year. But it feels as if I'm carrying a weight.' Mouth and eyes screwed up. 'It's just anxiety.' He picked up his newspaper and opened it at the page he had been reading.

Paul was slightly taken aback by the man's self-awareness, and by the list of symptoms which seemed to tally neatly with habits he had observed in himself. And what did he mean, 'that's what I recommend to you'? 'But Hazel,' Paul said, betraying impatience, 'did you know Hazel?'

Vic lowered the paper so he was looking over the top of it at Paul. 'She's *your* sister.' Then he seemed to relent. 'She was Bea's friend. Funny you coming after she's left.' He smiled unexpectedly, revealing a whole new set of wrinkles. He didn't seem to expect it himself, because he raised the newspaper again, covering most of his face. 'Don't worry,' he said, 'best not to. Take it in your own time, that's what I would say to you. You're not in a bad place.'

Paul hadn't had time to absorb this before he heard the front door open and close, and Mr East appeared.

'Hello, Vic, all right? Mr Feather? Come into the office.'

Paul followed him, and duly got his cup of tea, and his seat in the comfortable chair. East sat down opposite him, on the other side of the desk, stretching out and leaning back as far as his straight-backed chair would allow him. 'Sorry I'm late, case conference. I hope Vic kept you occupied.'

Paul smiled, feeling a little more at ease again. This office was not unlike Victoria's, in the library. 'Certainly. I took him for a member of staff and he took me for a future resident. It was a little disarming.'

'I expect it was.' He spoke without inflection, and Paul recognised with some surprise an air of tired animosity in him. 'Why do you want to find Hazel?'

'She's my sister.'

'That hasn't made much difference for the last three years.' Still no inflection. It was like waiting for a punchline. 'I had a glance at her file, to refresh my memory. She talked about you, wrote to you. You didn't want to see her then, did you?'

'I don't quite see what you're saying.'

'Hazel left us a while ago, but I still feel some responsibility for her.' Open hostility would have been easier to handle, but any accusation remained implied. East's tone was official. Distant, but not rude, as if he was mentally checking regulations as he spoke. 'It may not be the best thing for her, to have you reappear. You know, I presume, that she tended to idolise you, and fantasise about you. She's got over you now.'

'I'm not some lover, who's best forgotten. I'm her brother.'

'Quite. Her only remaining family. For a while you had a great deal of significance to her, more than a lover. Were you aware of that? She decided that you could help her.'

'I don't wish to discuss this with you, Mr East. She's my sister, and I wish to see her.'

She's my sister. I'm her brother. She's my sister. He had acknowledged her three times, but each time without much

60

self-belief.

'I'm quite sure you have no legal right to prevent us from meeting.'

'That's correct. I'm just trying to give you a sense of responsibility, just in case you don't already have one.' East sighed, as if it took too much effort to sustain animosity. 'As it happens we don't know exactly where she is. She was unusually fortunate in that she was able quite quickly to take on a flat because of her parents' money.' He paused. '*Your* parents. But she hasn't been there for some time.'

'You don't know where she is? Is that normal?'

'Mr Feather, she left this place. That's why we call it a halfway house, because it's halfway into the community. There was a short stay with a friend, a period in a hostel, then the flat. We helped her to find a place that she liked. She's found a job, writing. Her GP knows about her situation, she's not on any medication, and we think she has recovered. She is confident that she has, and so are we. There's really nothing more to say. She's a capable woman. We miss her.'

'So how can I find her?'

'I don't know. As I understand it, she's not in her flat much. You could talk to her neighbours, stake the place out if you like.'

'Who's Bea?'

He paused again, and leant back in his chair. Tiredness now seemed to take over completely. His mouth moved, and for a moment Paul thought he was sneering, but it moved again, and he realised that his teeth were tugging at the skin inside his lips. 'A friend of Hazel's,' he said. 'I suppose you could talk to her parents, they might even be interested to meet you. Bea would never see them when they visited, so Hazel always talked to them for her. They got on quite well. It was good for her, your parents being dead, you not being much in evidence. The contact was important, for everyone.'

'Can't I get in touch with Bea herself?'

'She died. Took some pills. She killed herself. She left here a few months before Hazel, wouldn't take her parents' money, couldn't get what benefits are available, got into . . . a mess.' East pronounced the word fastidiously, as if he was only using it for

Paul's sake. 'Her mother still came here afterwards, to see Hazel and talk about Bea. They got on well. You can have her address if you like.'

Paul took the address from East and got up to go. As he put on his jacket and left, he felt himself watched no longer with any trace of animosity, however faint, but with curiosity. For some reason, he found this more disturbing.

In a different part of the city, Hazel stopped suddenly on her way to the station and took a camera out of her plastic bag. She seemed highly interested in a building opposite, taking several pictures of it. Passing in front of the building, oblivious to this, was a young woman in a pale-blue outfit. She wore a short, tight skirt and a matching jacket with large padded shoulders, a nipped-in waist and an extravagant flounce over her bottom. Her skirt was so tight that she seemed to be moving her legs only from the knees down. Her white stockings were patterned and her heels were so high and narrow that she stumbled now and then as she walked. Her face was a creamy pink mask, her lips bright red and her shoulder-length hair, brunette, was permed into tight, shiny curls.

On the tube, Hazel took a notebook from her bag, opened it, and then paused, with her pen in her hand. Although she considered for some time, she only came up with one word 'Neanderthal'. She put her notebook away. She was wearing a burgundy polo neck, grey trousers and a sports jacket, all of which were too big for her.

Paul's mood didn't improve back on the High Street. Oddly named. Why is a street thought of as high? If only it were, elevated above the crowds, inhabiting the sky. He took refuge underground, finding, with something like despair, that it was the rush hour.

Sitting on a bench on the platform, his back pressed against the wall, his fingers gripping his plastic seat, he tried to be unobtrusive. He had just heard that his train was going to be delayed because of a person on the line. When he eventually approached the edge of the platform, he saw a mouse nosing around beneath the rails, apparently unconcerned by the thunder approaching overhead. Here was a role model to envy.

Things got worse on the train. Paul became aware suddenly that it was three days since he had seen a newspaper, and he began to worry that he might be missing useful material. Perhaps something vital that would give coherence to the whole enterprise. He regretted the missed opportunity with the *Daily Mirror* earlier. He was in danger, he felt, of becoming rusty, just as he was in danger of becoming unfit. He had completely forgotten, for instance, to mention to East his points about the environment of the house, the stress it was likely to induce, the dangers involved in bad lighting and the wrong kind of carpet. Another missed opportunity. He could have been reasonable and logical, with a very large number of facts at his fingertips. East would have been on the defensive.

Newspapers surrounded him now. Paul was able to read fragments over the shoulders of people on all sides. 'Two English girls'. What? Kidnapped? Raped? Murdered? Smuggling drugs? The fact that the word 'English' was used suggested that what had happened had happened abroad. Foreigners had almost certainly done something to these girls (who might of course be women), but what? In moving his head 180 degrees, and with the help of peripheral vision, he could see several references to sex and death, some economic news, and one case of appalling cruelty. His expertise at gleaning the essence of stories was here only enough to tantalise him. Sex, death, cash and cruelty. These were just the staple elements of his research, nothing without the detail. He found that he wanted to read over every shoulder at once, to avoid missing something crucial. Could he ask to borrow a newspaper if someone was reading it at the time? Paul didn't think his social skills were up to this, but he tried to weigh the embarrassment against his growing unease. His hotel was still seven stops away. He felt an urge to snatch a paper from a stranger's hand. Hazel instantly and vividly came into his mind. Creating a scene. How could he even contemplate doing something similar? He concentrated on the reward he would give himself when he reached the news-stand at his station. He would buy everything, absolutely everything on offer, and take it all up to his room. The train slowed down again. Six stops still to go. Why was he so frightened? Best not to think about Hazel. Emulate the mouse. Concentrate on breathing evenly, on not doing anything foolish, on not thinking about madness. He would never forgive himself if his control broke down. He clutched his strap more tightly, leaning his head against his arm and closing his eyes as people moved past him. His head rested on his hard bicep. He swayed slightly from side to side as the train jerked away again and began to pick up speed.

Brother and sister travelled beneath the city, passing close by each other, moving in different directions, in adjacent tunnels. Paul, in a state of barely-controlled anxiety, Hazel, pleasantly composed. Hazel had heard the same announcement concerning a person on the line, and she was daydreaming. Her fantasies about suicide invariably involved water. She is walking down a crowded shopping street when it begins to rain. The rain hits her skin, she feels its wet touch, and she starts to dissolve. It's not like acid, it doesn't burn her. Her flesh runs like paint. Her features blur to a blank face. People gather as at a car accident, and watch. She vanishes. Alternatively, like a monk setting fire to himself, she will stop in the middle of a shopping centre and invert a bucket of water over her head. Wicked Witch of the West. She will bubble and boil and collapse in upon herself, reduced to a sticky puddle of matter. It will cause a little comment. (People are trying to *eat*.) Then efficient cleaners in uniform will come and remove her unsightly remains, and everyone will go about their business, only slightly diverted.

Edmund Staples had several fantasies, some of them suicidal. There was a clear picture in his mind. He is in a warm bath, watching the blood sluggishly emerge. It looks as if it is being slowly pulled in a steady string from his veins. Once it is out it disperses in a cloud, in shades of red and pink. He imagines no pain. He lies back comfortably, watching his life drain away. He had considered this. He had lain in a hot bath with a razor blade in the soap dish beside him. It was reassuring, to have this option available to him. No matter how bad things got, there was always this clause in the contract, waiting to be invoked.

In different moods he thought of something less discreet, less lazy. The high building, the bridge. Falling, of course. He imagined that as he fell, face down, arms and legs flying up behind him, sky diver, the wind, the momentum, would draw his mouth into a rictus grin. He imagined the air battering him. He imagined he was falling, desperately grinning, not on to pavement or water, but into an outstretched hand, like a mattress of springy, padded flesh.

Bea took several painful days to die, having misjudged her overdose, of liver failure.

Nine

In the library, Paul could relax. Soon he would consult the dictionary he had taken from the shelf, but first there was a package he had brought from home. He had scanned them all and discarded most of them, but this one had attracted his attention. The usual padded envelope, but no note, just A4 sheets.

Relaxing, in an environment he trusted, with a piece of research material in his hands, he began to read.

POLAR BEAR

'What you have to know about me,' said Bel, 'is that I am the product of a completely ordered world.'

'Completely?'

'Completely.'

'Are you sure?' I was quite proud of my scepticism, pleased that, through everything, it had remained intact.

'Of course I'm sure.'

'Because I don't know if any such thing exists. I've never met it. I'd more or less decided that there was no such thing.'

'You've never had Sunday lunch at my house.'

'No.'

'Then you'll have to take my word for it.'

My scepticism succumbed gracefully. I had no wish to offend this woman. I was doing my best at this point not to offend anybody.

'Daddy's perfect carving. The buzz of the electric knife. Mummy's roast. She doesn't choose her roast for the value or the quality, she looks for symmetry. Chicken is easy, but she has to search a bit for beef or lamb. Vegetables arranged in pretty patterns. I used to think she got a ruler out to measure between knife and fork, and a protractor for the glasses. That's how it looked. She must have hoped for twins, to complete the effect. Andrew and me weren't symmetrical. She should have had identical twins, who she could have dressed identically, and sat directly opposite each other. We didn't really fit. The atmosphere, Joan, you can probably guess.'

I nodded, I could guess. I didn't mind being told, however. After a period of intense interest in myself, I was finding it refreshing to listen to other people. And other people, I was finding, were usually more than happy to talk about themselves.

Bel continued. 'Sepulchral. White tablecloth, silver, pink napkins. Subtle restraint. Mummy is a very suitable case for treatment. There's a condition, isn't there? Obsessive neatness? But I'm only telling you this because I know I can trust you not to spread it around. In fact my worst nightmare is sharing therapy with my mother.'

We were cooking. It was our turn. There wasn't much room in the small kitchen, but we weren't in each other's way. I was peeling potatoes into the sink, Bel was chopping vegetables on the surface behind me. It was early afternoon, but the light seemed to be having trouble getting through the net curtain. All the time that Bel was talking, she was concentrating on chopping the vegetables. First she washed them, then she chopped them, then she washed them again. There was a little pile of carrots in front of her, perfect matchsticks in a delicate orange bonfire. We had been planning to cook the meat in Guinness, but instead we had been passing the can between us, taking regular swigs. Bel's cat watched us with interest, following our movements.

'We'll use stock,' said Bel, 'no one will notice.'

'Are you sure?'

'You don't know these people. Only Vic ever complains, and even him only if it's foreign. They like my cooking. Alan will be nice about it, of course, and Vic will say it's very tasty, June won't say much at all, and Ian will be sycophantic. You wait.'

*

The time isn't supposed to be important in this house. Part of the point of this house is that there is no fixed schedule. Independent living means creating your own schedule. Self-determination, in this theory, involves wearing a watch. Nevertheless, the time is always the same. Six-thirty. After Neighbours *and the* News, *before evening classes or group meetings, or further television.*

'Mmmm.' Ian beamed at Bel and Joan. 'Delicious. You are clever. I can really taste the Guinness.'

Those who didn't cook are washing up, and Bel and I are in the sitting room, in the old, deep armchairs. Bel is explaining things again. She enjoys this role, showing a novice the ropes.

'The mess, you see, is precious. Not a lot of mess at home, as I think I said. Everything just so. And there wasn't much leeway, I don't have to tell you, in the hospital. I think you'll find your own room, Joan, your possessions scattered, a liberation.'

Bel's face is turned slightly towards me, but her eyes are on the television. As Vic, Ian and June enter, loud music announces that something is starting.

'I suppose the mess is something personal.' *I speak as the credits end.* 'It's your own.'

'Sssh.' *Vic frowns at me, Ian glances an apologetic smile my way, and Bel turns wholly towards the screen.*

Soap operas are especially popular. In the hospital reactions would often be out loud and unrestrained, as if people were testing their responses to see how they sounded. 'He's evil.' 'She shouldn't be doing that.' 'That one has a good heart.' Here the etiquette demands silent attention. I look from face to face, and at the cat on Bel's lap, buzzing with contentment.

✻

The floor in Bel's room is hoovered and bare, the blankets tautly stretched over the bed, the wardrobe and drawers shut. It is what I imagine a cell looks like. On the desk is a short letter, and in the bin beneath it are several screwed up balls of paper.

I enter the bedroom, stepping softly because the television is in the room below, and sit down at the desk. I glance at the letter in front of me, which takes only seconds to read. Then I begin picking among the rejects, taking them out of the bin and unfolding them. Soon, including the original one, I have four in front of me.

Dear Mummy,
I told you that's how it would be if I came. I didn't want it, but I knew it would be that way. You tell me I think about things too much, expect things to happen and then make them happen. If I could change, I would. How easy it must be, to be you! Nothing to worry about, except polish and dust, and surfaces in general. And pleasing Daddy. Pleasing Daddy isn't one of my options. Don't expect me to explain. I think there's a deal that has to be made, I think for me to get better I have to not see you both.

Dear Daddy,
I'm sorry I broke that glass. I know it wasn't very 'constructive', but what you said wasn't right. I don't want to cause you pain. Communication is our problem. Lack of it. I just have nothing to do with your lives

69

anymore, no connection. So I run out of words. It's very hard to talk to you, is the point. If you've nothing nice to say, say nothing; that was what you used to tell me, wasn't it? You made sure I had nothing nice to say. Do you want to know the truth? I worked it out on the way back here. If you would die, a nice quick heart attack, then I'd live with Mummy quite happily. Will you do that small thing for me?

Downstairs the television was still audible. It was safe to assume that Bel would be there at least until I heard the credits. The next letter was longer. The sloped handwriting was more cramped, hard to read in places.

Dear Mummy and Daddy,
Why were you so interested in those nature pro-grammes? We used to watch them together, after din-ner, with cups of decaff or tea, and a bar of chocolate shared around. A few squares each, on a plate. Polar bears, leopards running after antelopes, close-ups of insects. Do you know what I think? I think even you, both of you, nurse secret dreams of different lives. My mother the bird, and my father the alligator.
*   I had a plan. I read that in Panama people are allowed to keep lions and pumas and so on as pets, and it gave me an idea. What I wanted to do was bring a polar bear home, have it come in after dinner as we were all settling down for the TV. Can you imagine? They look cosy, but they aren't. It would lumber around the room, smashing everything, while you shrank back into the sofa, trying to disappear. You'd run out and cram into the downstairs toilet, because it would be too big to get through the door. Just its paw would get through, crashing through the panel like a horror film, claws like sickles, milky white. I doubt that you'd be able to squeeze back far enough, so you'd get a few lacerations each. You'd stay there, behind the locked door, bleeding over each other, peering through the hole in the door and listening to the bear ripping the house apart room by*

room, until finally it would exhaust itself and go to sleep on your double bed.

Would that disrupt things a little? I don't know. I don't know if it really would. You'd just worry about your carpets and sheets mum, dad would wonder about the insurance. We're covered for fire, flood, and earthquake, but what about polar bears? After it had been quiet for a while, the police would come, or the army. They probably wouldn't get a tranquilliser gun in time, they'd have to kill it, it would be too dangerous to wait. Maybe it wouldn't mind being killed. It wouldn't be happy where we live would it? It would be lying there in the midst of clouds of duck down, great white beast, dreaming of ice and drifting snow, a tight circle of guns all trained on it . . . and then someone would shoot it in the head, in the middle of its dream, so that it wouldn't even know it had died. Maybe it wouldn't mind.

I carefully screwed up the three rejects again, and replaced them in the bin. Downstairs, the television was as noisy as ever. I reread the letter on the desk.

Dear Mummy,
I'm so sorry that the glass was broken. Anyway, I'm sorry that it upset you, and caused such a commotion. My God, you'd think it was a family heirloom, the way Daddy reacted. I was especially sorry that we didn't get a chance, as a result, to get out into the garden. It must be at its best. Next time, I hope. Thank you for the cuttings anyway, which look very nice in my room. Andrew seems to be well. You come here next time, I'll make you a meal. My cooking here is appreciated. Lots of love,
Bel

*

Two days later, 'My parents are coming at the weekend,' Bel said, 'but I don't want to see them. Will you see them for me? I thought you mightn't mind.'

I said that I wouldn't mind. I was thinking that my interest in other people could develop into a genuine hobby. And after all, I told myself, I'm doing my best not to offend anybody.

In return, I made her listen to my dream. In the first weeks I dreamt mainly about the hospital. The sign in the Common Room there was a recurring image, but it was always jumbled.

> *The year is Tuesday.*
> *The season is February.*
> *The month is 1990.*
> *The day is Winter*

Alan said this was a transitional phase.

*

Mr and Mrs Standing seemed pleased to see me. They took me to a hotel for tea and sandwiches.

'So you're Bel's chum, are you?' said Mr Standing. 'We're very pleased she's made a friend, aren't we, dear?'

'We're very pleased,' Mrs Standing agreed, her face melting with gratitude.

'How, in your opinion, is she?' asked Mr Standing.

'I think she's very well.'

'Splendid. We quite understand that she may not be up to company, just at the moment. Splendid. She's lucky to have a friend like you.'

*

When Bel's cat went to sleep, it wound itself into an almost perfect circle. A furry, black-and-white cushion, rising and falling gently, purring quietly like a phone left off the hook. Its face was always invisible, burrowed snugly into its body, but the one thing which broke the circle was an ear, pink triangle poking out like an aerial, listening for danger. I observed. It was a time when I hoped to find lessons in everyday things.

✳

We went swimming together, coping with the difficulties we encountered together. Bel, bony and large-eyed, me, shorter and boyish, feeling self-conscious about our bodies and our space in the changing room with its doorless cubicles, and the pool itself, with its covertly staring boys and men. New rules of behaviour to learn. The water made no demands, however. We churned through it, and it was patient, it hid us and enabled us to be bold. We jumped off the high board hand-in-hand, and when we surfaced again in the choppy water we rejoined hands, grinning triumphantly.

As we sat in the café after our swim, we even exchanged friendly words with two young men, and admitted that we might see them at the pool the following week.

Afterwards we went to the precinct, and sneered at the clothes together. Bel even listened for a while to me on the subject of clothes. It's an area of expertise, we all have at least one. We browsed in a department store and I bought a gift for the house, a dolphin which would splutter and flipper its way along the bath.

We walked through the furniture department, surrounded by three-piece suites grouped around coffee tables. Synthetic, velvety materials in mauve, TV chairs which tilted back and produced footrests, materials guaranteed to burn slowly without giving off toxic fumes. Bel stopped and grasped my arm, squeezing so hard that it hurt. 'Look,' she said, excited, 'it's him. What's he doing here?'

'Who?'

The question seemed to change Bel's mood. 'My father. He's been following me.'

I followed her gaze, and saw a man on the other side of the room, closely examining a scatter cushion. I had met Mr Standing twice by this time. Was it him? It was impossible from here to know.

'I'm not sure . . .'

'Why can't he leave me alone?'

Bel released my arm, walked towards the man, then began to run, barging past a couple talking to a salesman, falling over an armchair and picking herself up, knocking a vase off a table. Caught between following and retreating, I watched the scene develop. This wasn't a place that I wanted to be. Bel had pushed the bending man on to the sofa, and he was raising the cushion over his face to protect himself. In two months in the house, I had already come to some important decisions: I was going to listen to other people, to watch for lessons, to avoid giving offence. I wished to learn quietly.

Bel was shouting at the man now, punching the cushion, and several salesmen were approaching. People at the edge of the department were stopping to watch. Measured aims, I thought, crossing the room. Suites were left at unusual angles, as if intended for families that preferred not to look at each other. Achievable goals, I thought. A salesman grabbed Bel and they both fell on to the sofa, on to the man with the inadequate cushion. They were yelling at each other. I wondered what my best response to this might be. Should I join the mêlée, the three of them now struggling on the carpet, halfway under a coffee table, or should I join the people behind me, gathering in a semi-circle, at a safe distance, pointing, sighting down the line of their accusing fingers, all trained on Bel?

So much depends on the correct response.

*I sat on the sofa the three bodies had just rolled off, picked up a magazine from the floor, (*What Today's Woman Wants*) and began hitting the salesman with it. Alan is a teddy bear, but I don't agree with him that this was a setback in my transitional phase. He wasn't there, in the centre of the department full of prototype sitting rooms. I tried to explain it to him: it felt like a stage-set, as if we were rehearsing still for our portrayal of normal family life. The public didn't like us, but the public notoriously prefers a musical, or a farce, and will go a long way to avoid anything approaching reality.*

When Paul had finished reading he gazed up at the high ceiling, considering. The story of Joan and Bel and Alan. He was used to fitting things into larger schemes, finding patterns and drawing conclusions, perhaps it was why he was so ready to believe in conspiracies, but for some reason, he found himself unwilling to examine this document too closely. He turned to the dictionary with a sense of relief, but with Joan still partly occupying his mind.

Ten

report – *v. trans.* 9.c. To fire (a gun); to be the cause or occasion of firing.

Libraries have nothing to do with violence. Paul felt dissociated from what he was reading, these words he had sent to Mr Walsh, which now seemed like some not particularly subtle hint. Libraries are considerate, imposing rules of silence so that you don't have to speak to anyone, erecting partitions on desks so that you don't have to look at anyone, even providing cubicles, so that complete isolation is available on request. The Reference Room was surrounded by these cubicles, each labelled by a letter of the alphabet. For a moment when he had first come in, Paul had thought that each one was full of information relating to its letter. He had nearly walked into the one marked 'R', expecting to find there every wrinkle and resonance that he was looking for.

report – *sb.* 5. Relation, reference, bearing, connexion.

The library was a haven. It was a world of relations, references, bearings and connexions, but not of things. A world of allusion, at one remove from actuality. Things between which relations and connections existed, things referred to, things with bearings on other things, all these were missing. Everything enjoyed the luxury of being theoretical, contingent on a reality which existed elsewhere. There were bridges, but there was nothing at either end of the bridges. Suspended in mid-air, they led the traveller from one absence, to another absence. If there was an assassin – surely still an unlikely theory – then there was no place for him here. There was room only for the concept, for words which might have some relation to an assassin, could possibly refer to one, have some bearing on one or connection to one. Only words. And there were rules to prevent the words from even being spoken.

report – *sb.* 2.c. A formal statement of the results of an investigation, or of any matter on which definite information is required, made by some person or body instructed or required to do so.

Libraries are formal places. They depend on formal statements and definite information. There is a predictable and meticulously observed pattern to a library, allowing the reader to pick a particular book from a huge collection with very little trouble. Books here could be measured in metres rather than in numbers, yet any one of them could be pinpointed in minutes. Order was the key. That was how the dictionary itself worked, making sense of language, cataloguing it and translating words into other words, each one traceable by the simplest of systems. This was how Paul thought of his report in his more ambitious moments. A formal statement of definite information, one which would allow the reader easy access to a vast range of knowledge. He could imagine no higher aim than to impose a pattern, logical and reasonable, on the hostile, chaotic mess of experience. Paul did not exactly think that he was achieving this, but he felt that in some small way he was working towards it. In any case, it comforted him to have the idea in mind; a Platonic ideal of the report.

report – *v. trans.* 2.d. To say factually.

What could possibly be simpler, or more attractive? Paul liked to think of himself as the conductor of an orchestra of facts. Facts were versatile, and could be played in an infinite number of arrangements, always creating different tunes and harmonies. A librarian, he thought, played a similar role. That was why he found it so difficult to understand Victoria. If he was her, he wouldn't change jobs. If he was her, in fact, their relationship might be easier. He would work in complete contentment in the library, she would please the Foundation and herself by exhausting her travelling expenses. There was a pleasing symmetry about this idea, but at the same time a world of confusion beneath it. His use of pronouns was faulty for a start. If he was her, then he would have to be female. This need not be a stumbling block. It was possible that he wouldn't have much difficulty attuning himself to what is supposed to be feminine. Victoria would certainly not have a problem with traditionally masculine qualities, such as assertiveness. It was intriguing to think of the different ways in which their roles might alter. Mostly, it seemed, for the better. Gender was a subject his research had barely touched on, perhaps because one of the beauties of his work was that it so rarely pertained to himself.

He realised that he had strayed a long way from facts. Here was another problem: for a man who loved facts, he was easily tempted by speculation. Who would he rather be than himself? How could he be different? How should he have changed events in the past?

He picked up the heavy volume of the *OED* he had been working with, and walked alongside the shelves until he found its place. His mind was still on Victoria, reaching up to replace a book in the university library. A colourful picture: blonde hair, red suit, white shirt. This library was gloomy, only permitting light grudgingly, through small windows. He had missed her last night, alone with a TV in his hotel bedroom. His mind had lingered on her. He had phoned her, but got no answer, left no message in response to the brisk request on her machine.

He returned to his place, noticing as he did so a blue-uniformed security guard leaving the room by the door behind the issues desk. A folded piece of paper lay on top of his notes. It had his name on it.

'But . . .' The word was a quiet exhalation of air, just enough to make someone sitting nearby frown at him. He unfolded the paper.

'Faith, Fear and the Search for Hope.'

Paul stared at this for a few moments and then, as a possible pattern began to occur to him, a particular set of references and connections, he dropped the note and ran for the door through which the security guard had disappeared.

He found himself by the turnstiles in front of the lift, watching the doors sliding shut. A shrinking slice of blue was just visible. He pushed through the exit gate and leapt at the button, slamming his hand on it just too late to prevent the lift from beginning its descent. He took a step back, looked around, and then barged through the swing doors to his left. A short corridor, and then the stairs. He was fit again, fit enough, he could beat the lift, this was the crisis he had been preparing for. His good hand sliding over the banister, anchoring himself on the turns, he took the steps three at a time, breathing fast but evenly, feeling full of vigorous purpose. What a good way to solve a mystery! Physically, with fast reactions backed up by muscle, a strong arm. Paul evaded a couple coming slowly up the stairs, burdened by books, almost danced out of their way, self-conscious urgency giving him grace, and he had reached the bottom of the staircase, the final two steps, before he fell, tripping over himself in his enthusiasm and launching himself into a sprawling, skidding bellyflop on to the polished floor. He ignored the pain. He ignored the signals from his toe, wrist, chest and, here was a new one, his back, as he lifted himself and set off again like a sprinter, a clumsy one, slipping wildly, barely recovering his balance, his momentum beyond his control as he shot through another set of swing doors like a macho cop bursting into a suspect's hotel room, and flailed towards the figure emerging from the lift, grabbing its shoulders with an urgency that had more to do with his desire to stay upright than any kind of violence.

The woman in the blue dress looked at him in horror, shaking off his hands as if he carried some disease. He stumbled and fell against the wall, where he was able to lean, managing to keep himself from sliding down it towards the floor.

'Take my bag,' she said, offering it to him at arm's length, 'please, take it, my purse is inside.'

They stared at each other for several moments, she fearful, he wide-eyed, panting, unable to utter a word. Slowly, as if not wanting to startle him, she withdrew her proffered handbag and began to back away, step by step, as one might retreat from a fierce, if rather bewildered, wild animal.

Paul had a half-hearted look around, and saw no sign of the security man. He took the journey back to the fourth floor very slowly, trudging up the stairs one at a time, giving himself time to compose himself. He was surprised by his actions, by his relish at the idea of a confrontation. This wasn't like him at all. He was not himself. He was surprised, too, by the vulnerability of the body he had taken such pride in. One reason to have a good body was to be able to forget it, to take its competence for granted when it was needed. Something had gone wrong with this idea. He barely felt competent to continue climbing the stairs. He did however, one at a time, a steadying hand on the banister, breathing deeply, attempting to keep his spine erect, and his thoughts eventually began reluctantly to turn to the note which had been left on his desk, its frightening implications, which almost certainly had something to do with violence.

Bored, she looked out over Adam's limited but perfect view. A paved path led from the house across the lawn to the vegetable patch, Mr Standish's allotment. The grass was framed by flowerbeds planted at regular intervals with bushes. The allotment, deemed unsightly by Emily, was fenced by bamboo hung with leafy runner beans. At the far end, just visible, was a well-cropped hedge.

Cats liked this garden. They patrolled it day and night, stalked birds and each other, and basked, limbs splayed, in the sun on the path. Hazel had already watched one fight from Adam's desk. A tortoiseshell eyeballed a black challenger swag-

80

gering towards it. At the conventional distance, both froze and, like Japanese duellists, crouched, staring at each other for long, silent minutes. When they sprung they whined piteously, as if anticipating hideous pain.

She waited patiently, but apparently it was too hot for a performance today. She looked down at her photographs, and her pad of A4 paper, and pushed them aside. She was bored with Adam's father. It was time, she felt, for a change.

Things weren't always like this. Paul was prankish once, fond of attention, given to unsuitable behaviour. His thoughts wandered as he walked, and for a little while he stopped conspicuously turning his head this way and that.

He is standing on his head, singing. The smiles of his mother and her friends are turned upsidedown. He has an excellent view of ankles. One man has little gold diamonds on his green socks, visible between dark trousers and black shoes. Even aged six, Paul finds this timid flamboyance odd. Why not green trousers, with gold diamonds shining all over them? Paul as it happens is wearing green shorts, and a red T-shirt which has fallen around his chest. Thin ribs stick out beneath smooth white skin. His father has recently died, but he is singing 'Happy Birthday'. (One or two voices begin to join in and then quickly fade away, embarrassed.) Shoes are also interesting. He can see brush strokes where polish has been applied, and he can see spots of dirt that have been missed. High heels look especially high from his vantage point, and fragile. How is it possible to stand on them? Who would choose to try? His favourite shoes are dark, unshiny brown leather. He has finished his song, but he is still standing on his head, hoping that they will now continue what they were doing, allowing him to watch from his unusual angle.

He fell into memory easily: bad memories, concerning the incident, his mother's subsequent strokes, Hazel's illness, and good memories, concerning the more distant past. Why should this be so? He dismissed this question. He preferred not to ask himself awkward questions. He was going to visit Bea's mother, therefore mothers were on his mind. In this way the present had a connection to the past. No mystery.

Bea's mother lived in a wealthy area. Houses well set back from the road behind walls and large gardens. His phone calls unanswered, Paul had fallen back on his imagination. He was expecting a formidable woman, tennis-club member and giver of dinner parties, a woman with a strong forehand and a good line in small talk. He had been wondering how best to present himself, how to make the most favourable impression. It was possible after all that Hazel had given him a bad press.

Hazel, of course, is watching him through a crack in the door, big, admiring grin on her face, even though he has won their game. The game is Dares. They have become very involved in it over recent weeks, and skilful at choosing tasks. The trick is to think of something challenging and outlandish, but not quite difficult enough to be rejected outright. As the game progresses from day to day, they explore and stretch the limits of what each is prepared to do.

Irritatingly, Paul couldn't remember his mother's reaction. Was she laughing? Was she angry? Or was she just silent? He resented his bad memory, felt cheated of something that belonged to him, disturbed that he could not remember whether she was offended. It was pleasing, though, that he had performed the dare. He liked the boy who was able to do that, causing a minor sensation, gaining face in the eyes of his sister. Bringing his attention to detail to bear on the present, Paul could find no such audacity. How would he go about causing a sensation now, and impressing Hazel, or Victoria? By lifting a heavy weight? By doing a large number of press-ups in a minute? In his maturity he discovers purpose only in physical activities, in pumping iron and in the discipline of exercise. No wonder Victoria thinks he is interested only in making love, not in love itself. He takes a boyish pleasure in daredevil leaps and breathless chases. In other areas he fails. He compiles a report for three years before he finds he doesn't know why he is doing it, or who he is doing it for. He becomes more preoccupied with memory, and with speculation, than with the present. He realised that introspection had crept up on him, but it was too late to stop now. The present then, this must be the implication, holds no attraction. He tried, in his methodical way, to summarise, because there was always consolation to be found in an orderly approach. One could at least identify the limits of the problem: he lacks purpose, that's all. And self-belief. And courage. And human contact. He lacks love.

Before he turned into the drive he saw, parked further up the road, a red Cavalier. It couldn't have followed him from the library because he came by tube. It is a popular car. He never thought to look at the number plate of the one in Aldesham, or of the one in the university car park. Nevertheless, he was sure it was the same one. The driver was no more than a shape, a shadow. As Paul stood and stared, sinking under waves of self-pity, the car's headlights flashed, like a nod of confirmation.

Yes, it's just as bad as you thought. All those fears that keep you awake at night? They're all coming true.

All the determination he had discovered in the library had left him. He felt unequal to this latest development. The unfairness of it seemed to him outrageous.

Paul walked quickly up the drive and pressed the bell, leaving his finger pressed on it for ten seconds, wondering whether, if nobody answered, he would be able to escape through the back garden. His mind was back on his mother, and on violence. The incident that occurred four years earlier meant that the two were always inextricably linked now. The unlikely had become the actual, facts had betrayed him, just as, he stretched painfully to relieve the ache in his back, just as his body had betrayed him. He heard someone approaching behind the door, and he took his finger off the bell. He breathed the words, 'Thank God.' Shelter. He almost thought it was going to be his mother, but instead the door opened to him and revealed Hazel, mirroring his astonishment but adding to it a smile of pure delight, as if he was the answer from a gracious God to a not particularly hopeful prayer.

✳

INCIDENT

This happened. She was driving to the library, up a hill made narrow by parked cars. She went carefully, because children sometimes ran out from between the cars, and because the road was narrow. It was a sunny day, a bright blue sky filled her windscreen, and her window was open.

She was approaching the corner when around it came a shiny blue Ford Fiesta coming much too fast, swerving on to her side of the road, into her path, announced by music blaring from its windows. She remembered these details afterwards. Something about the music made it seem unreal, she said, first it was very quiet and then there was this noise. It was like that film where the helicopters go to war to the strains of Wagner. The car was like a cross between a loudspeaker and a compact tank, and the flash she caught of the driver's face didn't reassure her.

It swerved back out of her way, but not far enough, because there wasn't much room or time in which to man-oeuvre, and her bumper caught the Fiesta and engraved an almost straight grey line in its shiny paint. She could have driven on at this point. The Fiesta slammed to a stop before it had completely passed her, but she could have simply driven on. She looked in the mirror at the man getting out. Her son's age.

'Fucking bag!'

That is what he said. Almost an oxymoron, 'bag' being a fairly cosy term of abuse. She told me it was all in the way he said it, shouted it. Teeth. Screwed up face. A monstrous look about him, like something not human.

This face is the last thing she remembers. A witness remembers the rest, a child standing between parked cars who, in the world which existed before the Fiesta stopped, might carelessly have run out into the road. She got out of the car, and the young man punched her, and when she fell down, he kicked her. Wordlessly, with a look of concen-tration. Soft sounds. Short kicks and long ones, with a backswing, carefully placed. Kicking people was a skill he had developed. She moved her hands and arms to protect

84

her breasts, and he would kick her stomach. She tried to cover her body, and he would kick her face. He gave little grunts as he worked. When the other car appeared, and he decided it was time to go, he had his leg drawn back and he was aiming at her head as if, the child said, as if it was a football.

A lengthy period of treatment reaches a turning point.
My doctor, teddy bear, his velvety voice:
'What would you say, Joan, was the cause of your breakdown?'
Myself, fragile, my shivering voice:
'Despair.'

Eleven

'Prove all things; hold fast to that which is good.'

This was the thought in Edmund's mind, at the moment that he flashed the headlights. But it was qualified, there was a suggestion of doubt, of a rising intonation, a question mark at the end of the phrase, as if, while he was affirming his faith, he was simultaneously asking, 'Yes, but *how?*' Internal interrogations. He had hoped Paul would confront him, as he had tried to in the library, and so remove the need for thought, for hesitation. Disappointed, Edmund was now at a loss.

Trace it back, trace it back. The answers lie in the past, where the present was made. Test the past to vindicate the present. Back to this, his only reliable resource: memory. He would prove all things. He would begin again.

Discrete images, resolving themselves into a narrative.

Dinah, entering Hilary's study cautiously, bringing his lunch. Nights there was his act on the table, stomping around like a child in a tantrum, but days were worse, because he was less predictable. He'd be scribbling his latest glosses into his pad of A4, or he'd be bent over the Bible on his desk, face between his hands, fingers clenched in his hair, staring down like a microscope, trying to glean every last nuance. This was how he spent his time. He was a watchman before; he used to sit in offices at night reading, talking to himself, boring his workmates, drinking. Nothing had changed much.

Then, sometimes, he'd make an effort to be a father. You could see him, making the effort. He could be jovial. He loved magic, the fan of cards offered eagerly, the sleeves rolled up and the big bare hands displayed. Some of his friends from his church wouldn't have touched cards, but he wasn't a man for conventional prejudices. He'd be delighted when the Jack of Diamonds turned up facing the wrong way. He'd be watching faces, waiting for the astonishment which was duly displayed, every time. He'd draw a lesson: proof of miracles, evidence of his latest theory on predestination. He loved to dazzle, and those heavy hands, palms large enough to hide packs in, did move surprisingly fast. That was the other side to him. Entertainer. But the mood was fragile, and from there back to tyrant was a short step. Ex-watchman, he was vigilant. He had a burst of fury ready for any little crime: eating too fast or too slow, staring at the table or looking around the room, spending too little time or too long on homework. He was the household God.

He divided the family with his heavy hands. His oldest son, apostate, left home when Edmund barely knew him. Escape was always on Dinah's mind too. At the time of the crucial events Edmund was fifteen, she was nineteen, and she was the one Hilary's finger usually pointed out. 'He was humiliated and tortured for *you*.' More than once, when she came home late, he knocked her down. His blows looked awkward, but they were effective, heavy hands moving with surprising speed, up from his side, swinging round to club her in the face. His follow-through was like a tennis player's, his hand up by his shoulder. Top-spin forehand. Edmund remembered the very last time it happened, seeing her tumbling back into the front door, slamming it shut. By this time, her plans to join her older brother were already laid. Edmund had looked down from the landing. They were like a couple of mis-matched boxers, her on the floor staring up at him, and he knew that it was time to make his own arrangements.

What did he do? What choice did he have? There could be no

revolution, the regime was too repressive to allow it. In any case, Edmund didn't want to be a dissident, he swallowed all the ideology, he just wanted some personal freedom. All he did was create small spaces he could mark out as his own. Discreet, sanctioned escapes. He joined the Scouts, and learnt the pleasure of predictable rules, and a uniform. To wear the same clothes and behave in the same way as everyone else was like a holiday. Who could tell him apart, in a hall full of green shirts and yellow scarves? How could he put a foot wrong, with the rules so clearly defined? Conforming was a great luxury. (Later, he was to find the same thing in the army. The strict regulations which punished anyone who trespassed outside them, even to the extent of wearing a beret at an unofficial angle.) School was harder. He never really knew what to say to other people, or how to behave with them. He never learnt the trick of being liked. Best to contain himself, he thought, tread carefully on alien territory.

Dinah had a long face. Mournful all the time. He'd nag her to tell him about their mother.

'She used to kiss your eyelids before you went to sleep. Lay a hand on your forehead as if you had a fever.'

'Do you look like her?'

A long face, and fair, almost colourless hair. Big blue eyes. Edmund didn't think people would call her pretty. Too pale. She nodded, in answer to his question. 'And I've had her influence,' she said, 'so it's taken me less time to learn. Your problem, Edmund, is that you're too young to remember her properly. It's hard for you to learn how to live.'

That's what she said; but he was more resourceful than she knew. By the time she finally left, without warning or any word of where she had gone, his plan was already settled.

A Friday morning. He saw that her bedroom door was open, and he knew straight away, spontaneously, that he was on his own. He went back to bed in the room he shared with Michael, and prepared himself, tried to psyche himself up. It was summer, and school had finished, so there was nothing in the way of his plan. He didn't know what he was trying to achieve.

Withdrawal, that's all. He hated Hilary, but to hate him seemed to be the same as hating God, so he had no weapons except passive ones. He gave up speech.

What a good experience it was. He felt he should have done it years earlier. Nothing in the world quite so liberating. Lonely, obviously, but no more so than he was used to. What a surprise. He was ready for an ordeal, for struggle, but instead he enjoyed it. Nothing is ever what you think it is going to be.

They had an undercooked frozen meal, packet to oven to plate in twenty minutes. Hilary dribbled lamb rogan josh and spouted the most incredible rubbish about Muslims and Hindus. He called it his latest field of enquiry. Silence gives you the gift of distance. Freedom from the tyranny of the correct response. While Hilary held forth, Edmund just concentrated on his food and allowed the voice to blow around ineffectively, like a wind around a house. Concentration improved. He made discoveries. Absence of speech made him see and hear more clearly: he noticed contradictions in Hilary's declarations, saw his vulgarity all the more clearly as he chewed simultaneously words and mouthfuls. It may sound absurd, but there are any number of good excuses for Edmund: it occurred to him for the very first time that Hilary might have made some mistakes in his interpretations. Not just about other faiths, but about his own. This was a serious shock: if Edmund could prise Hilary and God apart in his mind, then he would be free to hate his father without restraint.

Hilary dribbled curry sauce, pontificating, unaware that something critical had happened.

Still, as two days and then three days passed without comment, he was beginning to get uneasy. He was expecting confrontation. Fantasies of himself holding out bravely, like some martyr faced by the Inquisition. He might have welcomed suffering. Dramatic, pain-drenched fantasies. He had not yet understood that a process of change was underway, one that would leave nothing unaffected.

'Edmund,' Hilary pushed away his empty plate and looked at

him. 'What's the matter with you? You've been like a mouse for the whole meal.'

'For the whole day,' said Michael.

'All week,' said Ruth.

He looked at each of them in turn – nice touch this – belying his nerves, and pressed his lips and shook his head.

'What?' said Hilary, banal as ever. 'Lost your voice? What on earth's got into you?'

So he took out the pad and pen he had prepared for this moment, and wrote 'I have taken a vow of silence'.

Michael and Ruth giggled, and then looked at Hilary apprehensively, ready to take their cue from him. He was still looking at the note, as if it was taking him a very long time to read it. He looked at Edmund. Eyes cross-hatched with red veins. 'When did you last speak?' he said finally.

He wrote 'Three days ago'. Steady hand.

'It's true,' said Michael. 'He hasn't said a word to me for at least three days.' Edmund was surprised he had noticed. He almost liked the little creep. At the centre of their attention, he found his uneasiness evaporating. This was something to relish after all, the reluctant admiration of the twins, the unprecedented uncertainty in Hilary's observant eyes. Unsure how to handle being out of the spotlight, his father was hesitating. Now he leant his head on his hand, and covered his eyes with his fingers. His mouth was a hard, slightly down-turned line. This was how he prayed, looking like a man trying to contain his impatience. Pious pause. They waited, well used to long hiatuses in meals, conversations, even sentences. They had been known to go on for several minutes, with no one allowed to move or speak until Hilary looked up to give the latest bulletin. This time though he raised his head after about thirty seconds.

'All right,' he said, with the air of someone who has consulted an expert, and had his views confirmed. 'Nothing wrong with that at all, as long as you're planning to take it seriously. Now go and do the washing up with your sister.'

Edmund did as he was told, but lingered in the doorway as Ruth ran along in front full of questions, long enough to hear

Hilary instructing Michael to watch him carefully, and be sure to report any lapses.

On the evening of the seventh day of the vow, Hilary didn't leave the house after supper, cooked inexpertly by Ruth. Instead, he invited Edmund into his study. A confidence boost. He hadn't expected unusual privileges; the most he had hoped for was a little peace. Someone was smiling on him. Someone more senior than Hilary.

'I wish to tell you about your grandfather,' he said. 'His name was Eusebius, as you know. But do you know what it means?' He barely paused. 'It means "pious". Do you remember him at all?'

How to forget him? A man with a name like a skin disease and a voice like a frog, who seemed fantastically old, and who used to take Edmund's face in his hands and kiss him on the cheek, near the mouth. Odd combination of wetness and dryness, saliva and cracked lips. Edmund asked him once where his mother had gone, a question that even then he didn't dare to ask Hilary. Eusebius told him she had gone to be with God, which made sense. Obviously being with God would be better than being with Hilary, but why on earth couldn't she have taken him with her?

In answer to his father's question, Edmund shook his head.

'I owe everything to Eusebius,' Hilary said solemnly, 'just as you owe everything to me. That's why I'm so proud of what you're doing. It's no accident that I named you Edmund, you know. There's much to learn from names. Yours means happy protection, or shield. You are the shield of the faith.'

Later, Edmund looked up Hilary's name. It meant cheerful.

They sat together in the study, Hilary at his large desk, gesturing over it, Edmund in the armchair, old brown leather. Hilary loved his study. Leather and wood, books. He probably thought it lent him gravity. He probably would have administered punishments there, headmasterly, if that hadn't always been a case of impulsive, on the spot, hitting out. The armchair was never quite comfortable. The back was too low or too straight, the cushions too small.

'Keep still while I'm talking to you.'

Edmund just in time bit off a meek 'Sorry'.

His father was droning on about Eusebius, the church-going and scripture-reading habits he had instilled, which, of course, had been no more than a useful foundation for the promising young pupil. The general idea Hilary was trying to impart was that he had grown beyond his teachers.

'When I was your age my path was just beginning to reveal itself. I could see my way forward, a difficult way, one which involved the ghastly everyday world of pain and work, but one I accepted. It was my task to live a religious life while playing my part in this irreligious world. Perhaps now I would choose differently, perhaps I would choose not to play any part in this world. In India there are people who become holy men at thirteen, and swear never to speak another word. They make stranger vows, never to sit or lie down. I've seen television programmes about them, these silent people, leaning on swings, grinning. Faces smeared in ashes. One vows to raise his arm in the air and not lower it again. It shrivels, and becomes withered. They look mad, but they aren't. They leave the material world behind while still living in it. They are looking for freedom from the cycle of death and rebirth. Because what is it for? Living and dying and living again? The only answer is to abdicate, to step out of the struggle. They believe this requires suffering. Mortification.'

Edmund looked suitably solemn. He was remembering his sister's words: It's hard for you to learn how to live.

His father paused, his tongue moving in his mouth, sucking this last word like a sugary boiled sweet. There was something in his tone. A tiredness, a wistfulness. 'You have chosen well,' he said. 'My influence has worked well in you, better than I had hoped.' His eyes seemed to return to Edmund from a great distance. 'I expect you have a goal in mind, that you wish to achieve through adherence to your vow?'

A slow nod. He had identified the tone: envy. His father envied him.

'Good,' Hilary continued. 'Always strive for enlightenment.'

Edmund nodded again. This was not the goal he had in mind at all. He even smiled. To deceive Hilary gave him a remarkable, thrilling sense of power, a brand new sensation which he felt tearing at the pristine boundaries of his world. He need not settle, he began to realise, for the passive option of withdrawal. His plan could be much more ambitious.

Outside the house, Edmund shivered, and turned on the ignition so that he could bring some heat into the car. What was the purpose of this reminiscence? Did it make him feel more ready to confront Paul? He tried to explain himself: it was good practice to look at how he was made, moulded, prepared. Through testimony: justification.

Prayer didn't help. Where once his prayers were confident, now they were requests for clarification.

How have I arrived in this place, with this intention? What should I be feeling now? I feel regret before I've lifted a finger. I feel doubt. You conjure me. Here is the Jack of Diamonds, appearing with predestined ease, every time the trick is performed. You conjure me, and I duly appear in the appointed place.

'You've not given me an easy way.' He spoke out loud. He looked down the road towards the high-walled house, his words only a little louder than the silence.

Twelve

Hazel overcame her surprise first. Paul, for all his anxiety, had frozen on the doorstep, and she had almost to pull him by the wrist over the threshold and into her arms.

'Don't just stand there. Have you grown shy?'

She was grinning with delight. He was allowing himself to be manhandled, but wasn't really helping. Surprise seemed to have made him unable to move or act. As she kissed him and hugged him, his expression was that of a man giving the probable every chance to reassert itself, before he accepted the unlikely.

'I didn't expect this,' he said.

'Poor Paul,' she disengaged a little, but still held on to his arms, like a mother looking at her son, 'and you hate the unexpected, don't you? You look quite haggard.'

As she led him to the kitchen, he glanced into the sitting room, and caught sight of a high-backed burgundy sofa, as long as a rowing boat. It floated in a bright rectangle of sunlight on a pale-blue patterned carpet. Hazel led him on through the hall, but this stately picture stayed in his mind and began to reassure him. He might for now be powerless in the face of unpredictable events, but this place at least could be a haven. This walled house. He couldn't imagine it being invaded. No one unsuitable could sit on that sofa.

The kitchen continued the theme. Heavy pine furniture, clean

94

white surfaces. Not a place for anything untoward.

They sat down on opposite sides of the table. 'This is where Adam and Bea used to sit for their meals,' said Hazel. 'They're brother and sister too. But Bea's dead now.'

'I know.' Paul adjusted his seat, and told her how he came to be there. 'Is Mrs Standish out?'

Hazel shook her head. 'Out in Formentera. I'm house-sitting.' She was abruptly impatient with explanations. 'Paul, why are you in such a state? When I opened the door you looked terrified.'

'Oh,' he rubbed his eyes with his fingertips, shifting position again, wondering if he should risk upsetting her, wondering also if she would still be there when he moved his fingers. 'It's a bit hard to explain.' He moved his fingers. She was looking at him expectantly.

'Try.'

That word made the difference. He lowered his hand and returned her look, seeing her face for the first time. He had last seen her, Boyd had reminded him, a little less than two years ago. Brothers and sisters who become separated, ignorant of their relationship, are supposed to find each other attractive. He looked at her as a stranger. Large eyes, high cheek-bones. Her lips a little fuller than his, although that might be less to do with genes than with his habitual purse-mouthed expression. Her chin not as square as his, her skin smoother, as if less marked by experience. Why should that be so? His hand moved up to his forehead, and he traced the lines that Vic had noticed. Odd that his flesh should expose him in that way. It seemed unfair: shouldn't Hazel, with her history, have the worry-lines? But then he remembered his sense of desolation as he approached the house. How could Hazel, smiling airily at him, match his recent experience? They were a similar height, but of course she was slighter. What on earth was she wearing? This was nothing like any of the many dresses of hers he had seen. White, pink striped, with pink flowers within the stripes. It wasn't even a very good fit. This concerned him, because he was convinced of the importance of appearances. So could he be attracted to her? No. Her smile was too broad, her manner too demonstrative.

95

He preferred a little gravity, more poise.

'Try,' she said.

It seemed that she was telling him that she wasn't to be treated as fragile, that there were no subjects it would be better to avoid.

'I bet you're dying to tell.'

The words however, were still difficult. It was a ludicrous thing to have to say. Victoria was right, at the heart of paranoia was a monstrous egotism. He adjusted his chair again.

'Someone wants to kill me.'

Hazel was smiling. 'Even if I wasn't an expert in body language,' she said, 'even if I didn't know a host of non-verbal hints, I'd see through you. Do you know what you're doing, Paul? Every time you touch your chair, you move it an inch or two away from me. If we talk much longer, we're going to be at opposite ends of the room. I think what you need at the moment is more space.'

Paul was disconcerted when Hazel made a detour to the garage to pick up a heavy roll of hosepipe. She had him pass it to her through the kitchen window, where she connected it to the tap. Paul put the hose in the hand that emerged from the window, and heard a cheerful 'Thank you!' Wasn't mental illness associated with abnormal responses? Surely this banal activity was an abnormal response to the news that someone was trying to kill him?

'We'll have the sprinkler in the middle to start with.'

Obediently, Paul carried it out into the middle of the garden. Just as he set it down, it began to spin round, soaking him before he could run out of its range. There was delighted laughter from the house, and then Hazel reappeared, carrying a mat and a basket in which Paul could see secateurs and a trowel.

'Sorry,' she said, responding to his expression with mock seriousness, 'I just couldn't resist it. Here,' handing him the secateurs, 'dead-heading first.' He followed her to the rose-bushes along the edge of the garden, and she lopped off a withered bud. 'Now please tell me all about it, Paul, I know you want to. What reason could anyone possibly have for wanting to kill *you*?'

Paul tried to brush the water off his clothes, and shake it from his hands. 'Religion,' he said. He was aware, as if observing the emotion, of being slightly stung by her emphasis.

Hazel nodded, without looking up. 'How did it happen? Whose toes have you stepped on?'

It was sunny, but too late in the day for warmth, and Paul's damp shirt was sticking to him and making him shiver. 'It's some nutter,' he said, and then he dropped the secateurs and took hold of a rose branch, pricking himself on the thorns, and pulled. His hand scraped along the stalk and he pulled off some leaves and the flower. He dropped to his knees and took hold of the central stalk, pulling again, and digging at the same time with his other hand, getting his legs involved, using his strength. *In a crisis I'll be strong.* It was a much harder thing than you might expect. He tipped his head back, staring at the sky, pulling with his whole body against the clutching roots and the sucking weight of the earth, and when the bush erupted from its bed he fell back with a cry that sounded like pain. The bush, scattering earth, was thrown from his hands. It landed behind him, upsidedown on the immaculate lawn, exposed like some frail, spindly creature unused to daylight.

Hazel had watched all of this quietly, making no effort to intervene, squatting by her bush, impassive.

When he had lain on his back for some time, panting, his breathing gradually slowing, she came and knelt beside him on the grass.

'Now tell me,' she said.

And he did. Still shivering, like someone who has witnessed an accident or an explosion, he began to talk. Falteringly at first, and then more confidently, sitting on the grass with his arms around his knees, he discovered that he was full of words, and full of the hope that to explain his predicament might reduce it to a manageable size. *Explaining* was everything; any situation which could be explained in terms of cause and effect must surely be redeemable. He described the work he had done on fringe religions, cranks and con-men, personal development, self-help philosophy. He mentioned his aptitude for finding overlaps and making connections. He explained how he roped in Paganism and Satanism, as well as some of the trendiest new things. 'And to pull it together neatly I centred it all around Jerome. Have you heard of him? Not the Saint. The sinner, in fact.'

Hazel, studying the brown-edged, crinkling petals of a rose, shook her head. This was good too, to be able to expound on his work in this way. Victoria's tolerance for it had always been low.

'Faith,' he said, 'is what I'm talking about. Faith and fear and hope. What I called, although I'm not exactly claiming copyright, "Faith, Fear and the Search for Hope". The Walsh Foundation turned all my research on belief-systems into a pamphlet, and published it under my name. I'm assuming that a follower of Jerome read it. Some fanatic. He's after a sort of revenge.'

'Who was Jerome?'

'A flash in the pan. Just an evangelist-type operation, travelling show. He had a clever knack though of stirring up a bit of controversy and media attention wherever he went. He had charisma, I think. And then he died, or was killed, in a storm of accusations about drugs, varieties of fraud and God knows what else. Headlines everywhere you looked, building him up as the Devil himself, you know how they do. And the story broke as I was writing the pamphlet – that's the point, Hazel – so I gathered all my arguments around him, and basically used him as an emblem. He was perfect.' He tried to keep the pride out of his voice. 'I analysed what actually made audiences respond to him.'

Hazel was watching him closely. 'And your answer was faith, fear, and the search for hope?'

'Yes. Or at least my answer, after some audience analysis, and setting aside the factor of the preacher's eloquence, was the equation that faith in these alternative religions is mostly just a combination of fear and hope.' He remembered the pleasure he had found in coming to this summary. 'I could give you several examples,' he said.

Hazel dropped a handful of shrivelled rose petals. 'That

98

sounds like you, Paul.' She drew $F = Fe + H$ with her fingertip in the earth. 'Crazy for answers. Like "fanatic". One little word to wrap it all up.'

Paul brought her up to date with the events of the last . . . how long? The fall on the university steps, the security guard, the ubiquitous red Cavalier. To shatter the life he had carefully created for himself had taken only just over a week.

'I think I met your man,' said Hazel, straightening, showing interest at last. 'He said he'd come to see Mr Standish, but he didn't seem to know why. Tall man, good looking but a bit skeletal. Long white raincoat and, now that I think about it, a blue suit. I wonder if that was his security guard's uniform? I wonder if he likes uniforms? I found him intriguing. He was just about as nervous as you were when you got here.'

'He was sitting out there watching me.'

'You mean he's still out there?' Hazel's attention was now fully engaged. She stood up. 'Well, we must talk to him.'

'*Talk* to him?'

'How else do you expect to deal with him?'

'The police.'

'And they'll tell him to stay away from you, they might even give him a court order, and he'll ignore them totally if he really cares about this.' She seemed abruptly to lose interest again. 'Let's not start arguing yet.' She fetched the uprooted rosebush. 'I'm going to replant this. I still want to know why you're here, then we can decide what to do next.'

She dropped her mat on the ground, knelt on it, and pulled on thick gardening gloves. Her dress overflowed the mat and lay on the earth. Paul watched her, with the curious feeling that there was a strategy involved in what she was doing, beyond just an effort to calm him down. Let's not start arguing *yet*. So far, she had made him do all the talking. Her composure was calculated, she was holding something back.

'This is like prayer,' she said happily, digging the trowel into the dry earth. 'I love it. Any evangelist I followed would be a gardener. The colours in this light. Bea was in love with the garden. She could tell me what it was like any day of the year. You plant something, she used to say, you care for it, and look!

99

Life. It was a way of being with her mother too. She used to say that if only they didn't have to speak to each other, they could get on fine. She could show her mother a plant that was doing well, and they'd smile, or if something wasn't thriving, they could console each other, silently.'

Paul said, 'Did you send me that thing? That story about her?'

Hazel ignored him, trowel in hand, reflective. 'Speaking to anyone was a problem, even to me. Her eyes slid away, she couldn't bear to meet people's eyes.' She glanced back at Paul, smiled, and glanced away again before he had to decide where to look. 'Do you like gardening? What *do* you actually like, Paul? Do you know I don't know anything about you any more? How is your eye-contact?'

Paul was still sitting behind her, not helping her replace the bush he had vandalised. He looked out into the middle of the garden where glittering loops of spray were creating small rainbows. Outside, a killer was probably still waiting for him. Staking him out. Assassin. Meanwhile here, at the bottom of the garden, he was getting to know his sister again, and she was playing verbal games with him.

'Walsh wanted me to find you,' he said, still not looking at her.

The name was like a spell, clearing his mind. Walsh was one of the business Emperors that Victoria seemed to admire. Walsh could take responsibility, take control of the situation. It was clear now that those pages of the dictionary had no bearing on some fanatical, half-mad assassin. The suspicion had only arisen because of Boyd's stupid, sinister pose. Paul decided he would mention Boyd's threats to Walsh. The name was like a blessing. He said it again, in a tone of pleased surprise, as if he had just spotted him walking across the lawn towards them. 'Walsh.'

'Why?'

'Why what?'

'Why should he want you to find me? Does he like reuniting families? What exactly does his Foundation do?'

Hazel wasn't watching him, still concentrating on digging. 'You've never heard of it?'

'Tell me what it is.'

'An independent research body. It has a variety of private accounts and some government ones.' It was what he always said. The words had ceased to mean much.

'What kind of accounts?'

'Oh, I don't know. Reports usually. The Food Safety Council, London Regional Transport, government departments. A variety.'

'And what is your report about?'

It was what Victoria had asked, in the coffee bar, and what he had found himself, in his own front room, asking Boyd. Boyd had said it wasn't necessary for him to know, but surely once it had seemed clear? It had grown, and changed. Where had it started? Something about . . .

'Patterns of behaviour,' he said. 'Violence. That's where it began. But it grew, you know how one thing leads to another. It snowballed. I don't know exactly. I'm just one part of something larger that Walsh is doing.'

He waited for some further reaction, some snide comment, but nothing came. He spoke to her bent back. 'I don't know exactly what he wants from you, but I assume it's something to do with mental health, actually. I mean he's probably doing some work in that area. I hope you don't mind. You can always tell him you're not interested.'

'I might, if that is what he wants. But I have a feeling he's after something else.'

'What, exactly?'

Hazel finally looked around. 'Haven't you guessed? I'm just a part of the background, Paul. He's studying you.'

The sun was much lower now. From downstairs, the wall made it impossible to see if the car was still there, and from upstairs the trees blocked the view.

'How are you now?' said Hazel. 'I don't think you should worry about our assassin. I think he's a bit half-hearted, or you'd be dead by now. Revenge is a complicated thing, he may not have got to grips with it yet. Why don't you change your clothes? You're still damp.'

Paul ignored her, so she left the window, with its festoons of pink curtains, and sat down at the dressing table. She surveyed the creams, perfumes and powders, and then unscrewed the gold cap from a small, round glass bottle. She held it close to her nose and sniffed, then nodded.

'This is Emily's favourite.' She dabbed a little of it on her wrists, looked at herself in the mirror, and moved her hands through her short hair.

Paul turned from the window, saw her adjusting her dress, and said 'Why are you wearing Mrs Standish's clothes?'

Hazel laughed. 'You had me worried. I was beginning to think you imagined this was my own taste.' This touch of vanity allowed Paul to smile uncertainly in response. Hazel got up, and walked over to the wall of mirrored wardrobes opposite. Several reflections began to lecture Paul. 'Don't you remember how we used to dress up in our parents' clothes?' she said. 'Sometimes we give up children's games too easily.' She opened two long doors. 'Mr and Mrs Thomas Standish,' she said, gesturing inside.

'I see,' said Paul, sitting down on the big double-bed. 'You are what you wear. Bit of an old idea, isn't it, Hazel?'

For the first time, she looked impatient. 'No, no, no, that's not it at all. You're longing to get me defined, aren't you? The way you defined all those people who believed in Jerome. Am I a nutter like your friend outside? Or am I just rather superficial? Have you worked it out yet? Have you weighed up the evidence?'

'I'm not trying to work anything out.'

She raised her eyebrows. 'I've got a strong feeling that's all you ever do. No wonder you're nervy.' Her irritation had disappeared. Paul felt he would be more comfortable if she would lose her temper, stop appearing to be so controlled. 'Not clothes,' she said, 'people. What I'm interested in, is how people cope. I'm after the centre, if you want to know, not the surface. I'm like a method actor. I'm Robert de Niro, in fact.'

She sat beside him on the bed, and he tensed slightly, but she lay back, stretching out her arms. 'It started in Malory, and developed in boarding houses I stayed at for a while. There are funny people in those places. I never felt quite comfortable.'

'Do you mean halfway houses?'

'No, I don't. I mean ordinary people. Is that the phrase you would use? Bed and breakfasters.'

She told him about the ordinary people she had met. Office workers, tube travellers, the unemployed. A woman with a nervous giggle, like a tic that she couldn't control. A man who used a new toothbrush every day. Another who had papered his entire room with pictures of football teams, although he'd never seen a game in his life.

'If anyone did those sort of things at Malory there was a group discussion about it. I began to get interested, and taking an interest, you know, is supposed to be crucial.'

When Mrs Standish asked her to look after the house it seemed ideal. Then her friends did the same.

'They ski, her friends, and have Easter breaks, so I've had almost year round accommodation. Non-stop house-sitting.'

'Non-stop moving.'

'Non-stop observation.' She moved up the bed, away from Paul. 'I'm an anthropologist looking at the fresh remnants of vanished tribes. I can see the ghosts of the departed family. During the day here, it's Emily, moving from room to room, doing chores, small jobs. She watches daytime television, makes the beds, loads the machine, does her hoovering, her ironing, her dusting, her polishing. At six or seven the front door opens and I see her husband return. He walks into the kitchen smelling the smells, wondering what's for dinner. I know all about him. I'm Adam coming home from school, sitting down with some toast in front of the telly. I'm Bea, masturbating behind her bedroom door, the small sounds of the world shut out by her sobbing breaths. These sit-com families translated into real life. Stern father, scatty mother, crazy kids. Guilty secret. I know all about them, I can feel Emily's shape on the mattress,' she moved her hand, as if feeling it, 'her husband's in his favourite chair. I know what they wear, what they eat, what they read, how they make love, what they dream.'

Paul had returned to the window. 'My research,' he said, 'leads me to believe that most people have dreams about being someone else.' He was thinking of his empathy with the woman washing her car. It wasn't something he wanted to share with Hazel. 'We'll leave through the garden,' he said. 'Over the fence and across next door's.'

'I don't want to be anyone else.' She moved to the edge of the bed, looking up at him. 'When I've got to know you again, perhaps I can house-sit for you Paul. How do you shape your days?'

His back was to her, he was still staring out, trying to see something through the foliage of the trees. 'I'll take you to my hotel, and tomorrow we'll see Walsh.'

'Are we going to share a hotel room, when you can't even sit on the same bed as me without getting nervous? Are you sure you even want to be seen with me?' Still, he didn't react. 'Do you know what I did that day you left me on the way to the opera?'

He didn't answer.

'I went to the cinema.'

He turned from the window. 'Then you had your day out.'

'I waited till it got dark, and then I hunched up in my seat and cried all through the film. Not because I'd missed the opera, although I'd been looking forward to it, or even because you'd left me. It was because I thought I'd let you down. That's why it's hard to forgive you, because you made me feel responsible.'

Paul was staring out of the window at the trees. He was no longer feeling reassured by the size of the house, and the solidity of its furnishing. It was here after all, that Bea had had the breakdown which had led to her suicide. Hazel probably knew the secret to that, but he never would. It was here that Hazel had decided to challenge him, having apparently stopped holding back. He was adrift between decisions, caught between Walsh's directive and an assassin somewhere outside. For all the skill he had developed, there was no escaping this confrontation.

'I wasn't responsible for what happened, Paul. I was over-wrought, upset. It was a difficult time. *You* were responsible, Paul, because you were supposed to be the capable one, only you were too busy protecting yourself. You failed me. You

104

should have warned me you couldn't cope.'

His back to the window now, he waited silently for her to finish.

'And you haven't changed, have you?'

He didn't speak.

'Silent as a therapist.'

'I've talked enough, Hazel, I don't want to talk any more. It's not something I do.'

This statement hung between them for several seconds. She looked up at him, the agitated italics of his forehead, speculative.

She was leaning forward and upwards like an inquisitor, the straight line of spine, neck and eyes pointing at his face. Hypotenuse. Abruptly she relaxed, leaning back on the sagging mattress, on to her elbows.

'I know what it's like being you,' she said. 'Withdrawn, hard work filling up your days, creating nothing. Touchy about your space. Some tidy love affair that's been effectively over almost since it started. I'm right, aren't I? Observation, you see. Sherlock Holmes, that's me. But you haven't any idea what it's like to be me, have you? I mean, have you? Your precious research doesn't give you a clue, does it? And what *would* give you a clue, you ignore, you suppress, you pretend doesn't even exist. Your research is an elaborate diversion, removes the need for you ever to look at yourself. What's the matter, Paul? Scared of what you might see?'

'We should go,' he said quietly, 'he's out there. We should really go now. When we've seen Walsh, we'll split up. We'll stay in contact now of course, we'll try not to lose touch again.'

'Each in our separate lives again, including our shy assassin.'

'Walsh will be able to sort all this out,' he said, 'track this man down and deal with him, arrange protection if necessary.'

'He may not want to. It seems to me that he started this by publishing your research. Have you asked yourself why he did that? Here's a man who's interested in violence, and who has created a situation in which someone is trying to kill you.'

'What are you suggesting?'

Hazel knelt by the bed and took from beneath it a cardboard

box containing photograph albums and pads of paper. 'I'm not going to be led by you, Paul. What are you going to do, rip up another rosebush? You're just going to have to let events carry you along for a while. I'm afraid it's out of your control.'

Thirteen

Hazel was wrong, Edmund understood revenge perfectly. He was familiar with the whole process: the anticipation, the anti-climax, the bitter-sweet aftertaste. He planned to act when it was dark.

He curled his upper lip into his mouth, found a way beneath the skin with his teeth, tugged at it, and unpeeled. Sweet, sharp pain. He was sitting cross-legged in the Cavalier, his long, white raincoat flowing over his knees, his shiny black boots on the floor in front of his seat, like two offerings to a bony, over-dressed Buddha. Frowning, his mouth the slightest, meniscus curve, he moved the piece of skin around on his tongue. It would be better if Paul would come out now. It was hard to believe that it wasn't the next thing that was meant to happen. He took the skin from his mouth and rolled it on his palm, moving it up and down different lines before dropping it. With his long fingernails, delicate instruments, he continued the slow work of skinning his lips.

He would complete the story. In order to test everything, to see that the structure was sound before proceeding. And then it would be dark, and he would act.

Discrete pictures: him up there on the table; Dinah knocked down in front of the door; him smugly holding court in his

study. The Jack of Diamonds, inevitably produced, and repro-
duced, playing its part in the elaborately conceived scheme it
can't comprehend.

Hilary had a new hobby-horse. In the insulating bubble of his
silence, Edmund listened to him pathetically droning on. He
had to listen, because he had become his father's ideal audience,
a silent listener for his self-glorifying rambling. Edmund put up
with it, not just because it suited the plan he was developing, but
because the more he heard, the easier it became to reject Hilary,
to separate him from his own beliefs. It became simple, pleasur-
able, like prising off a scab.

Hilary's new hobby-horse, his latest field of enquiry, was
reincarnation. For some reason (forebodings of death?) it preoccupied him at this point. It was clear he was half persuaded by
it, despite a lifetime of beliefs to the contrary. Edmund thought
it was pitiful, and fantasised happily about being the quality
controller of souls, the one who stands in the great car park of
Purgatory, directing the dead to their new bodies. No, I'm
afraid it's back to the vale of soul-making for you. What fun.
Every rapist a rapee, every fat businessman a Third World
peasant, every football hooligan a feeble girl, every drunken,
bullying hypocritical father . . . well, the attraction is clear.
Only the laziest and most desperate, Edmund felt, could be
convinced by it. He was temperamentally far more suited to
heaven and hell, the straight-forward, one-chance-is-all-you-get
approach, concentrating your thinking, making you opt defini-
tely for right or wrong.

He was seduced by a plan. There was Hilary, firmly in the
wrong camp, and there was Edmund suffering his lectures. The
plan started as a tiny seed, and grew. Could he? Surely not. But
could he? There were several trains of thought, but they all led
to one conclusion. There was more than one question, but there
was only one answer: Hilary.

Even if it hadn't been so logical, Edmund might have been
seduced all the same. He wasn't exactly putting up a determined
resistance. This idea slipped inside his weak objections as if

they weren't there, it peeled off his reluctance and revealed that he was asking for it. Once the crucial change in his thinking had occurred, the urge became overwhelming. He could hardly contain himself. There was something about Hilary dying that transcended logic. It became the next step in Edmund's personal development. Without his particularly noticing, it stopped being a question of whether he should die, and became a question of how to make him die.

Hamlet did it.

When he studied the play at school, Edmund was struck by the scene in which he's on the point of killing Claudius at prayer, and then relents, preferring to catch him in the midst of his sin. He wrote an essay on it, a revealing document. '*Cogent. You show a good understanding of the character.*' Of course he did. He *was* the character. He knew it was no delaying tactic, he could see it was a cool, logical, delightfully ruthless decision. Catch him in his sin, before he can repent. Send him straight to hell.

He started indulging in Shakespeare-induced fantasies.

Hilary is on the table, kicking aside a dirty plate, staggering and recovering himself at the edge, daredevil comedian, arms waving as he tries to find his balance on the edge of the drop. Enjoying the faithful spotlight as ever, he is in Falstaffian mode, not yet ready to swing down into his contrite humiliation. The twins, of course, still maintain their cautious, compound attitude of timidity and scorn. They don't seem to know any more which is real, and which is pose. They hold hands and catch each other's eye. Edmund stands a little apart, solemn and judicious in his silence. They don't imagine that his thoughtful eyes see himself behind Hilary, giving him a hearty shove between the shoulderblades. The kitchen floor splits apart, revealing the abyss.

'. . . *trip him that his heels may kick at heaven*
And that his soul may be as damn'd and black
As hell, whereto it goes.'

109

The comedian tip-toes on the edge, and his desperately flapping arms keep him upright, this time. He completes the remainder of his performance, sinking on to his knees, and on to his belly, degrading himself by degrees.

Edmund was much taken by the idea of a fall. Not just for its Biblical connotations, but for the element of uncertainty it involved. Cats, he had read, tend to get injured in falls of between three and nine floors, but above and below that they're all right. Perhaps from ten floors they just resign themselves to fate, go limp. In a drunken, loose-limbed state, he speculated, one might survive a serious fall unharmed, or one might just break a bone or two, or one might be disabled for life. The point is that your own efforts are unlikely to have the slightest effect on the result. It's like a paradigm of the human condition. Not just the outcome, but even the manner of the thing are in God's hands. His choice. And there was the drama of it too, that was attractive. He imagined the horror on his father's face, his hands groping up towards heaven as if he was searching for the rungs of a ladder.

After seven weeks of silence, Edmund found himself in a state of resolution. It was a wonderfully peaceful condition. Over the previous weeks he had fluctuated from exuberance to nervy jumpiness, from rage to cool disdain, all of it uncomfortably contained in a silent show of indifference. This new, quiet assurance finally matched his outward behaviour. It was good to achieve equilibrium. With the decision came calm. This is what he had always found: doubt only produced fear and unhappiness. Once the choice is made, once you opt for certainty, then you can be perfectly peaceful.

The act was performed in darkness.

He lay awake in bed, listening to Michael's steady breathing, waiting for the sound of the front door. What thoughts entered his mind passed through it without snagging his attention. He observed them without emotion. Hilary would have approved, because this was a state of near trance. Edmund's eyes were open, but he saw nothing. He was aware of his body, its weight on the mattress, the weight of the sheets, but he felt no particular connection with it. It lay still and heavy, the human cloak. Only his sense of hearing was alert, supernaturally acute, stretching beyond the house and outside, into the streets, and half a mile up into the sky, where an aeroplane was passing, quietly flying away, leaving the city.

What did he feel then? Edmund felt that God was speaking to him. In the sound of Michael's breathing, in the soft, slowly diminishing sigh of the aeroplane, and in Hilary's amplified footsteps, in the street outside.

There was the scraping of the lock, and then a little splash of metal as the keys were dropped. The scraping again, the turning of the latch, a pause, and then the door shutting heavily. Michael's breathing remained steady. Getting out of bed, he could hear Hilary's breathing too, uneven and hoarse, more like sighs and growls than breaths. Edmund's uniform for this night was black: black sweater and trousers, black trainers. It gave him strength, reinforcing his purpose, as if with it he had added something to his personality, discovered a solidarity with others, also dressed in black. He became something more than himself. Hilary's nemesis, but more than that too, he was one of those scary youths one sees on the streets, or one of those callous young murderers the local newspaper is always so full of: the harmless young man, misunderstood and underestimated, who abruptly one night becomes a beast, a fiend.

He stepped silently on to the landing and waited out of sight at the top of the stairs.

Hilary came up slowly, his tread heavy and his breathing laboured. One hand resting lightly on the banister, his eyes on the step in front.

He spoke his first word for seven weeks.

'Father.'

Three steps from the top, Hilary paused and looked up, his mouth slightly open, his shoulders moving. The dark shape in front of him was a figure out of his nightmares. If he had been carrying his gun he might have used it, instead he held both hands out in front of him, in a gesture caught between self-defence and surrender. Edmund lifted his foot without hesi-

111

tation and kicked between his hands, not with the toe of his shoe but with the whole sole, his bent leg crashing forward like a piston, into the middle of his father's chest.

It was everything he had hoped for. Hilary leant backwards into the air, big hands grasping at nothing as space swarmed around him, his lips moving quickly, in soundless, blubbering protest, and then he fell, arms flailing stupidly, into the darkness. It was everything he had hoped for, but he hadn't fully imagined the impacts. He bounced twice, once on his side, and once on his face, and he landed up on his back.

Edmund kept still for ten seconds, looking down at the jumbled body below, the idol finally toppled. At first in his elation he wanted to jump after him, through the air, straight to his father's side, but something happened as the seconds passed. He kept looking down, he wouldn't let himself look away, and something happened to his elation. He thought he was becoming composed, as he followed his father slowly down the stairs, but by the time he reached him, and knelt beside him, Edmund's hand was over his face and his mouth was open, and he was panting, as if breathless.

He was still alive and, as far as it was possible to tell, it seemed that he wanted to say something. He was grotesque. His nose had broken in the fall, a jagged bit of bone was visible. Gasps for breath intermittently bubbled through blood at the back of his throat but, with his ear close to his lips, Edmund thought he distinguished two words.

'Hank odd.' Hank odd? He lowered his hand, and smiled uncertainly. Now Hilary really was burbling. He tried again. 'Thank odd.'

Not 'Thank God'? Edmund took hold of his shoulders. 'What are you thanking Him for?'

He was confused. At that moment, shuddery and a bit queasy, he was feeling some remorse, but gratitude wasn't what he wanted to hear. He let go of his shoulders and altered his position, to speak directly into his father's ear.

'Don't thank Him too soon,' he said, his voice croaky and uneven. 'There is memory in Hell. Don't think you'll forget this life.' He was getting carried away. 'Maybe Hell will be no different at all.'

Edmund didn't know where the words came from, it wasn't the way he usually thought, but he and his father stared at each other for a moment, equally dismayed at this idea. Edmund was still staring as his father's eyes began to lose their focus. His mouth sagged sideways, and the skin of his face began to lose its shape as his muscles began to give up. Very quickly, his flesh seemed entirely inflexible, like some synthetic material. It was mottled, mauve and blue. Very quickly, it grew cold. Edmund saw all this happen, and felt it, the skin was cold when he touched his father's cheek, but still it took him several moments more to understand that he was dead. He hadn't seen death before, hadn't realised that it was as great a miracle as life. When he took his hand away he left white fingerprints, like incriminating evidence. Why did he touch his father's cheek? He had no idea.

In the car, waiting for the moment to go to the house, he reached that point. And now it was dark.

'Prove everything.' Paul was there and Edmund was there with him, pregnant with destiny. Not much room for doubt. It was all proven, wasn't it? *He will certainly visit the following address.* And what did he do? He visited it. He was in there, he should have come out again ages ago, but he was in there anyway, as predicted. They were each playing their allotted parts, revenger and victim, just as he and his father once had. Edmund could only feel he was behaving responsibly.

His memories having come to their natural conclusion, he unfolded his legs from the seat, put on his boots, and opened the car door, surprised by the advent of cool air. As he stood up, lifting his stiff body, his knees cracked loudly, with the hollow sound of corks fired from a gun. He felt a little dizzy after his long confinement, and put a hand on the car's roof to steady himself. Paul had entered the house in the late afternoon. Now it was evening. Edmund turned his back, stood close to the trunk of a tree, and unzipped his fly. The urine came immediately, in a fast stream which spattered his clean boots. The smell made him feel faintly sick.

His frown had returned, the slightest downward curve of the lips. He reached into his car, opened the glove compartment and took out his father's gun. It gleamed dully in his hand, as if brand new. He had had plenty of time to clean it in the hours that he had been waiting, and he was a man who believed in being utterly conscientious over whatever task he was engaged in. He headed down the road, feeling liberated now that he had left the car. He had finally, he felt, made his choice, rejected doubt and opted for certainty. This was nothing to agonise about. This was a deserved death in a dark house at night. He had been here before.

Fourteen

It was almost exactly six hours since Edmund had called, and the girl had told him that Mr Standish and family were away. It was a pleasing detail. As he walked up the drive, his long, light raincoat floated behind him just as he liked it to. He felt like an angel, and looked like a Sergio Leone gunfighter. Now was surely the right moment. Stupid to fret, stupid to doubt. Lights greeted him on the ground floor and, without slowing down, he side-stepped the porch, took out his gun and reversed it in his hand. Through the window he saw an empty room, pristine, like a shop display. Now he paused. Sofa in a floral print, matching the curtains, books bound in red leather, pale-blue carpet, magazines fanned on the surface of a French-polished coffee table, arranged between placemats for drinks and two silver-framed photographs. A boy and a girl, grinning. Edmund stood looking in for longer than he had intended, but when he did finally smash the glass, it was with the uninhibited swing of a fast bowler.

When Paul came out of the shower, he couldn't find his clothes. A cloud of steam followed him into the brilliantly lit bathroom, and he peered into it here and there for a few moments, thinking that his jeans and shirt were lost in the fog. It cleared quickly however, sucked away by the clattering fan, revealing bare, cream fixtures. He shouted for Hazel and then, holding a furry blue towel around his middle, went in search of something to wear.

She was in the main bedroom, surrounded by photograph albums and exercise books, wearing his grey striped shirt and blue jeans.

'We have to go, Hazel. You said you'd come.'

She turned her head towards him. 'I lied.'

Her mischievous expression turned to complete surprise as she took in what she saw. 'My God, what a body. What have you done to it?'

He pulled the towel a little closer around him. 'It's just the fall I told you about, the two falls.' He looked down at his chest and arms. In fact, although his skin was still a bit mottled, darker in places than it should have been, grazed here and there, there wasn't much left to show for the damage that was done. There was still, however, something left to feel. His wrist, now in a pressure bandage, was much better, but various bruises still ached, and his back, somehow damaged in the fall in the library, protested painfully if he didn't remember to keep it scrupulously erect.

He straightened, and then found time to register in turn what he saw: cross-legged, diminutive figure, in his clothes, in the midst of a swamp of documents. Books and papers. They used to do homework together, on the floor in the sitting room. She would lean over to look at what he was doing, making admiring noises at the incomprehensible work that lay just three years ahead. Now she sat there, pretending to be him. He began to speak and then stopped himself, deciding it was best to ignore his confusion, and her words. He had only just been reminded, after all, that confrontations were invariably best avoided. He had a nostalgic pang for the comfortable quiet of his Suffolk cottage. Get this over with. Get this over with as quickly as possible. It's only an episode, untypical, nothing to do with real life.

Inside the nearest wardrobe he found rows of blouses, skirts and dresses. He opened the next one. Mr Standish's shirts, trousers and suits.

Hazel shook her head as he sorted through them. 'Predictable. His wife would be a better fit for you, Paul, in more ways than one. Have a look at my picture of her.'

'Would you give me my clothes back, Hazel, please?'

'First I want to show you something,' she said, reasonably. 'Just relax, enjoy yourself, you know that poor man isn't going to come breaking in here.'

She paused for him to respond, and then continued smoothly when he remained silent. 'I wasn't talking about your bruises, Paul.' He was putting on a baggy blue shirt, and finding a belt for the trousers, and it took him a moment to realise that she had abruptly returned to the beginning of the conversation. 'I wasn't talking about your battle-scars. I meant your body, the *shape* of it. I've never seen a body that shape before, except in the cinema. Are you familiar with a well-known cure for depression? This is according to one of my doctors. Hearty, rugby type: to restore self-esteem and improve general outlook, exercise regularly and take good care of your appearance. How's your self-esteem, Paul? How's your general outlook? Are you keeping everything under control?'

He hesitated, 'I don't know why my body is of so much interest to people,' and then, with an exaggerated sigh, sat on the edge of the mattress, gingerly, above her, and stretched to take the photograph album she was offering.

Emily was wearing a tweedy skirt and a pale-green shirt. She had on gardening gloves and was carrying a small wicker basket. The camera had taken her by surprise. Her eyes were wide and her mouth was slightly open, splitting her nervous smile. Paul read aloud, in a flat voice with an edge of scepticism:

'Girlish mother of two, Emily is frightened of adulthood, responsibility and freedom. She loved her daughter very much. She was frightened of her too. Of course she blames herself for Bea's tragic suicide.'

'That's the wrong tone,' said Hazel, with a touch of petulance. 'It's supposed to be the same sort of way they introduce a Miss World contestant. Enthusiastic. Imagine a big round of applause at the end.' She clapped a couple of times. 'You see what I mean about her and you, though, don't you? You do give me the impression that you're a frightened man. Am I right?'

She gave him two seconds. 'No. Don't answer that. I know: talking isn't one of the things you do.' She found another photograph. 'Here's one of my most recent ones.'

It was the immaculately presented woman she had seen the day before. In the glossy photo she looked still more perfect, her clothes shining, her hair symmetrical, her skin smooth and polished like fresh, pink plastic. Frozen in the image, she was almost extra-terrestrial. The long, narrow heels looked like a natural extension of her feet. Hazel hadn't added to the one word caption she had thought of at the time.

'Neanderthal,' Paul read. 'What's that supposed to mean?'

'I've been trying to work out who she is,' Hazel said, ignoring the question, 'and all I can think is that she's made herself up. This is the way she wants to be, or needs to be. I admire her enormously, I'm never that thorough.' She found another photo in the box. 'Here's her male counterpart. He's not nearly as interesting, but that's because men are more limited.'

It was a picture of a man in a bulky leather jacket, tight, faded jeans and cowboy boots. Beneath it she had written:

'According to Suetonius, the Romans made it illegal for men to wear silk.'

'I follow people,' she said, 'the way you used to follow football. I choose someone, and then I try to keep track of their difficulties and their qualities. I collect them, their ways of getting by, enduring.'

'Can I have my clothes back now?'

'You haven't explained about the body.'

'I work out a bit. I do some weight training.'

'It's just like the leather jacket you see, or the pretty blue suit, almost self-parody. That's why I'm interested.'

'I've looked at your pictures, can we go now?'

'Who else asked about your muscles?'

'Boyd, the man from the Foundation.'

She reached up and followed the shape of a bicep with her finger. 'You refuse to tell me why?' He was managing not to withdraw his arm, when her mood abruptly changed. 'Oh Paul, look at your face! Stop worrying, I'm not trying to get into your knickers, it's purely aesthetic. Clever stomach creases, smooth curves, amazing bulges. We might be sitting in a bedroom together talking about your body, but I have no designs on it.' She smirked at him. 'I don't want to get into bed with you, if that's what you're afraid of. If you'd ever listened to me when I needed you to, you'd know that's never what I was after.'

Paul shook his head and raised his hand, as if to ward off the threatened reminiscences. 'Let's just forget about it.'

'Do you know what I wanted? I wanted to be like the twins who develop their own language, so that they understand each other, and no one else. You've read about them. And then they grow up telepathic. I could be in pain on the other side of the earth, and you'd know about it, and you'd find me. You were going to fix me, the way you used to fix models, and the Christmas tree lights, and the car.'

This was distracting, this continual slippage into the past. It made it difficult to operate competently in the present. Paul had a vision of his childhood room, with fourteen perfectly-constructed Airfix models of aeroplanes hanging from the ceiling. Blue underneath, khaki on top. Tanks, cars and boats on the shelves and the desk. His father had helped him with the first one, a Spitfire, which had its own protected airspace above his bed. In his dreams he drove, sailed and flew in beautiful, flawless vehicles, alongside his father.

'I was going to *be* you,' she said, 'because you were so solid and stable. We were both going to be you.'

Paul nodded, earnest, trying to match her attitude, but she was a step ahead again, her mood changing again. She smiled at herself, spoke lightly. 'It was my mistake, not yours. I didn't know how pointless it would have been to be like you. But I know where I am now. All that's left now is the ordinary problems.'

'What are they?'

Hazel took her photos and put them back in the box. 'You know what they are, Paul, just the usual stuff. Depression, anxiety, an inability to deal with everyday life, the things that everyone feels.'

'Everyday life at home is mostly all right,' Paul said warily, suspecting a trap, 'apart from an irate postman. I've got it under control. It's this city that I find appalling to live in.'

Hazel nodded as if this was barely worth mentioning. 'I bet it reminds you of mum. I saw two fights yesterday, one in the tube, one in the middle of the road. Someone jumped out of a van in a traffic jam, and someone came screaming out after him waving an iron bar.'

This was a good feeling, swapping tales from the front-line. 'On the tube yesterday,' he said, 'I had an anxiety attack. Did you ever feel anything like that? That time I was with you? I mean, I was short of breath, I could feel my stomach tightening, I actually didn't know what I was going to do next.'

'Perfectly average urban angst. Poor Paul, you're scared stiff, aren't you? I bet you felt waves of misanthropy too, didn't you, welling up inside you. I tell you, if you *didn't* feel those things now and then on the tube, that would be unusual. You didn't know what you were going to do next. I wonder what might have happened? I have a friend who only discovered he was ill one day when he got a lighter out and walked down the aisle setting fire to people's newspapers. Wanting to do it is normal, wanting to do almost anything is normal. It's when you do it, when the self-censorship breaks down, that you have something to worry about. Everyone is walking around the world with absurd fantasies in their minds.'

Downstairs, faintly through the closed door, there was a smash of glass.

'Jesus Christ!' Paul stood up, bouncing slightly off the mattress, his flesh bouncing too, his entire body trembling with a Parkinson's shiver that seemed independent of him. His well-developed muscles could not control it. The physical confrontation he had looked for in the library terrified him here, in this strange house at night, this foreign ground, when his body too felt almost foreign to him in its unfamiliar fragility.

'Sssh,' said Hazel, still seated. 'I imagine he'll look downstairs first, since we left the lights on. How are you on drainpipes?'

'Drainpipes?'

'Go to Adam's room. He used the one outside his window to get out late at night when he was a boy. He told me about it, how he used to wander round the garden in the middle of the night. Luckily, unlike you, I'm a good listener.'

'Come on then.'

She was gathering up the photographs, and the books. 'I'll be right with you. I don't want to leave all this behind.'

'Hazel, he's *down* there.' Paul was having trouble containing his terror in a whisper. 'He'll be coming up,' he squeaked, 'he wants to *kill* me, and maybe he'll get you too, don't you understand that? He's down there *now*, aren't you afraid of dying at all?'

She continued to gather her research materials. She looked up with a brief smirk, as if he had given away something he had been trying to hide. 'It's wonderful for your research, though, isn't it?' she said.

Still, she hurried because she understood that he wouldn't go without her. They left the bedroom together, and then both paused on the landing, as if by agreement, straining to hear him below.

A door slammed suddenly, and she saw his shoulders jerk in response. He reached out to the wall to steady himself. Now they could clearly hear footsteps on the tiles in the kitchen.

Hazel remembered lying in bed at night as a child, listening to the sighs and whispers of the house. No one had ever explained to her satisfaction what the noises were. The house, she liked to assume, stretched and shrugged and flexed its muscles at night, loosening up after the exertions of the day. Now it was as if the house was as tense as they were, waiting for something to happen. There were more movements downstairs, disjointed and hard to place. Paul's breathing was fast and shallow, hers, she heard it and approved, was deep and slow. She pointed at the door and he went first, tip-toeing clumsily, looking, in his outsized clothes, like a comedian.

From the sounds that she heard she was able to picture the

intruder. He wasn't nervous any more. He was pushing doors open casually, impatiently. He wanted it over with.

Adam's room. Paul began to fumble with the window, with the catch that needed to be unscrewed. His fingers seemed to have grown fatter and less able. Hazel stood by the door, looking through the crack on to the landing. She turned to Paul to whisper encouragement, and when she turned back there was a face in the stairwell. Skin tight over bones, eyes expressionless, deep-set. She watched, and more became visible. Mouth slightly down-turned, a tall, thin figure. He was moving quietly up the stairs. A blue uniform was discernible, beneath a long white coat. A gun was held loosely at his side, in his large white hand.

Hazel, engrossed, didn't hear Paul's sigh of relief, or feel the draught of cold air on her back. He had to touch her shoulder. She looked round, not with alarm, but with the irritated glare of someone whose concentration has been disturbed.

She walked with him to the window. 'Go first,' she whispered, and then, to forestall argument: 'See if it'll take the weight.'

One floor up, not as high as all that. Twenty feet perhaps. Stories entered Paul's mind concerning death by falling: a lunatic who thought he could fly, suicides, research related to vertigo. The film, *Vertigo*. A fragile . . . steeple? Unlikely camera-angles. As he leaned out and took hold of the pipe, and felt the first warning twinge from his back, he began deliberately to recall information relating to murder, trying to spur himself on, remembering photographic evidence of bullet wounds, stab wounds, bludgeonings. The pipe was black and cold, not plastic but sturdy metal, attached to the wall with strong brackets. Lead pipe, *Cluedo*, what a mess it might make of a skull. 'It's fine,' he said, 'follow me.' But as he leant out and felt the cool air circulate around his face, what flowed into his mind, expelling everything else, was the episode on the steps, the dizzy, stretched half second of suspension above nothing, the imprint, like a heat scar, of a flattened palm on his spine. He gripped the wide pipe with his right hand, and, straddling the window sill, looked back over his shoulder.

Hazel wasn't even watching him, she was back at the door,

her briefcase of photograph albums and exercise books under her arm. She could hear the man moving around in the main bedroom.

Paul swung his other leg over, and lowered himself, reaching his right hand out to the pipe, until he was hanging spread-eagled, one hand on the pipe, one on the sill, with his body and face flat against the wall. This, he noted, seemed to be an ideal therapy, stretching his spine luxuriously, causing the pain in his back to subside. His arms were strong, he was still fit, he could hang here, twenty feet up, for some time. Could it even be a cure? His wrist suddenly went into a spasm, and he let go of the sill, and promptly felt the pain reappear in a jagged rip that swung across his back like a perforation as he swung across the wall. Startled by this new agony, he felt his grip on the pipe loosen. If he were about to die, he wondered, what should he think of? What should he say? He slid down a foot as he swung, his fingers scraping down the metal, but he got his left hand to it before he fell and clutched it, hugging it to him, pressing his cheek against it. First it seemed hot, then very cold.

What should he say? He should say: *No.*

His fingertips were scraped and cut, his wrist hurt, and his back didn't like this latest position, with its novel strains and pressures, but he found that his newly vulnerable body was up to the test. He lowered himself hand over hand, using his feet to share the weight.

Hazel leant out of the window above him. 'Catch,' she said, and dropped her case down to him. She had just heard the light switched on in the next room. She seemed to be halfway down by the time he had caught the case. Where he had used strength she used agility, swinging down incautiously, as if this was her habitual exit from the house.

'Run.'

Finally, she seemed to be sharing his urgency. They ran together, she ran, and he moved in a peculiar loping hobble, not down the garden but straight into the bushes that bordered it, like thieves.

Edmund reached the window as Hazel hit the ground below.

He watched the two of them run, and in the short time available he aimed his father's gun first at one, and then at the other, but he didn't fire. He couldn't tell which was Paul, and which was the woman he had spoken to earlier. This was the excuse that he gave himself. In fact, however, this wasn't the climax he had hoped for. It was a disappointment. He had enjoyed stalking them through the house, but the only appropriate ending would have been to corner them, and meet them face to face. Not this dormitory dash out of the window. The time had become unpropitious. He might have chased them, possibly it was his duty to chase them, using the pipe as they had, but, breathing in the cool night air which seemed both to fill him and leave him hollow, he became aware that he was tired, and ravenous, and he found that his certainty had evaporated. Can certainty disappear? Doesn't it cast doubt on whether it existed in the first place? It was possible that he hadn't tested everything quite carefully enough. He was back where he started, wavering again, purposeless, somehow drained of will.

*

TRANSITION

'*This is where we live. Scuzzy around the edges, you'll have to excuse that. This is Harry, say hello to Harry.*'

'*Hello Harry.*'

'*Harry doesn't say much. I'm Danny, which you know, because you will have been told. And this is it. I don't know what you expected? I hope you didn't expect the Ritz.*'

We are in the sitting room. Harry is in an armchair which may once have been brown leather, but has become a many-holed, peeling suede. There is a thin carpet on the floor which doesn't quite reach the walls, and so rumples and creases like a loose pair of tights. A table, brown formica, with three chairs, plastic pale brown seats. Three. One for the new occupant.

'*I'll think about it.*'

'*You get your own room, that's the main thing, Joan, isn't it, your privacy. There's a mirror.*'

'*I'll think about it, that's all I can say.*' *I'm already thinking about it, I'm thinking: Let me out of this place. There is a smell which I haven't yet identified.*

'*I don't know what you expected?*'

I shrug, as if I didn't know either. In fact this is pretty much what I have come to expect.

'*You haven't seen your room yet.*'

'*This is fine, this is probably . . . I'll think it over anyway, and let you know.*'

✳

I creep around these places with a sinking heart, these dismal places, and I try not to let my feelings show. Some of them can tell anyway, they have eyes, they catch that first reaction, that wince, that disappointment as fears are justified. Sue said, Treat my floor as home, but she is often around during the day and my typing disturbs her, and the small difficulties of living with someone have begun to multiply. We are no longer students, after all. Yesterday I woke up with a trodden cigarette butt near my nose, and I don't think it was an accident. I tell her about this dump I have just seen, and she tells me, as if she knew about it, that if we complain it will be improved. We have a right to complain, etc. She reminds me of where we lived as students, how cosy it became. I tell her about Harry, tell her that I think he is a psychotic type. She says he's quiet, what do you want, he won't bother you while you're working. She gives the word a certain emphasis. Working.

✻

'Well, you surprise me, I didn't think that you liked it. I didn't think we'd ever see you again. I'm glad you decided, though, because this is an okay place. It's a friendly place, and that's important. You know, parties, friends round, whatever you like, that's fine.'

'I expect I'll be working a lot.'

'Working, of course. What work is that?'

'I write.'

'A writer?'

'Just technical stuff, for technical magazines. Occasional stuff. Nothing very exciting.'

'Technical, that's interesting.'

'But I write at home, so I'll be here a lot. Typing.'

'That's good, because we're here a lot too, so the company will be welcome, it'll be nice to have the company. Although you'll be wanting peace and quiet of course, which is fine because you have your own room, so you have your privacy.'

✻

There is a bed in one corner of my room and a table in the other. On the table a mirror, leaning against the wall. A chair and a shelf. Through the window I can see the yard which belongs to the ground-floor flat. I looked in the window of this flat as I waited outside the front door, and I saw, through flowered curtains, a gas fire, a television and a tall light with an orange shade. Homesickness caught me by surprise, as if it had been lying in wait. In front of the

126

*mirror is a pot of orange face-cream, half used. I don't
know if this is a present or an oversight. I can't imagine
Danny or Harry using face-cream. It smells of apricots.*

*Still not a word from Harry. He is making me nervous. I
am expecting him to come out with a long speech, a protest
about something, off balance and ferocious. Or to turn his
head on one side and fix me with his eyes and say, like Gary
Gilmore, I know you, I know who you are.*

*I've bought a rail and hung all my clothes on it. I've
taken a drawer out of the chest of drawers in the kitchen,
put my underwear in it, and put it under my bed. I'm going
to get a bedspread, and a tablecloth.*

✻

'You've done wonders, I'm not joking, it's like a different room. You've almost put me in the mood to do something with my own room, which is the first time I've felt
like that. It shows that all it takes is a little attention.'

'It's not much.'

'It's not much but it doesn't take much, does it, to turn
things around.'

'I like a room to be comfortable, it can get depressing
otherwise, if I'm working in it all the time.'

'I can understand that.'

'So a bit of colour.'

'You've polished the mirror.'

'Yes.'

'Did you see the cream that I left out? The one before
you left it in the bathroom. I thought you might want it.'

✻

*Harry came in. I was writing about a conference that I
attended, speeches and so on, and Harry came in and
watched. In fact he didn't come in, he just stood in the
doorway. Hello Harry. No answer. Harry doesn't say
much. His hand was on the door jamb. Little white curls of
dead skin all around his fingernails. Is that what he does all
day? Sit in his chair and bite and pick at his fingers? We*

looked at each other, and then he looked around the room,
slowly, and then he went. He probably thinks we have
come to an understanding now. What he doesn't know is
that I have more plans for this room. I saw a bit of carpet
that I could use, cheap because it was the end of a line, and
has been on display. Patterned. And after that, the walls.

Danny has apparently been negotiating with our neigh-
bours. Outside my window, in the yard below, he is cutting
the wild grass with a pair of rusty-bladed shears. He has
uprooted the grass which grows in the cracks between the
paving, and now he is working on the small, rectangular
patch of lawn. He squats, and then he kneels, his thin
sweater close against his skin. When he stands up, stretching
his back, stretching his whole body, he sees me watching.

*

'I hope you like it. I suddenly thought, when it was too
late, that you were probably vegetarian.'
'No.'
'Or Jewish.'
'No.'
'It's nice to have a reason to make an effort. The kitchen
isn't much, but it's enough. It doesn't really take much,
does it, except a little effort? I just haven't tried before.
Harry's not fussy.'
We were eating chicken, roasted until it was dry and
almost flavourless. Danny's enthusiasms were beginning to
affect me. Recently I caught myself feeling glad when he
interrupted me working. He has told me what Harry does.
He cuts pictures from magazines and puts them in his scrap
books. Before he sticks them in, he copies down any text
which is on the back, so that it won't be lost.
'It's very good.'
'Thank you. It's good to eat together, better than snatch-
ing meals. And I don't mind the shopping, the supermarket.
I like it, in fact. You know what supermarkets are like,
clean and light. Like your room.'

*

128

The wallpaper is white, with narrow pale-blue stripes. The bedspread is blue, with small white roses on it. The carpet is grey and blue and red. The tablecloth is navy-blue. On the table is my typewriter and papers. My clothes are pale colours.

Sue came, and I gave her tea in my room. I have a kettle. Danny didn't speak to her at all, he just nodded when she came in and pretended to be reading when she left. He must have been pretending because I've never seen him reading before. He is the kind of person who says he doesn't have time to read. We have argued about it. In my room Sue gave me a big hug. 'God,' she said, 'is it hell?' She walked around the room. Gingerly touched the part where the damp has made my wallpaper start to bubble and turn brown. Paused by one of the thin patches in the carpet, and again where the frayed edge does not reach the wall, revealing bare floorboards. I sat on the bed, and she sat at the table. We made conversation until she left.

She left behind a newspaper which she had read on the way over. I read it in the sitting room, spread out on the table. On the inside back page I saw a picture of a seven-year-old boy who was looking for parents. Five of his seven years had been spent in care, although he still saw his grandmother. He was, it said, lively and likeable, given to bad moods. I took the paper into the kitchen to show Danny. Only because I found it interesting. As I read it to him Harry, in his armchair, was attacking a finger with his front teeth, holding it in one hand like an awkward piece of meat.

Something unexpected had happened. I had discovered curiosity. After a short time, I became impatient with technical writing. I lost my job when I sent a photograph of Harry to Glaziers International *magazine along with a piece about links between severe depression and auto-cannibalism.*

Alan's feeling was that the transitional phase was coming to an end.

Fifteen

Victoria had skipped quickly through the Health
Questionnaire. Illness, having no place in her plans, bored her.
After the usual childhood episodes, she had succeeded in avoiding it. Hospitals were foreign places, doctor's waiting rooms no
more than boring preliminaries on the way to contraceptive or,
occasionally, antibiotic pills.

Have you now, or have you ever had:
Recurrent Cough, Coughing Blood, Pneumonia,
Bronchitis, Asthma, Hay Fever, Shortness of Breath,
Pleurisy, TB History, Chest Infections, Hoarseness,
Throat Troubles, Sinusitis, Chest Pain, Irregular Heart
Beat, Heart Troubles, High Blood Pressure, Dizzy Spells,
Fainting Spells, Frequent Headaches, Leg Pains or
Cramps, Trouble Swallowing, Stomach Pain, Frequent
Indigestion, Stomach Ulcer, Change in Bowel Habit,
Weight Loss/Gain, Black Stools, Rectal Bleeding,
Anaemia, Tumour or Cancer, Jaundice (Yellow Skin),
Diabetes, Urine Sugar/Albumin, Blood in Urine, Frequent
Urination, Burning on Urination, Awaken to Urination,
Prostate Troubles, Gynaecological Problems, Abnormal
Periods, Kidney Stones, Venereal Disease, Skin Troubles,
Eczema, Drug Allergy, Nose Trouble, Ear Trouble or
Deafness, Eye Problems, Excessive Worry, Numbness or

Tingling, Mental Illness, Epilepsy (Fits), Paralysis, Arthritis, Back Trouble, Broken Bones, Breast Lumps, Breast Discharge.

Her pen had slid down the 'No' column, filling it with ticks, defining herself, by a process of elimination, as a wholly healthy human being. Every bone and every organ, the steadily circulating blood, all of the surrounding flesh. She found however, that she wasn't reassured by this catalogue of wellness. If anything, it made her uneasy. She hadn't known she was so ostentatiously healthy. She had turned the page, her hand moving slowly about her body, to find herself confronted by a new list. She had begun to read, her pen pausing and hovering uncertainly over the questions that followed, as if afflicted with a stutter.

Do you suffer from recurring dreams?
Are you afraid of the dark?

'I want Hazel Feather's file, now, and I want you to prepare an official version on Edmund Staples, quickly, for my approval. I want it ready by the time they arrive.'

If anyone really had called him 'Buzz' Boyd, he probably would have hit them. He was short tempered, and the Walsh Foundation wasn't an organisation much given to staff tribunals, disciplinary procedures, or any other democratic trappings. Its hierarchy was feudal, and in the absence of the King, Boyd enjoyed playing the despotic Baron. As he walked on through the ranks of desks which surrounded his office, moving from administrative staff to his team of personal assistants, the bright young graduates who he changed from year to year in order to sustain eagerness without encouraging ambition, Boyd was pleased by the quietness that moved with him. Voices diminished and conversations paused within his aura. To one or two he nodded, but he didn't allow any change of expression to compromise his grave demeanour. His progress was funereally slow, and there was nothing to be heard in his wake but hushed voices, the whisper of papers and the dry, insect-like chattering of keyboards. He glanced back over his shoulder at the bent

131

heads, the uniformly dark colours. All the staff in his office obeyed a seventeen-page dress code. He entered his room, and no one saw his smile. *Dress code.* There was a construction that Hazel would enjoy.

L-shaped, his office inhabited a large corner of the building which housed the Foundation. Following his usual habit, Boyd slid open the window behind his desk and stepped out on to the balcony, grasping its curving railing and leaning forward at its centre, like a Captain on the prow of his ship. He wasn't looking down at the street, the small cars and the smaller people, he was looking up, at the gleaming, opaque windows all around him, towering over him. Icebergs in the grey sea. His favourite, in cold metallic blue, caught the sun at this hour, a dazzling decoration on its middle floors.

The Walsh building, in comparison, was compact, even squat, and its grimy red, asymmetrical, corniced and crenelled façade made it stand out like a fairy-tale dwarf, Rumpelstiltskin, among flawless Princes and Princesses. Not a particularly sea-worthy ship to Captain, but Boyd, leaning out over the elaborate wrought-iron railing, wouldn't have chosen to be anywhere else. The handsome skyscrapers were mostly split up, a floor here, a suite of offices there, some of them deserted, the rest divided between a heterogeneous jumble of companies of different origins, types and sizes. The Walsh building however, attended only to its own business. It sprawled below ground as well as above, narrowly missed by a tube line which intermittently made its bowels almost as noisy as a ship's engine room. Up on his balcony, looking at his lanky, more glamorous neighbours, Boyd had a sense of solid foundations, of strength.

He switched on the dictaphone and opened the file which had arrived on his desk, turning pages as he spoke into the tape.

'Hazel.'

Stickler for detail, he mentioned the date and time.

'What shall we say about her? Hazel Feather. What do we know about her? RMI. This isn't an honour of any kind, it means recovering from mental illness. It doesn't have an expiry date, the way cancer does, five years clear and then you're cured; it's more of a stigma than that, it hangs around you, harder to shake off, this blot on your papers.

'History. The doctors' synopsis: a grandparent subject to colourful manic periods; father died early; a mother pursued by depression.

'Symptoms. Hazel's symptom was loss. Loss of interest, loss of energy, loss of appetite. All draining away, all the good parts of life, the ones that actually involve living. And not to be replaced by sleep, because she lost that too, poor profligate. Stalked in small hours by large nightmares, some of which were going to come true. So she left college, went home to mother, just as mother, slowly recovering from her first stroke, suffered her second. She couldn't speak. She couldn't move much. After a while, she died. More loss. A life beginning to be defined by absence.'

Boyd paused, impassive as ever, listening to the quiet whir of the tape. He turned several pages at once.

'An unremarkable set of circumstances, an unremarkable response. The secret must be in the detail. I want to know you, Hazel, I want to find my way inside you. I won't have you holding back, I want everything. There's not enough here to have snagged Walsh's interest. I want the whole story. The key must lie in something intangible, not in your illness, certainly not in your photograph collection. A question of an attitude, an approach.'

The rest of the sleepless night was a mixture of embarrassment and frustration. The police, when called, soon established that Edmund had gone, pausing only to take some cold meat from the fridge. Lengthy but imperfect statements were taken in the sitting room which had once, only a few hours earlier, been so reassuring. Unpredictable events, it seemed, knew no decorum, recognised no barriers. Hazel was asked to ring the Standishes' hotel in Formentera to verify her position, while Paul tried to look at home in Mr Standish's clothes. It was hard to look at home while he was subject to uncontrollable fits of trembling and stuttering which, he felt, must make him look like a man with abominable secrets to conceal.

When they finally left, at four o'clock, Hazel stroked his head solicitously. 'Told you we shouldn't have called them,' she said. She lit another cigarette, and he noticed that she had only half a packet left. 'But you were right not to tell them that you knew anything about him.'

'Walsh will want to do it his way,' said Paul, in the insistent tone of a believer affirming his faith.

She knew London. Mostly he found himself walking behind her, allowing himself to be led. His treasured autonomy, he felt, was becoming increasingly fragile. And she was a difficult person to walk with down a crowded street, because she would frequently stop to slip a small camera from her bag, and take a surreptitious picture. Also, a surprising variety of shop windows seemed to engross her, and she had the instincts of a tour guide, unwilling to let anything slip by without some rubric. He was forever running into her back or stepping on her heels. Outside a department store: 'Easy pickings there, unless they've changed the security.' A coffee shop: 'This was where everyone met when I was at college; best ice cream for miles.' A second-hand bookshop: 'I worked here for a while, when I gave up the writing.' Paul hustled her on.

'Don't you want to hear about my life?' she complained.

Once she arrested him with an urgent hand on his forearm, and said, 'Can we follow him?'

She was looking back at a man, not distinctive from behind, who had just walked by, but she seemed to accept that it was not the right moment, because she did not go after him. Still with a hand on Paul's arm, she made no movement at all. They were, to his discomfort, a small, conspicuous island in the flow of people. Crowds always worried him. 'You have the perfect job,' she said, unaware of his restlessness, 'but it's wasted on you. You don't look at anyone, do you? I've noticed. It's absurd, but you have no curiosity. I should get you the sack, then I could have your job. I'd be much better at it.'

'No, you wouldn't,' said Paul, and then regretted his snappy tone. He moved her to the edge of the pavement. 'What was it about him?'

'Nothing. Just a big smile that made me want to know him

better. What I'm interested in is knowing people better, I thought I'd explained that. I catch smiles. I have an album of faces. I like to shadow people, sometimes for long periods, getting under their skin. And then perhaps meet them, chat them up, in a sense. I'm *for* interesting people, I'm in favour of them. They're worth a second glance at least. Hamlet kept tables you know, where he wrote his observations. That's all I do, watch people, write things down. I bet Shakespeare did too. He'd have used a camera if he could. What do you think?' She looked at his blank face. 'Come on then,' finally letting go of his arm, 'it's this way.'

She led him into smaller streets, taking turnings with a confidence he envied, still providing an intermittent commentary. He even admired her walk, her casual stride. In Aldesham, moving between home and the village, this was his gait too, but in London it changed entirely, his step was shorter, his pace quicker, his direction erratic, and he was conscious of the space he occupied.

Hazel stopped. 'This will be it.' She looked at him with the same expression as when she had stroked his hair after the police left, so that he felt simultaneously comforted and irritated. It was the same way Victoria had been after his fall down the steps. What was he, an invalid? A child?

Hazel was still looking at him. 'Are you ready for this?'

He didn't answer her, but for the first time he moved in front of her, pushing through the glass-panelled swing doors, only thinking as he approached the woman at reception that Walsh would probably be busy, might not even be in the building.

'Paul Feather,' he said, 'and Hazel Feather,' and stopped, stymied for a moment by this unfamiliar coupling of their names, this link from a collection of vivid, largely uncomplicated memories ('Happy Birthday' sung standing on his head), to a continually surprising present.

The receptionist, who, in white shirt and red scarf, may or may not have been in a uniform, was talking into a phone clenched between shoulder and chin. Her hands were draped over a keyboard. 'Wait a minute,' she said, and looked up.

'Yes?' she said. 'And you are?'

Paul repeated their names, and she pressed a button on the keyboard, and looked at the short list that came on to the screen. 'Feather. Feathers, P. and H.' Her manner changed a little. She almost smiled. 'That seems to be fine, Mr Feather. The waiting room is up the stairs, on the left. I'll call Mr Boyd for you in a few moments.'

She was returning to her conversation when he interrupted her. 'We'd like to see Mr Walsh.'

She allowed one corner of her mouth to move marginally upwards. She looked past him. 'It's on your left,' she said, 'I think your wife has gone ahead of you.' She moved round in her seat, her face angled again into the receiver.

Hazel was waiting for him at the top of the first flight. 'Do you think we should split up? We may not have much time.'

For a moment he misunderstood. 'There's the waiting room, it's just behind you.' He could see it over her shoulder, book-lined, with several profoundly comfortable chairs.

'You'll never discover a thing if you let yourself be bullied, Paul. Take charge of your life. Come on, follow me.'

She moved away before he could comment on this contradiction. Taking charge of his life hadn't been an option for some time. It seemed to be only a question of whose orders he obeyed. He watched her continue up the stairs. The receptionist conveyed her imperatives, and Hazel hers, even the room itself seemed to be speaking to some part of him, attempting to dictate. Every choice available was someone else's idea of the right thing to do, not his own. He chose to follow his sister's lead. A triumph, he thought, for autonomy. The second floor emerged directly on to a large open-plan space, serried desks, bent heads, turned backs. Paul's glance passed over it swiftly. Was that . . .? No, it couldn't be. Follow Hazel, he told himself, don't add any further to the confusion. They kept climbing. In Paul's back it was spring, little buds of pain blossoming up and down his spine, a whole flowerbed coming into leaf just above his pelvis. He straightened, shoulders back, trying to keep his torso erect and still. It made him feel like a robot.

The door from the stairwell on the third floor led into a passage. Hazel smiled pleasantly and held the door open for someone coming out as they went in. Without hesitation she then walked into the room he had just left. With hesitation, Paul followed.

They found a small office, with a large desk and a large window, covered by a grey Venetian blind. It was shabby in the old style: formica, anglepoise lamp, big electric typewriter, dusty filing cabinets.

'What are we doing here?' said Paul.

The filing cabinets were like wardrobes in dark-green metal. Each drawer revealed rows of closely packed pale-green files. Hazel's hand was running over their tops, her fingers scurrying among labels, as she searched for 'F'.

'I know what you're up to,' said Paul. 'Waste of time. Why would my report be in this particular office, or even in this particular building? Do you have any idea how big the Walsh Foundation is? My report . . .'

'Here it is. It's a fat one too.' Hazel extracted the file from the cabinet, cradling it to prevent anything from slipping out. 'But what makes you say it's anything to do with you? It's me they want to see, isn't it?' She opened the file, and revealed the contents page.

1. *The Feather Report.*
2. *Paul.*
3. *Hazel.*

She flicked through the sheets. 'I remember that headline,' said Paul, peering over her shoulder. 'I told you. It's the stuff I've been sending them.' At the same time, she said, 'See? One of my photos. What did I tell you?'

They looked at each other, confused. Paul's research was in the second section, and some of Hazel's photographs and writings were in the third. These sections were appendices to the main report. The subject of the main report appeared to be Paul and Hazel.

They heard someone coming up the stairs. 'I'll put it back,' she said, 'we'll wait in the waiting room, this is bad for your nerves.'

Boyd, filling most of the corridor, met them as they came out of the room. 'I believe you're both trespassing,' he said. He extended his hand to Hazel. 'I'm pleased to meet you. Paul has done well. Shall we go up to my office?' Her hand was enclosed almost entirely in his. He held on to it for several seconds, looking at her as if he had apprehended a prisoner.

'Very little goes on in this building without my knowledge. Some would say very little goes on anywhere without my knowledge, but they flatter me, of course.' They were sitting around a low table in his office. Boyd was relaxed in a wide, brown leather, swivelling chair, Paul was on the edge of a hard, straight-backed one, trying to maintain his upright posture. He found some consolation in his view of Boyd's head, which was very nearly bald, covered by a thin and imperfect screen of dark hair. A tape-recorder lay among the coffee cups, its red light gleaming, and Boyd had on his lap a pad of paper. At the top of the pad he had drawn a feather in a box.

'Now, I'd like to hear about your adventures since I last saw you,' he said. 'Please don't leave the office in the meantime, Hazel.'

Paul, reluctant at first, discovered fluency as he became involved in his story, and discovered structure as he told it, a sequence of cause and effect. This inspired him as it had when he had told Hazel his story in the Standish garden. By the end the tape, which had initially made him self-conscious, had become his perfect audience, the record he felt that not just his experience but also his eloquence deserved. He was barely aware of Hazel's movements. He didn't notice her occasional amused glances in his direction as she paced around the office, sitting behind the desk, taking up a stance on the balcony remarkably like Boyd's own.

Boyd continued to make notes for a few moments after Paul had finished. Then he stared at his pad, puzzling, as if seeking the best response to what he saw. He appeared to come to a decision, and when he finally spoke, his young voice was amused. 'Don't worry, Paul, you're not paranoid, there really is someone out to get you. And are you all right now, after your falls and stumbles?'

'Not really. My wrist is still weak, my leg hurts, my chest is sore, my back aches. When can we see Mr Walsh?'

'Oh dear, that body you've taken such good care of. Although I must say, I can think of nothing more futile than people standing round a coffin nodding and saying, "Well, he took good care of himself didn't he?" Do you see what I mean? I'm sure *you* do, Hazel. But still, I think you should be pleased, in a sense, that all your suspicions were justified. That's why we like you here, Paul. We like your reliability.'

Hazel was sitting now, in a chair like Boyd's. Higher than both of them, Paul felt able to be assertive. 'What can you tell me about the man who has been following me? How is he connected to you?'

'It's a shocking development, isn't it?' Boyd looked less than shocked. 'We have been aware of his existence for some time.' He got up, put his head round the door for a moment, and spoke to an assistant. 'His file is on the way. Edmund Staples. He's been complaining to us ever since your pamphlet was published, and we've done a little investigation into him. He's a colourful character. I think I can recall the salient points.' Boyd placed his hands together, as if praying, and began to recite a selection of facts. Edmund's fundamentalist upbringing, his entry into the army after his father's early death. His discharge, on the grounds that he didn't fit their psychological profile. 'That's a euphemism they like to use, it tends to apply to men who enjoy shooting people a little more than is customary.' His involvement with various sects, of which Jerome's was just the latest in the series. In Jerome's demise he found what he needed: a cause. 'And someone who's dead can't really let you down, can he?' Boyd finished with a friendly smile. 'He can only *be* let down, or slandered. That seems to be where you come in, Paul.'

The file arrived, and Boyd handed it to him. 'Perhaps you'd like to keep this one.'

'What are you going to do about it?'

'The Walsh Foundation likes to clear up its own problems. We'll do our best to trace our friend Edmund and deal with him appropriately.'

'"*Deal* with him", Boyd?'

'Deal with him, Hazel. Appropriately. Treat him, re-educate him. I think there is a moral responsibility involved, don't you? The Foundation has charitable extensions, we can accommodate Edmund, I don't see that as a difficulty. I imagine we'll even be able to compensate you, Paul, and indeed you, Hazel, for the distress you must have been suffering. The scene in the Standish house does sound alarming. Make sure you send us the bill for the window, Hazel, won't you?' Boyd drew a line beneath the notes on his pad, and then placed it face down on the desk. 'Now that's enough of that, isn't it? I must say, it's very good to have you both here. Very congenial. Strange, isn't it Paul, to think that only, what, ten days ago, we were no more to each other than voices on an answer-machine. While you, Hazel, were a complete mystery. And now here you both are, here we all are, in the heart of my lair.'

'And where is Walsh?' said Hazel. She was taking something out of her bag as she spoke. 'May I?'

Without pausing, she took three pictures of Boyd. Two shots of his head, which sagged chinless on his shoulders, like a partly-deflated football, and one of his body, slightly slumped, in his wrinkled V-neck sweater, his thin tie. He didn't try to answer her question, he just sustained for the camera his slight smile, the only expression his slow face had used since they arrived. He *tried* to sustain it. Paul, at first embarrassed by Hazel's action, was fascinated to see the smile waver, to be followed by a hint of indecision. The curve of the lips subsided, the face itself seemed to subside, a further deflation. Hazel took three more pictures at this, and then stopped.

'My X-ray camera,' she said, replacing it.

The tone was now cold: 'And what caption will you give me?'

Hazel shook her head. 'Trade secret,' she said, 'unless you'd like to tell me what keeps you going?' She looked at him brightly. 'Or how you cope with loneliness? What does a man like you do for sex?' She shrugged at his silence. 'How much do you know about me?' she asked. 'Why am I here?'

'You're here because Mr Walsh wants to see you. I'm afraid I'm not in full possession of the facts, surprising as that may seem. And Mr Walsh, before you ask, isn't in the building. Hasn't been for some time. There is what is known as a vacuum at the top. The Walsh Foundation is a headless body and, as a result, perhaps not as co-ordinated as it should be. Hence our difficulties with Edmund. Mr Walsh will be ceding control to me, of course, but it's a gradual process. He's reluctant to accept the inevitable. You and Paul, in fact, represent his final project. Everything else is in my hands.' He picked up the tape-recorder, weighing it in his large palm, as if to demonstrate. 'He seems to have taken a special interest in the two of you, and his precise motives, I very much regret, are not clear to me.'

Paul stood up. 'Someone was going to shoot me,' he said. His hands were shivering, he wanted to hit Boyd, or turn over his desk, this man who had threatened him, and was talking about a killer on the loose as if it was a small administrative error, less important than office politics. 'You must have encouraged him, you must have given him information to help him find me.'

Boyd stood too, and stepped up to Paul. For about fifteen seconds the two men stared at each other. The proximity, the physical presence, scared Paul as it had in his kitchen (I'm bigger than you, stronger . . .), but he didn't move away. He raised his hand. He didn't want to hit Boyd now, just to touch him, as if to feel him, the shape and texture of him, might make him more knowable.

It was Hazel who ended the long moment. 'This is pointless, Paul,' she said. Her matter-of-fact voice eased the tension, made Paul feel, for all his rage, as if he had been posturing.

Boyd nodded, his smile beginning slowly to return. 'She's right,' he said, 'slander is pointless. The thing to grasp, if you can, is that Mr Walsh still hopes to see you both. You'll find him in his cottage in Norfolk. Ours not to reason why, eh Paul?' Watching them both, he seemed to come to an abrupt decision. 'That's all we can usefully discuss at the moment,' he said. 'My assistant will give you directions for finding Mr Walsh.'

They found themselves abruptly outside his door, without having had the chance to ask about the large file in the faded office on the floor below.

141

From the balcony, he watched them leave the building. There was a delay of several minutes before they emerged. Hazel stopped and looked up at him, shading her eyes. She had known he would be there, Captain at the helm, conductor at the podium. Their eyes met over six storeys, he encountered her searching gaze, and then a cab drew up, and he looked past her: as they entered the flow of traffic he looked further down the wide road where angry cars were subdued by congestion, halted and released, halted and released, from here to the fringe of the city, and beyond, as if being marshalled in some intricate scheme, on a vast scale.

Sixteen

This was when they had only met once before.

'Easy enough to forget a chequebook. Just bring the money next time, sir, that'll be fine.'

'You make decisions about people quickly, Tod.'

'Yes sir, right away, most times. Ain't no art to it. There's two kinds, far as I can judge. There's wholesome, and there's unwholesome.'

Paul smiled indulgently. 'Maybe so. But how do you tell them apart? That's the problem you see, Tod.'

'Easy, Mr Feather, if you don't mind my saying. The first kind, wholesome, they put their litter in the bin outside the shop there. The second kind, unwholesome, don't. Just drop it in the road.'

'That's it?'

'Like I said, ain't no art to it.'

'I *loathed* him. He is the type of man I loathe. I couldn't stand him, I could hardly stand to be in the same room. So full of his fat sense of himself and his little circle of power. That weighty manner he loves is just indigestion, you know, and that's the reason for his nasty face, too. And doesn't he love his voice? Doesn't he love to pronounce and periphrase? What's my caption? I don't know. You know the picture with the thin straight lips, when he was trying not to look annoyed? His narrow eyes? How about: *A Martyr to Constipation*? What do you think? Paul? What do you think? He despises you, you know that, don't you? But then he despises almost everybody. He's a thug, and I loathe him. I *loathe* him.'

Paul was uncommunicative in the taxi, first unable to think about anything but the meeting they had had as they left the building, and then antagonised into silence by Hazel's excitement. He had still said nothing more than 'This way' by the time he reached the door of his hotel room. He unlocked it and walked in, his mind on what needed packing, and it took almost a minute to discover that Hazel hadn't followed him. He turned to find her standing in the doorway, gazing expressionlessly, as if taking snapshots with her eyes.

It was as if a cyclone had hit a small newsagent's, swirling at its centre for a few minutes, picking up sheafs of newspapers and stacks of magazines, whirling them round the room like water around a plughole, and then suddenly dropping them so that they fell at random, in sluttish, orderless tangles, covering every available surface. Bed, bedside table, chair, desk, floor.

Hazel's expression was hard to read. Amusement or concern? In either case, Paul wasn't pleased. 'What does this remind me of?' she said.

'Don't start, just don't even fucking *start*. I've had enough from you already. More than enough. I should never have got into this, I knew anything involving you meant trouble. Three years with the Walsh Foundation I've had, perfectly happy, then you turn up and everything falls apart. You think you know better than me after three *days*, don't you?'

'Don't swear, Paul, it doesn't suit you. You're much too repressed to be a good swearer.'

'Will you stop patronising me? You've done nothing but since we met.'

'I know, and you were expecting it to be all the other way round, weren't you?'

'Fuck *off*,' said Paul, infuriated at how sulky it sounded. She was right, the word just didn't come naturally, but he didn't have any other words to choose. After years of successfully avoiding confrontations, he didn't have the vocabulary for his anger. '*Don't* come and see Walsh, I don't want you to, I'll explain to him.'

'I want to come. I don't go along with things, Paul, that's not how I work. I make choices. Boyd or Walsh aren't in charge of my life, *I* am. You're summoned up here, followed and chased down a drainpipe by your poor fanatic, and now sent back where you came from, blindly obedient from start to finish. Tell me one thing. Where did Edmund get his information if not from the Foundation?'

'I don't know or care. It's not Walsh, it's just Boyd. It can't be Walsh, don't you know anything about him? He's establishment. I think he owns one of those American TV stations. You heard Boyd, it's just some kind of internal politics.'

'Your faith is as strong as Edmund's, isn't it? Anything said against Walsh is sacrilege. But you saw the same as me: *The Feather Report* isn't by either of us. It's *about* us.'

'I've had enough, I'm going. But first I want my bloody clothes back.'

'And then this last thing, your girlfriend . . .'

He made a grab for the collar of her shirt, *his* shirt, but she moved away as he caught it, 'What are you afraid of?' and he slipped on a magazine, falling into her, circling her waist in a kind of rugby tackle, falling on to the side of the bed with her and then toppling off the edge, landing beneath her, 'What are you afraid of?' pushing her off, furious now, buttons flying into his face and several different parts of his body flashing warning bursts of pain, chest, wrist, back, knee, 'What are you afraid of?' but she wouldn't come off, she was snarling and fending off his arms, and Mr Standish's baggy shirt was impeding him, his hands were disappearing in its sleeves and she was like a wild animal, clutching his ribs with her knees, snarling and asking over and over 'What are you afraid of? What are you afraid of?' and he couldn't shift her, he couldn't move her, he collapsed suddenly, totally, beneath her and said: 'You.'

There was a quiet cough. He looked up and Hazel looked round, to see a figure standing in the doorway.

'I could come back later?'

'Come in, Victoria, come in, just a bit of rough and tumble.'
Hazel lifted herself off him, brushing dust off her trousers.

Then he realised two things: first that she hadn't been snarling, but laughing, and second, that he couldn't get up.

'I can't get up,' he said.

Victoria and Hazel looked down at him.

'Oh God,' said Hazel, 'I'm sorry, I forgot all about your injuries.'

'Is it your back?' Victoria nodded, answering her own question. 'I thought you were holding yourself more than usually stiffly. What should we do? Should we lift you?'

'You should both just leave me alone. I think I'll just stay here, thank you, I could get to like it down here. I think I'll just stay here for a bit, until I'm feeling stronger. You two just carry on. Perhaps you could pack for me, Hazel?'

It was quite pleasant on the floor. In this position, from this unusual angle, he was permitted to watch without speaking.

'Are you looking up my skirt?' said Victoria.

'Not at all. Just at your ankles.'

Her stockings were white, with small white flowers scattered here and there. Hazel was wearing his grey socks. Paul closed his eyes, too tired suddenly for observation, almost too tired for thought. Victoria had just been hired by Boyd for a company which, she had found out, was a subsidiary of the Walsh Foundation. They had met her as they left the Walsh building. Why would he do that? To find out more about Paul perhaps, or just to needle him, make him anxious. Paul decided to try not to think. This was his position for exercises. Usually he would lie still for a while, breathing slowly and evenly, relaxing and loosening up tense muscles before he began. Much good it had done him. In spite of all the training his body had received, it had stumbled without distinction through the physical demands made on it. He felt like a knight from the age of chivalry, furnished with gorgeous, elaborate armour, unhorsed in battle. What happened next to such warriors, in the age of chivalry, was that helpless, unable to rise or even wriggle, they got hacked to death by peasants armed with sticks and hoes and rusting axes.

146

Best to lie still. Best not to move at all. Safety in stillness, as in silence.

Victoria was speaking to Hazel, about him, as if he was no longer there. 'This isn't unusual. I saw him at work once. A pile of newspapers spread out in front of him, and he was grabbing at them, turning pages frantically, as if he was in a race, tearing out bits, bending right over them and scanning them, pulling them apart then pushing them aside, right off the desk, to make room for the next one, and the next and the next. He couldn't get enough. He looked like a greedy man at a feast, guzzling, stuffing himself, desperate to get everything in. It's not pretty.'

Hazel was moving around the room, sifting the debris for possessions. 'Comes as no surprise,' she said. 'I'll tell you some time about a man called Harry.' She gingerly lifted Paul's left leg to retrieve a book hiding beneath a magazine. 'Did you bring much, Paul? I assume you travel light?'

Paul opened his eyes and watched Hazel gathering his few belongings for him. 'I meant to ask,' he said, 'do you remember me standing on my head, on Mum's birthday, when I was about six? You dared me to. Can you remember her reaction at all? Was she upset? Only it's been on my mind. I hope she wasn't upset.'

Hazel looked down at him in surprise. 'Upset? She laughed, of course, of course she did, she loved it. You were the one, you were the daredevil in those days. Did you forget that?' She sat down on the bed. 'What's wrong with you, Paul? What's happened to you? You've retreated, like Mum did. Did someone attack you, and you didn't tell us?' She turned to Victoria, tactfully silent in the background, turned back, shrugged. For the first time, there was no confidence in her. 'Look at you,' she said.

147

Seventeen

By now he was ready to find shelter. The raincoat he was fond of was beginning to let the water in, and his hands inside his deep pockets were becoming damp. It was hard, again, to know what to do next.

Edmund had given up doubt around the time that he killed his father. Freed from it, he had felt no pangs of withdrawal, he had only wondered why he had allowed it to bother him for so long. Cautiously returning to speech, he continued to avoid it. There was no trick involved, no sleight of hand, it was just a question of maintaining a rigorous watch over himself. It had reappeared only recently, tentatively with Jerome's death, and unmistakably with the notes that he had been receiving, that seemed to anticipate and develop his own thoughts.

He pushed doors open carelessly, moving from room to room, impatient. He stood at the window again, watching the retreating shapes. And again, and again, aiming first at one, and then the other. The arm raised, the familiar weight in the hand. The pale light over the two grey figures on the blurred grass. One limped slightly, that must be Paul. Now they were outside the light, but he could still see them, now shadows behind the tangly black leaves of the bushes, now lumpy targets as they rolled over the low fence. Now the gun hung at his side.

He relived the sequence without any attempt to recompose it.

In the last scene he looked upwards, where the view was infinitely clearer. Pinpoint stars, pure white on darkest blue. What he regretted was loss of clarity.

He remembered a sermon he had once heard. 'God loves doubt,' the Minister had said, 'and doubters.' He had scorned these words, and not returned to that church.

He was walking now, having abandoned the hired car, walking with his possessions in an Adidas bag, and waiting for purpose to re-establish itself. Waiting, in fact, to somehow acquire purpose. This in itself was unusual. Regarding purpose, he was accustomed to being in the passive mode. It was something he expected to be given. He wasn't used to waiting, certainly not accustomed to actively looking. He knew that a solution was readily available. The map of his next moves was probably already drawn, was probably ready for him in the designated place, but he didn't want it yet. He wasn't too sure that he wanted it at all. He wanted to step off the established route first, to give doubt a fair chance to be vindicated.

He walked down the street in the warm rain. Walking, he felt, was important. He was exposed to events, accessible to them. Walking involved several interactions with other people in the space of a few minutes. He avoided umbrellas. Occasionally, he looked into faces. Once he said 'Excuse me', when he brushed someone's shoulder. He paused to look in a window, and someone had to walk around him. He crossed the road at the zebra, when a driver stopped for him. He walked briefly in the gutter to avoid the queue at the bus-stop, and was splashed by a passing cyclist who shouted something back over her shoulder. Like a shy man at a party, Edmund observed hungrily. But the rain was persistent and heavy, literally heavy on his drenched coat, and by now he was ready to find shelter.

A woman was reading a *Daily Mail* and dripping on to the pile from which she had taken it. Snoopy's kennel was awash. She glanced several times at the window, and once at her watch. Wet brown hair tailed over her neck and shoulders. Her coat, like his, was white, but of a different cut. He moved alongside her, making space for himself as politely as he could, and reached up for a magazine. He looked at it for a few seconds, turned a page, looked at the window, then finally at her. Her lips. Odd how the skin turned inwards, creasing and bulging as it did so. He could see the mark of her lipstick, red, could instantly imagine her applying it, her mouth inches from its reflection in an almost-kiss, the tip like a crayon moving along the puckered surface. This fantasy was almost tactile. He felt his penis begin to press at his briefs, and wondered at the effect of this isolated detail.

Lips.

Did other people walk around looking at each other, noticing these things all the time? Did it have a similar effect? He hadn't even registered the rest of her face yet. He thought, on impulse, that he might try something unusual.

'See that?' he said. He nodded towards the window, where the rain was becoming dramatic, battering at the glass in noisy, splashy waves.

She looked up, eyed him and his magazine, glanced again at the window. 'It's happened before,' she said, conceding a shrug and returning to the paper.

He moved away. If she knew how very easy he would find it to kill her, she would be less dismissive. Anyway, her face didn't move him as her lips had. It was too smooth. How did women make their faces so smooth? He found women difficult. Even their clothes. He looked at them, and didn't know how they worked. What is this woman wearing beneath her coat? Is it a scarf or a collar? Does the blouse wrap around or button? If it wraps around, what keeps it there? And what relation does it bear to the thing below it? When Hilary died, Edmund had expected Dinah to get in touch. He had imagined, in some detail, a reunion of the family. His mysterious older brother, who was undoubtedly rich and successful by now. Neither had ever contacted him. If the police had found them, they hadn't told him about it. His eyes slipped helplessly away from the woman's smooth face. If anything was going to sidetrack him from his predetermined route, it was unlikely to be a woman. He didn't know how to approach them. In his fantasies they were compliant, and already naked, saving awkwardness with clothing. In real life however, they carried their personal space

150

with them, as well-defined as the shell of a car. He gazed at that white coat, from which water dripped on to the floor at her feet. He would have to look elsewhere. Persevere. Things had to be given space in which to happen.

He had moved from the small Theology section on to Film and TV Tie-ins when a boy stepped into his path. He was small, but Edmund was unsure of his age. He was dragging a skateboard by its end so that its back two wheels left tracks on the floor.

'Do you read books?' he asked.

'*Read* them?' said Edmund, as if this was a slightly unconventional idea. 'Not much, not really. Do you? Can you recommend anything?'

'I want a book with a lion. Do you know any books with lions?'

'You don't want lions,' said Edmund confidently. 'Lions get fat and lazy. You want a tiger. You can't tame tigers, not really. They pace up and down, and look like they'd tear you to pieces if you let them.'

Edmund spoke with authority. Ever since he was a child and his father had sanctioned it as a place of entertainment and education, he had spent time in the zoo. The lions were unimpressive. Fat lumps of meat were thrown by enthusiastic keepers across a moat and into the tiered, bushy enclosure. Usually, they wouldn't stir. Occasionally a keeper would succeed in hitting one with a heavy-looking joint, and it still wouldn't budge.

'Lions aren't really cats at all,' Edmund said. 'They're big, lazy dogs.' The boy looked at him sceptically, but not altogether disbelievingly. Edmund was pleased with himself. He had engaged someone's interest. He laid a hand on his shoulder, having a feeling that this is what one did with small boys. 'Now your tigers,' he said, 'are quite different. They don't get fat, and they don't get contented either. You only have to look at them. They're angry.'

In fact they usually looked to Edmund as if they were going insane. Their swift, obsessive pacing, their indifference to taunts from watching children, their eyes, focused on another place.

151

He dreamt of setting them free, and taking them out of the city. They would trust him and follow him, loping along behind and around him, like a troop of bodyguards, and he would lead them to safety. Sometimes he was one of them, pacing relentlessly behind bars, swollen with rage.

The boy stepped away from the hand on his shoulder. 'Do they really eat people?'

'Yes, they do, of course they do. People are their favourite food. What's your name?'

'Martin.'

'We could go to the zoo together, Martin.'

'Do you work there?'

'No, but I'll take you there. I'll show you to the tigers.'

The boy stepped away again from the hand that was returning to his shoulder. 'I have to go.'

'Why do you have to go? I mean it, I'll take you there.'

'I have to go now.'

And he ran off, dragging the skateboard behind him.

Edmund wasn't too discouraged. He was pleased to have had more success with Martin than with the woman by the magazines. After all, small boys weren't strangers to him. He had slept in the same room as Michael for many years. And there was the army. Women were the problem. Their unfamiliarity. Ruth had been too young, and when Dinah was around, even though there were only two years between them, she had been different, more like a mother. Women were something he could work up to, he felt, if he was given time. The woman in the Standish house, for instance, had been friendly. In different circumstances, a different life could be lived. He was preoccupied with different lives. His fantasies, concerning his family, women, even tigers, all seemed to hint at possibilities that were open to him but just, temporarily, out of reach. There was an exception, of course, but he didn't want to think about that now. He was giving optimism a chance. It was all possible, if he was given time. Or if, he corrected himself, he *made* time.

Outside the centre the rain was much lighter, forming patterns in diagonal dotted lines on windows, like arrows.

Choice: left for the tube, right to follow Martin.

*

The skateboard, green fibre-glass, stickers, lurid pink wheels, disappeared into a crowd of adult legs. Whenever Martin looked round, Edmund wasn't in sight. He did look round at first, a few times, but he was soon reassured by the other people, and distracted by the colourful shop-fronts. He stared into the window of a Pizza Express, face pressed to the glass, until he had succeeded in annoying some diners. A man paused with a slice of pizza in his hand and stared back for a while, before trying to ignore him. Martin smirked. Feeding time. He still dragged the board behind him, because it was too crowded to ride. Adults looked down with growls when it collided with their ankles. Martin, purposeful, was unaffected and possibly unaware. He turned down a side-street of closely-packed houses and mounted the board. It clattered over the pavement. Another side-street and he was almost alone.

Unreasonably, it was sunny now. The only place in the world now for Martin was the park, because the air was so fresh and in the park the damp grass was glistening in a thousand places, as if scattered with fragments of glass. He paused on top of a hill, and then pushed himself off, crouching, streamlining his body, leaning into a curve, clutching the bottom of the board as he leaned, face in the rushing wind, fingers inches from the furiously spinning wheels. The hill levelled and sloped upwards and he rose slowly as the gradient did, tipping himself into the dangerous grass, before his momentum was exhausted.

Edmund was sitting in the middle of the bench, his arms outstretched along its back. He watched Martin approach and adjusted his position so that his legs were across the path. On the next bench a woman was sitting reading, her dog lying on the ground beside her.

'Have you been following me?' said Edmund.

'No.' He pouted with impatience. This wasn't what he wanted now, still exhilarated after his ride.

'You have, you've been following me.' Edmund smiled, as if to say that he forgave him. 'Gumshoe.'

'I haven't.'

'Oh.' He stopped smiling, and moved his legs. 'Go if you like, then.' But he carried straight on: 'I've got some time to kill, we could just chat if you like.'

Martin hesitated. 'If you just stay there,' he said. The man's bony face was disturbing, but in his tone there was a flattering nuance which requested Martin's attention. The woman was still on the next bench, the sun was out, he might have a story to tell his friends.

Edmund pulled his legs right up now and crossed them, clasping his hands over his ankles. He looked like a winged insect. 'You're very sensible,' he said. 'That'll be your parents.'

'Yes,' said Martin, nodding. 'I have very . . . sensible parents.' He tried out the phrase and liked it. Their invocation seemed to make him feel happier.

Edmund was silent for a minute, long enough for Martin to become restless again. 'Well, that's good,' he said eventually, 'that's very good.'

'Has something happened to your parents?' asked Martin.

'I wouldn't say anything's happened to them exactly.' He paused, and then snorted at his accidental comic timing. 'They're dead.'

Martin laughed too, uncertainly, and suddenly Edmund leant forward and snatched his forearm. 'It's not funny, Martin, it's not a joke. I killed my father, kicked him down the stairs, drunk as a cunt he was, head over heels he went, Martin, arse over tit he went, cracked his head open in two different places they told me. Broke his jaw and his nose and his arm. Fell to bits, you could say.' Martin pulled himself free and moved a step away. 'And what was I then? I was a gangling, unpopular fifteen-year-old. And what am I now?' Martin was backing away, but Edmund continued to address him. 'I'm not my father's son, not really. And I'm certainly not a soldier. Maybe I'm not even a believer. Do you know the pain of not knowing who you are, Martin? It's a weakness, a nausea, you can't quite focus, you can't quite think. That's how it was last night. Dear God,' he said abruptly, and he lowered his face into his hands, 'what is happening to me?'

Martin had gone as far as the woman on the next bench before he looked back, and he walked on almost immediately, and then began to run.

When Edmund raised his face, it took several seconds for his eyes to focus. He was confused by the fact that the skateboard was still at his feet. 'Sorry about the language,' he said, addressing it. 'Army habits.'

There was still time to kill. Resting his heels on the skateboard he leafed slowly through his magazine, looking closely at the bright pictures, bringing one right up in front of his eyes. He couldn't find the intriguing detail that he had observed on the woman in the shop, although there was much more to see. He pushed the skateboard to and fro. When the woman from the next bench walked by he made no attempt to hide what he was reading, but he didn't raise his eyes. Soon after she had gone, checking his watch again, he put the rolled magazine into the Adidas bag, and began to leave. He started walking but stopped again almost immediately. He looked up and down the path, and then back at the skateboard. He returned to fetch it and walked on, with the Adidas bag in one hand and the board in the other, its wheels staining his raincoat.

The station in mid-afternoon was almost empty. Smears and skid-marks of dirt covered the floor. The glass roof arched high above, ribbed with metal bars. Edmund checked the timetable and then headed for Lost Property. An unobtrusive corner door led to a small well-lit room cut in half by a low counter with a tough, ridged-rubber surface. Beyond it he could see a back room which was thickly hung with umbrellas, like some odd unseasonal decoration. He coughed loudly and a woman appeared. She saw the skateboard and laughed.

'Your good deed for the day, is it, dear?'

Edmund, disarmed by this, put the skateboard on the counter and left. His experiment with communication was over. He went straight to the left-luggage lockers, moving more quickly now, and he fumbled slightly with the key. To find his instructions was a great relief.

Paul, it transpired, was now in Norfolk.

155

He ran now, up the platform, until he found a non-smoking carriage near the front, and in the carriage he chose a window seat. As the train moved off he sighed, a long, slow breath, and began to relax. He hated to catch trains, but liked to travel on them. His eyes rested on the woman sitting opposite, but her face offered him nothing. Noticing his gaze, she bared her teeth in response, and her hand stopped on its way to her hair. She snarled at him, and showed her claws. He expected nothing else. He snarled back, 'Rrrrr,' and took a bitter pleasure in watching her get up and hurriedly, with backward glances, move away.

Eighteen

Victoria was reminded of the various changes, troubles, irregu-
larities and abnormalities on the Foundation's health questionnaire. What would they call this? Was this paralysis? Paul
looked back at her, puzzled by her scrutiny.

'What are you thinking?'

'Are you comfortable?'

He was propped on the back seat of her car by a blanket,
two pillows stolen from the hotel, and several cushions bought
for the purpose. He couldn't move at all, but he suspected this
was only because of the padding that had been moulded
around him. He felt like some piece of delicate equipment.
Fragile. Handle With Care. In fact his back was feeling fine,
but for now he didn't mind being spoilt. He was relishing
Hazel's contrition.

'Are you more comfortable in the front or the back? Do you
want your feet up? Victoria, do you mind if he has his feet up?
Shall I move my seat forward?'

He waved a weak hand at the box cradled in her arms. 'Don't
put it in the boot, it'll give me something to read as we go.'

Hazel leant in. 'You've no interest in it. Don't humour me.'

'I'd like a look. I was hasty. And anyway, I'm not sure I feel
like talking.'

'Wait.' She laid the box in the boot and rifled its contents before reappearing. 'I sent you "Polar Bear", you know that. This is more of the same. Still about people, and how they cope.' She threw the pages on to his lap. 'Bear in mind, I don't want to hear a word about it.'

Paul, disconcerted, wasn't sure at first what he was looking at. As they set off, he started to listen to Hazel and Victoria's conversation but, finding that it wasn't about him, changed his mind and began to read.

JUST BEFORE THE END OF THE WORLD

It was a slow line, subject to delays. Even at eleven in the morning people stood five deep in front of Joan, up to the edge of the platform. The train still five minutes distant. Being skinny, she could have shuffled further forwards, but she preferred to stand at the back, against the curving wall. Although she was squeezed in between two people, hands pressed at her sides, someone's breath on her cheek, she felt that she was apart, that she had room to think. Her thoughts were in the detached tone of someone introducing a piece of classical music.

'The trouble with my research is that it tends towards misanthropy. The trouble with misanthropy is that it so easily finds justification for itself. It becomes a way of looking, a distortion.'

Leaving the tube was only a partial release. She was still surrounded. As she moved up the stairs the conversation around her was of last night's television, the wildlife pro-gramme. She wasn't listening. Her thoughts were a dispas-sionate commentary.

'What I need is a job which doesn't demand this journey, something to do part-time from home, wherever home might be, or something involving irregular trips to different destinations. Photographer, caterer, plumber, gardener. I'm not choosy, so long as there is still the opportunity for research. Only not this repetition, this reeling in every morning, as if a hook is caught in the soft flesh of my cheek.'

*

The man had a fistful of poetry, alphabetically arranged, Muldoon to Spender, stashed in voluminous pockets. He produced it and offered it to Joan.

'Take these?'

'I don't think so.'

'Take them. A pound each. Bargain.'

'No.'

'Where's Alf? Alf gives me a pound each. Twelve pounds here.'

'Where did you get them?'

'They were a present.'

'What, all of them?'

'I don't like poetry.' *Thrusting them at her. Wild eyebrows, bad breath.* 'Take!'

Usually the shop wasn't a bad place. Often quiet, leaving her with the smell of the books, glimpses of the street outside, time on her hands to consider her research. Usually she was generous. She would take a cautiously-reviewed first novel, unlikely to sell, and hand over two pounds to its reviewer.

'Come back when Alf's here, then.'

Baffled, he took a couple of steps away from her, head on one side. He looked so honestly puzzled that Joan began to feel sorry for him. She was quite surprised herself to find that she had scruples. They seemed to have appeared, firm and fully formed, from nowhere. Drawing a line. Drawing a line at accepting stolen poems.

Sensing hesitation, he stepped back towards her, holding out the books again.

'Ten pounds. I'm robbing myself. Do you know why I want the money? What do you think I am, a tramp? I'll tell you what I don't want it for, not for alcohol, or nicotine, or any other poison.'

It was true that she had smelt stale food on his breath, not cider or whisky. And he didn't look much like a tramp. His long overcoat was shabby but clean.

'Why do you want the money?'

'My bet. I have £375 on at the moment, and I have an

arrangement so that I can add to it all the time. I'm betting that there will be contact with aliens before the year 2000. Do you know what odds they're giving? They're giving odds of 500 to one. I'm going to make a lot of money. And all of it, except enough for me to live on, I am going to give towards a cleaner environment. Now do you understand? It's like giving to charity. The poets would approve.'

'What if they don't come?'

'Who?'

'What if the aliens don't come?'

'They will. They are coming.'

'How do you know?'

'They told me.'

✳

Lunch was with Bernard, a young teacher she had met in the shop. They ate in a brasserie that neither could afford. Joan fitted in, she was in her black period, baggy black T-shirt and jeans. Bernard, V-neck sweater and check shirt, did not. His parents had recently died, and he was disposing of their books in slow, painful instalments.

'My consolation is that it will take a very long time to sell them all. They have more books than you do. A lifetime's collection. I'd like you to see them.'

When he spoke to her, he looked at his plate. When he ate, he looked at her. Joan told him about her morning customer.

'I gave him the money. Only because Alf would have if I hadn't.'

'You were wrong to do that. I don't like to think of him being paid for stealing, just as I am being paid.'

Joan's eye was caught by a disturbance at the bar. A minor celebrity had come in, and two or three people were clustering around her. Her companion was pushing them away.

She said, 'If I was famous I wouldn't have a home, I would stay in different hotels, a day, a week, never more than a month, always moving. I wouldn't allow anyone to push away people who wanted to talk to me. I would stand with my back to the bar, and be seen. I'd meet thousands of people like that, and remember all of them. I'm good at faces. Eventually, any bar, pub or restaurant I went into, anywhere in the world, I would find people I knew. I would continue conversations abandoned a year earlier. Ask after families, pick up brief romances, step painlessly in and out of lives.'

Their meal was finished. Bernard asked her to come to his flat that evening and, feeling trapped by her own words, she said that she would.

✻

Alf stayed on for a while in the afternoon. While Joan stood behind the counter, he stacked the new poetry volumes on the shelf, placing them at random, running a fingernail down a few spines to give them a used look. Seeing her watching, he winked.

'Twelve for a tenner, eh? Good girl.'

✻

Bernard was pleased with himself. He was waving a fat cookbook at Joan.

'I never thought I could cook until I found this. It was my mother's. You won't get it for a while, not till I've mastered it. We're having coq au vin. *Onions, bacon, chicken, wine, couldn't be easier.'*

'Can I see the books?'

'Later. What would you like to drink?'

Bernard had done something surprising. He had put on black jeans and a white shirt. There was a message here, that she would have to read. Although Joan had been home, she hadn't changed. This was a deliberate decision. She knew how pleased he would have been to open the door and find her in a black dress, short-skirted, with a little gold jewellery. She could imagine his reaction precisely. His awkwardness. His pleasure, not just at the way she looked, but at how it reflected on him. His assumptions, and their consequences. Clothing consultant was another feasible job, one that Joan felt she might excel at. She would visit people

161

in their homes and arrange their wardrobes, dress them according to what they wanted to happen to them. People would approach her as they approached therapists and psychics. In many ways, it would be ideal.

After they had eaten, Bernard showed no signs of moving from the table.

'I would like to see your parents' books.'

'You see books every day. Aren't you bored of seeing them?'

'The books might tell me about your parents, and about you. I'd be interested, as part of my research. I'm studying people. In the shop, in bars and pubs, and in their own homes. When I have enough material I'm going to write my own book, about how people betray themselves.'

Bernard, betraying some amusement, took her into the sitting room. Three walls were lined with books. The fourth was almost bare, empty shelves like ribs. As Joan walked around the room, scanning titles, partly with an anthropological interest, partly with an eye to their resale value, Bernard followed her. It was hard to concentrate on the books when she could feel him so close behind her. She imagined him stepping in her footsteps, mimicking every movement, every turn of the head, every half-gesture. She led him back to the door of the room and into the hall. He followed her. His breath tickling the back of her neck. She imagined that when she left he would follow her down the street, always a few inches behind, never opening his mouth, never quite bringing himself to touch her, always a few inches behind, like a ghost on a television screen. She was overcome by a sudden, overwhelming dislike. As she picked up her coat he put a hand on her shoulder.

'Stop a minute. Don't go yet.'

His fingers touched her bare neck, and changed everything.

*

On the tube home Joan rubbed her cheek, imagining Bernard and Alf and the man with the poetry as captioned photographs in her planned book. It was getting harder to imagine the captions. This, she felt, was a good sign, imply-

ing that she was beginning to engage more fully. She was learning new ways of looking. However, according to the man with the poetry, she would be lucky ever to finish her research. Apparently the world was likely to end soon, it was touch and go whether the aliens would arrive in time. Apocalypse would come not in flood or fire, but in fog. Thick, heavy clouds of it, poisonous and corrosive, unrolling around the globe like loft insulation. His winnings, he hoped, would provide protective clothing, until the aliens could begin evacuation. He had in mind those monstrous white suits, like spacesuits, worn with bulky hoods and huge gauntlets. So much, thought Joan, for the job of clothing consultant.

'Who was Bernard?'

'Oh God,' said Hazel, 'I *knew* that would be the first thing he'd say. He's just like our mother used to be. All "It's time you had a nice boyfriend" with one hand, and "But darling, not him" with the other. Bernard doesn't exist, Paul.'

'But this is you, isn't it? I thought you'd just changed the names?'

'It's not that simple. There are no names involved. I said I didn't want to talk about it.'

Victoria confirmed this without taking her eyes from the road. 'She did, Paul, I heard her. And I heard you say you didn't feel like talking.'

'I'm feeling a bit better now.'

A glance in the mirror. 'I think you've been feeling better for some time. I think you've just been letting us pamper you.'

'I deserve it. Someone's trying to kill me, after all. And my sister beats me up, and you turn up out of the blue.'

'I'm glad you put that in the same category.'

With only the back of her head to go on, it was hard to be sure that Victoria was joking.

'Whatever's happened, Paul,' Hazel said, 'you asked for it. It's your way of life that's to blame.'

'My way of life?'

'I said exactly the same to him.' Victoria again. 'And what's more he agreed. Just before he fell down the stairs. "You're probably right," is what he said, "You're probably absolutely right".'

Hazel turned in her seat. 'What's your average week, Paul? I asked you at Bea's house, and you never said. I mean before all this started. Go on, describe your average week to us.'

'My week? Why? What about my week? Why do I feel you're ganging up on me?'

'Just a typical seven days in the life of Paul Feather. I asked you before and you ignored me.'

Paul remembered. *How do you shape your days?* 'Research,' he said, 'exactly. That was my typical week, just research. God knows if I'll ever get back to it.'

'What else?'

'Just research. Reading, watching TV, writing it all up, sending off packages of it now and then. And my exercises. You can guess it all yourself. Nothing spectacular, nothing out of the ordinary. What are you trying to say, Hazel? You're saying there's not much to it? It suits me, that's all that matters. Any week would sound incomplete if you made someone itemise it. Tell me your week if you're so different.'

'I'm not saying anything. What makes you think I'm saying something, Paul?'

'All right then.'

'All right?'

'Tell me about your week, then.'

'I will. I look after the house, and make notes about the people in it. I take a few pictures, follow the likely ones, chat with them. Writing. Looking up friends. Seeing my lover, who bears no relation, of course, to Bernard. Making love to him. Don't look surprised, you never asked me, did you? You have no curiosity about people. Making contacts for more house-sitting and bits and pieces of work. Have I told you how I like temporary jobs? They keep me fresh, and keep me supplied with material. Reading – have I already said reading? The thing is, Paul, you have no curiosity about people, almost no contact with people at all. It's not just me, everyone is on the fringe of your life. Suppose you were going to die, would you keep spending your time the way you do? Exercising fanatically? What, is there some Olympic event you haven't told us about? Are you living a real life? Because you are going to die, Paul.'

They were on the motorway, they seemed to have been between junctions eight and nine for a very long time. At the brow of each hill another long, six-laned stretch reeled out ahead. One day, not very long in the future, someone would have to decide how many roads could be built, how many cars could be sold, how important it was that things should progress in this way. Someone would have to say, 'No, I'm sorry. There's no room for any more roads, no room for any more cars. Sorry.' For now however, it looked fine, it looked beautiful, and you could imagine things carrying on in exactly the same way indefinitely. Admittedly the stacked cushions and pillows limited his view. Green and blue, the wide ribbon of grey: a child's picture. For now it looked beautiful, and it was hard to imagine that there might be a problem. As far as he could see, there was still every reason to be optimistic.

Paul subsided into silence. Hazel's story had reminded him of his panic attack in the underground. He found it no better on the platform than in the train. Usually, when a train was coming in, Paul would be sitting on a bench, or standing with his back pressed against the wall. If, by some oversight, he wasn't, he invariably looked over his shoulder, in case someone was planning to push him. If it was rush-hour, and he couldn't escape people in close proximity, he tried discreetly to size them up. Is that person really reading the advert, or are they watching me, using peripheral vision? Hazel was the kind of person he was looking out for. She sometimes felt an impulse to push someone under the on-coming train. It was one of those fantasies she thought almost everyone routinely considered and rejected. (It never worried her, this vision of a platform full of people with fantasies of casual murder.) Edmund had considered it, but more recently, since doubt had entered his life, he felt a temptation, like a kind of physical suction, to jump beneath the approaching train.

Nineteen

Tod opened the door while Paul was still fumbling with the key. 'Howdy.' He looked from face to face with pleasure and tipped his finger up to where his hat would have been. 'Pleased to meet you,' he said, a little self-conscious with the two strangers, allowing Norfolk to briefly displace Texas.

Paul made the introductions. 'Tod's been looking after the house for me.'

'Have you been house-sitting?' said Hazel. 'What have you learnt about my brother?'

Tod hitched his thumbs in the pockets of his jeans. 'No, ma'am, jest looking in now and then, moseying around. Everything's been hunky dory, Mr Feather, but there's piles of post we're holding for you down at the store. Seems like the whole world's writing to you. You could come and pick it up whenever you like.'

To Paul's surprise, this prospect didn't much please him. Hazel answered, 'No, he couldn't, he can't pick anything up in his present state. I'll go down to the village with you and help you bring it back. How would that be?'

Paul stood at the window as they left, watching Hazel's mobile face and hands. She was an animated listener. When he turned round he found that Victoria had gone upstairs.

'I like your sister.'

'I can see you do. It makes you wonder why I lost contact with her for so long.'

'I always did wonder.'

'Don't expect an answer. I don't know, is the answer. I feel I'm losing my way a bit.'

'How do you feel?'

'Just the same, achy and sore, ready to break.'

'Do you feel well enough?'

'I want it to be this way.'

Victoria was stronger, Hazel was stronger too. Why? Where had he gone wrong? He placed his hands on Victoria's, used his weight to hold her arms down, asserting his physical advantage, pressing himself against her. And she smiled at him, enjoying the strength of his body, permitting it. She wrapped her legs around him and lifted her face up to his, her breasts squashed against his chest, her tongue entering his mouth. He felt the tip of her tongue moving in his mouth. Sensitive, he felt the tips of her nipples on his skin. Most gentle. Her hair moving away from her face. He let go of one arm and pulled her head roughly back down on to the pillow, raised his hips slightly, adjusting, holding back, choosing his moment. Her free hand, impatient, pushed him swiftly into her. He forgot his control, forgot everything, lost himself, until he came, much sooner than he had wanted, in a clumsy, sweaty rush of pleasure, forgetting, gasping as if hugely surprised, and forgetting everything, all the discrete things that he had been anxious to keep in a coherent fashion in his mind. All gone, like inks, beginning to create a picture, washed by rain to one colour.

Some time passed, nothing unwelcome had returned, and now her hand was guiding his, and he was saying her name, twice, three times, and her smile was growing and growing, losing its focus, and he saw nothing else, in the great luxury of forgetting himself.

Exhausted, he slept.

She watched him. His posture was dramatic, like Chatterton sprawled on his couch. One arm across his forehead, the other splayed out beside him. His arms, like his shoulders and chest, were shapely. She lifted the sheet slightly. His neatly creased stomach. Only his penis let the side down. Flabby, lolling against his leg, it spoilt the streamlined effect. She had been uncertain about Paul for a long time. But recent events. Hazel, the danger he had been in, altered circumstances. He seemed more interested in people now, less interested in things. She was still uncertain, but what had changed was that her resentment had gone. She smiled at this understanding, and reached down, and touched his unstreamlined, unshapely penis. Unlike Paul, Victoria was a great believer in change, and development.

Boyd contemplated his weekend.

'Get me Hazel's file again, to take home, and you might as well get her brother's as well. I want a One-Eleven on Staples on my desk on Monday.'

Boyd's typical week was even less eventful than Paul's. It was spent largely in his office. Not just in the building but in the office, behind the desk. He believed in position, in the weight and presence of a man in a particular place. He saw himself as a generator. He believed, although he would find a different way of expressing it, in waves of power emanating from a place of power. Electro-magnetic radiations that affect mood and health. Leukaemia occurs in clusters. Ley lines cause cancer if your bedroom happens to lie on one. There are elements in the earth that, over a period of time, may poison us. *Places* have power. The deep, intrinsic significance of the land. Have your eyes open for clues: if a cat sleeps there, you can too. Consult authorities, sensitive people. Boyd believed in these things, and drew conclusions. He distrusted ancient, intrinsic power, and considered how he could use it, make it new. Anything that he was aware of, was something that he could use. Can stress cause cancer? Boyd could create intense stress. He enjoyed his position. He was the centre of gravity for the Foundation. He was not unpredictable, even whimsical, like Walsh. Boyd sat in his place, he paced his office, he looked out over the city, and he generated stress.

Whenever he wasn't in the building, he was in danger of disorientation. He felt lost. He had created routines to steady himself.

168

After work, he would always visit the same restaurant and sit at the same table. The manager would bring the menu and a bottle of quite expensive red wine, would say 'Good evening', and would retreat without waiting for an answer. The waiter knew how long to pause before approaching Boyd for his order. Typically, pasta, veal, cheese. Boyd ate slowly, but without any sign of relish, or even of satisfaction. He drank his wine, always one full bottle, by large mouthfuls. He never sipped. While he ate, chewing slowly, he would gaze at other diners, and at the pictures which covered the walls. His large face hardly moving as he chewed, his expression not changing.

What does a man like this do at the weekends? He was married once, but not for long. There was a daughter who never saw him, even a grand-daughter, so a postcard had recently informed him. But he was alone, and even a loathsome man, a man who speculates about causing cancer, is vulnerable to loneliness. It was as if he was bereaved. What did he do? He took work home. He took home the files of people the Foundation had an interest in. He read them, annotated them (because he was a great taker of notes), and dreamt of plans. Boyd's plans were grand, large-scale things, intersecting and building one on another, creating unlikely structures, implausible results. Ambitious architect, he drew them up, and then revised them, and then elaborated them. The elaboration was what he enjoyed, the fine, idiosyncratic detail. He was more than ready to take over. It wasn't merely Walsh's physical state, he had grown – Boyd had chosen the adjective with care – he had grown *unconscientious*.

Boyd was nothing if not hard-working. When the Foundation was short of subjects, he took home the files of his own staff and pondered these, like an artist working on a miniature, for an exercise.

He wasn't however, a slave to his work. He had a hobby. His hobby was shoes. They were tailor-made for him, in black leather, brown leather and suede, patterned and plain, some with tasselled laces, a few with reckless two-tone panels. In many cases the differences were minimal, but each pair he

169

owned was unique, and he owned enough pairs to wear a different one to work every day for several weeks. He liked to inspect them, and ponder what to order next. They gleamed, and any one he picked up was likely to be perfect. He liked to examine it for flaws, and find none. He liked to imagine making his own shoes. He had gone so far as to buy the materials. They occupied one room of his house, which was towards the end of the Nash terrace overlooking Regent's Park. In this room he kept his leather, his strong shoemaker's thread, his nails and, central to the work, his rack of wooden lasts. There were models of his feet, and a few of various subordinates, precisely designed using measurements plundered from medical files. (No file was sufficiently confidential to exclude Boyd.) He had bought all the equipment, but having bought it, he had found that his enthusiasm diminished. It occupied the room, that seemed to be enough. It would all be ready, in pristine condition, if the urge returned. Occasionally, he toyed with the equipment, picked up a smoothly-curving last, with a name printed on it. Some time in the future, he might present a pair of shoes to somebody, out of the blue, for the sake of watching their surprise, receiving their gratitude. He would nod without a word, as if there was nothing out of the ordinary in such a gift.

He filled his time adequately, but not with any kind of communication. He would have liked a companion. A male friend, to share his meals and some of his free time. Weekends. J. Edgar Hoover had such a friend, and J. Edgar Hoover achieved a great deal, no matter what might now be said. Companions should be available, Boyd sometimes thought, in the same way that company cars are available, as perks for executives. They should be tailored to individual needs, their sophistication dependent on seniority. His would be quiet and interested, clever enough for his interest to be worthwhile, clever enough to be stimulating, in a self-effacing way. Boyd felt that if he achieved control of the project, he might manoeuvre Paul into such a position. If he survived.

Edmund? Edmund didn't have a typical week. He was so used to loneliness that he didn't have a name for it. While Paul slept,

Edmund rolled a bullet between his fingertips like a home-made cigarette. It takes such a very small thing. Doubt has spoilt everything for Edmund. He woke early this morning to find himself in the middle of a furious interior monologue. 'No,' he said. 'You can't do that. Why?'

There are sometimes similarities to be found between people who would deny that any similarities exist. Like Boyd, Edmund would welcome a companion, like Paul, he felt that his life was unravelling.

Mind the gap.
Let the passengers off first, please.
Move right down the train, please.
Mind the doors.

Tod and Hazel were unloading the van. Three large cardboard boxes of letters, magazines and parcels. Paul stood in the window to watch, thinking of the tube again, of panic attacks. A body on the line. The trouble with forgetting, was that it left you vulnerable when you began to remember again. Memories came into his mind, triggering each other, spreading. Hazel saw him and waved, appeared to say something, inaudible thankfully, and then returned to chattering at Tod. No doubt she had listened all the way to the village, and talked all the way back. This, Paul already recognised, would be like her. Listen, evaluate, reply. That had been the pattern: she had heard him out, made her judgements, and then begun to probe. They had taken a long time, she and Tod, more than enough time to talk about him, his habits, how he lived.

He felt a touch on his back and he jumped, a major spasm involving all of his upper body, so that he almost hit the window with his forehead. It was the shock that there should be someone there *behind* him, when he was behind the window, looking out.

'Tense again?' said Victoria. 'Already? You should stay in bed, you need a long, long rest.'

'I know,' he said. 'I know that already. What's happened is I've run out of any other ideas. I see myself in a medical

171

casebook: The Man Who Stayed In Bed. I see me confining myself in bed and refusing to get out. I could carry on my research as long as it was brought to the bedside. A fridge within reach. And one of those remote controls which does every appliance in the room. The slight pressure of a finger would bring me the world. And I'd still get my share of attention. TV would come to me eventually, inevitably. A camera crew after novelty at the end of the news. And then I'd watch myself. After the famine and the crisis, the man who won't get out of bed. I've thought it all out, you can tell, this is a serious fantasy. If ever I really had to see anyone, I'd be carried there. I see doctors talking about my case, research being done on me, that's the way I see things developing at the moment.'

As he spoke, however, he was leaving the bedroom.

The boxes were on the drive, and Hazel was squatting beside them, sorting through.

'Leave them,' said Paul, 'I'll deal with them.'

'Seems like the whole world's writing to you,' she said.

'Leave them for me to sort out. I'll give you a call if I need a hand.'

Hazel went inside the house with Victoria, and he took her place, sorting through the boxes. Newspapers stained his fingers as he looked over them. He found a cache of junk mail and was offered several cars and holidays in the space of a few seconds. He didn't pause over anything, he skimmed it expertly, ident- ifying it, placing it mentally in his scheme, setting it aside. Nothing was irrelevant, this was the glory of his research, and the key to the pressure it exerted. Once it had been about violence, causes and effects, now there was no limit to it. His heart sank at the sight of the boxes, and his depression grew as he examined them, because it all belonged, the whole world belonged and called out for his attention, his shaping eye. He took the matches from his pocket, and set fire to the torn remains of a large brown envelope. He hadn't built a bonfire, he had strewn everything in a ragged circle around him. He ripped up one of the boxes, lit a fragment of cardboard from the envelope, and eased it between the folds of several newspapers. He took another box and held it over the flames, then turned,

172

still squatting, and lit more papers and envelopes, a couple of books, pamphlets, a pack of assorted birthday cards. The flames moved up the box he was holding, towards his hand. He dropped it. Squatting in a bare circle of gravel, he was surrounded by a low ring of fire now, with fierce, lively patches and darker, smouldering areas. Flames smeared over cardboard, and flared over newspaper. He watched it all burn, now and then shifting things to encourage them to catch, turning to make sure that it continued all around him, unconcerned by the heat, interested in the changing patterns being created and destroyed, created and destroyed. He felt like a witch doctor, engaged in an obscure ceremony. Once, not long ago, he had felt himself to be an anthropologist, now he felt more like the studied than the one who studies. He was a member of a remote tribe, searching in a primitive manner for auguries, for reassurance, for a measure of protection in the face of encroaching civilisation and all of its attendant demons.

Twenty

Paul was trying to explain himself. It wasn't something he was accustomed to.

'I have cancelled subscriptions, I have asked to be removed from lists.'

'On account of me? On account of my back?'

'On account of me. On account, if you like, of *my* back. It's a weight removed.'

'Talk to me about weight. I should send you doctors' bills.'

'It will take effect . . .'

Paul felt hands on his shoulders. He turned away from the postman, to find Hazel behind him. She moved round him, said a word and shut the door.

Paul said, 'It's hard to take a step without something of this sort. It's what I have always tried to avoid. Friction. I know too much; and you can't know without being known. I have tried to make myself invisible here, and it hasn't worked. I'm on lists. I have made myself known. There is Walsh, of course, and there is Boyd, people working for them, but there are these other people too, the ones compiling the lists. I'm assessed as a consumer, as a future father and husband, my career prospects are judged, what I like to eat and drink is taken into account, the size of my house, my taste in books. People picking over facts. Assumptions are made, and acted upon. My ferocious postman thinks there is too much of this. I agree with him. There is too much information. I know too much, and there is too much known about me.'

Hazel stood with her hands on his forearms, and her back to the door, as if guarding it. 'I think the time has come,' she said. 'I think it should be today. Don't you?'

Victoria drove them to the station, and then left them. Few words were exchanged. The directions Boyd's secretary had given them involved several stages, train and coach and bus. They talked about Walsh. Or Paul talked about him, rediscovering an enthusiasm he thought he had lost.

'He is the architect, after all,' he said. 'He will have the answers. Look at the Foundation he created. He's a giant in his field.'

'What field is that?'

Paul shrugged. 'Knowledge. He will have the answers.'

'What answers exactly?'

Paul shook his head, frowning impatiently.

Later, as they came close to their destination, 'He won't be there,' he said.

'He will, because he wants to see us.'

'I don't know if he does any more. There are stories that surround him you know, myths. I read somewhere that he funds a private army. What's he going to be like? Anyone who controls Boyd would have to be pretty fierce. It's probably some kind of estate, with patrols. Do you think we're safe?'

They arrived in the middle of the afternoon. It was a large detached house in a row of four, on the edge of a small village. As they approached up the drive, two men came out to meet them, one in a white smock, who might have been a cook or a nurse, and the other a thin man, dressed in a baggy, double-breasted grey suit.

'For God's sake stop following me!' The man in the smock hesitated at this, and retreated uncertainly to the door, while the second man walked on towards Paul and Hazel. His left hand was in his jacket pocket, his right was held out well before he reached them. He looked like ageing royalty, frail, but conscious of his position.

'Walsh. Very good of you to come. Shall we sit outside?'

He shook hands with each of them. Prominent bones within papery skin. Ridged, yellow nails.

He walked slowly, with Paul and Hazel on either side of him, across the lawn. They went through a passage lined by trellises and overhung by a fruit tree, and came out behind the house. His smile was tentative, as he indicated seats. They sat at the table in the garden, and another man brought drinks. White wine for Hazel, and a dark beer for Paul and Walsh. Paul looked at the house, and saw a face move away from a window.

'They prefer me not to drink,' said Walsh, following his eyes, 'and they prefer me to stay indoors, but some things are intolerable. It's important, don't you think, to maintain a certain standard?'

Neither answered, and there was a silence. A sense that all three were waiting for something. A password perhaps, that would allow them to drop their masks.

Hazel tasted her wine. 'You know what I drink.'

He looked mildly surprised. 'I know everything. You must be aware by now.' He lifted his glass and lowered his lips to it. Took a long sip. 'I know you both intimately. How do you find the beer, Feather?'

'Fine.'

'*Fine*, you say. It's wasted on you. I have it imported especially. My neighbour, the MP, charming man, always visits when he's here, and I suspect that it's not purely my company which attracts him.'

He paused, perhaps to regain breath after the long sentence, perhaps to allow time for a response. There was no sound at all, except his throaty breathing. Paul wasn't sure what to say, Hazel was opting not to speak. So, like a good host, he continued. He spoke courteously, but with a hint of amusement, about Paul's uncultivated tastes – mentions of tuna and pasta – as compared to his own. 'I like everything to be perfect,' he said, and then corrected himself. 'That's not quite accurate; for me, everything *must* be perfect. So you were hardly a promising

176

subject. I must say, I congratulate myself, I really do, on scouting you out.'

His genial tone failed to break the ice. Paul studied him. It was hard to estimate his age. Short, light-brown hair, parted neatly. It was easy to tell that he would once have been suave, and poised. His age in any case seemed irrelevant, less important than the quantity of flesh remaining on his bones. Hazel was looking around, not appearing to pay attention. Paul understood. Listen, evaluate, reply. He imagined Walsh as an interviewer, with celebrated but reticent guests. Patient. Doing his best to draw them out. The secret of the interviewer's art is to ask simple questions.

Walsh asked if she liked the garden. 'How does it compare to Bea's?'

They duly looked around. Once it would have surpassed Bea's. It had been conceived on a lavish scale, with an eye to symmetry, complementary colours and textures, and the creation of specific moods. Once it might have been suitable for Walsh, perfect, but now it was ruined. The grass was brown and scrubby, the neglected remains of the flowerbeds were unattractively tangled, dying.

'Perhaps I should have employed the poor girl.'

They said nothing.

'Help,' he said abruptly, and paused to take a deep breath. 'You can't get help, can you?'

It occurred to Paul that Walsh was in pain. His throat was thin, which made it seem unusually long, and it moved freely inside his collar. When he turned his head stringy tendons stood out in relief. A question occurred to Paul: how does a perfectionist react to the imperfections of his body?

Walsh looked at them, looked closely from one to the other. 'Can you understand that I just wanted to meet you? Is that enough?'

He waited, but still neither spoke, as if silence was what they had planned before they arrived. His wet eyes in his tight, sallow face gazed at Hazel. Hazel didn't meet them.

He sighed. 'I dislike monologues,' he said finally, 'I become breathless. I had hoped to enjoy this meeting. So seldom that I

177

meet our people working in the field. The front-line. So few pleasures.'

He looked again from Hazel to Paul, as if hoping that this might placate them.

'For the most part, I don't even get proper reports. Boyd wishes to assert himself. I receive condensed versions, dry things with the character bleached out. But they couldn't condense you, Feather, couldn't rinse out the idiosyncrasy. I liked your *OED* pages. It seemed to me an original gesture. You saying, "Here, here is what we both deal in. Words. Take them, read them."'

Paul looked at him, and Walsh nodded in a friendly way, as if encouraging a shy child to join the conversation.

'I never meant to send those pages. They fell out, got mixed in. It was an accident.'

'I came to that conclusion after a while. They were simply how I made your acquaintance. Beginnings are unimportant. Lost very quickly in the mists of time and consequence.'

'What about the endings you create?'

'My point, my whole point, is that only one ending matters.'

This appeared to be a conversational cul-de-sac. Walsh continued hurriedly, not wanting another silence to develop.

'But you know that,' he said, 'your fear is what drew me to you. You were so *upset*. So I started reading the originals, unexpurgated. I had to insist, but there are still enough of my people there. To accommodate me. And I looked at your file. Your mother, of course, the assault. I follow my whims, I trust them. What interests me about you, Feather, is your fear. Then you, Hazel, cropped up very quickly. What interests me about you, is your different attitude. I divined these things, it's what I excel at. People. Naturally I thought it would be intriguing to bring you together. I'm afraid I have the perfectionist's love of control. Your fear, Paul, was the subtext of your work. Were you even aware that all your reports were about death?'

Another simple question, but Paul declined to answer it.

'In the circumstances,' Walsh continued, 'I responded. I have a personal interest in the subject.'

Hazel asked, 'What is it?'

'What?'

'Your personal interest.'

'In death? Yes. A personal interest. Personal reasons.'

'You're dying.'

He put a finger on his lips for several seconds, as if considering this, then turned back to Paul. 'You see? We share certain interests.'

Paul at this point got up, unpremeditated, and walked away from the table. There was a large pond at the end of the garden, and he walked towards this, and gazed down into the murky water for a while, until a sluggish orange movement revealed a fish. He watched it move through the near-stagnant water, appearing, disappearing. Near the surface, where the sun could reach it, it looked pale yellow rather than orange. He could make out individual scales, curled here and there like shavings of dead skin. He didn't want to return to the table, so he continued on the move around the garden, widely circling Walsh and his sister, the two of them with their shared interest in people, until he reached the house. Through the window he saw a man in a surprisingly small kitchen preparing a meal, pouring something in a long, slow stream into a saucepan. This was who he wanted to be, the man achieving something simple, but doing it skilfully, with care.

Paul sat down again, beside his sister. Walsh was talking again, explaining. The appropriate department, he was saying, had routinely followed up an intriguing paragraph in a newspaper. Walsh took an interest because of the man Jerome, because of the rumours surrounding him. 'My Foundation thrives on rumour,' he said. It became clear that Staples had killed his father. He liked the detail that began to appear, had his people look closer. Police and psychiatric reports, the army's assessment, the various enthusiasms. 'There are very few people and institutions that my Foundation cannot connect with,' he said. 'I have contacts everywhere, I *am* everywhere, in effect. I was a man of consequence. That is a phrase, isn't it? I *created* consequences, I was the stone that created the ripples.'

Once Walsh would certainly have been impressive, but the fragile fist on the table, a skimpy bird's nest, suggested only petulance.

'Do you know how much influence I used to possess? The most powerful people commissioned reports from me, and their actions depended on what they received. Boyd once called me the greatest manipulator of information since Goebbels.' He paused. 'A vulgar phrase, from a vulgar man.' But he smiled, in spite of himself.

'Lately,' he said. 'I have, to some extent, indulged my own interest. This is the privilege that a man in my position enjoys. I created an experiment, through an unlikely juxtaposition. Paul Feather, his sister, Edmund Staples. With those ingredients decided, I acted accordingly.'

Paul spoke again. 'What does that mean?'

'It means that we published your research, and then drew Edmund's attention to it.'

'Why?'

'Several reasons. Officially, in order to study reactions. Such information could be useful in hostage situations, or any number of terrorist scenarios. Also, I must confess, it was an ideal opportunity for a small wager, something that I can never resist. Boyd was sure Edmund would kill you. I thought not. Money changed hands.'

'This was a bet?'

Walsh nodded, casual, still watching, still studying Paul's reactions. He raised an open hand, as if to brush away objections. 'There was another motive,' he said, 'more pressing than either of these. I'm dying, as you've gathered. I have been researching attitudes to death. Yours, Hazel's, Edmund's. The deaths of your mother, and his father. Your own death, Paul, was the ideal spice to the mixture, the kind of inspired touch that makes my work unique.' He made a grating sound in his chest. Laughter. 'Staples was never going to be one to express his indignation in the pages of *The Times*, was he?'

He paused again, apologising for his joke with a smile that caused a blossoming of wrinkles all over his face, as if the many muscles involved were all visible beneath the skin. He looked like a man who had never apologised with anything stronger than a charming smile.

'You saw the file,' he said. 'There are two Feather reports. Yours and mine. You have been featuring in mine while compiling your own. There is some continuity. All three of us,' he included Hazel with a generous nod, 'are responding to the present, to what is in the air. Primarily, however, my subject is death. Approaches and responses. Something has happened to me, which was not planned. Old people always whine that their friends have all died. I will be one of those friends. My neighbours will mention it. Next door is the MP, who used to take an interest. Now it is Boyd he cultivates. I should have been spared, I wouldn't have minded my friends dying. I didn't expect things to happen to me. I *make* things happen. Used to make things happen. I liked everything to be perfect, and I made it so. Listen. I have begun to speak about myself in the past tense.'

More deep breaths as Walsh looked at them, sitting opposite him, unresponsive, and then he seemed suddenly to lose patience. As he became more animated, so it became more difficult for him to speak.

'How naive are you both? What do you imagine life is like? Civil? Decent? You two of all people. Know better. Life is grotesque.' His hand moved slightly on the table top. 'People are. Grotesque.'

Paul looked at Hazel. 'We'll leave now.'

'No.' Walsh raised his voice, and the word came out as a croak. He attempted to cover this with a bluff tone. 'Not one of your options. Because he's still after you, you know, we haven't deactivated him.' The words seemed to return his confidence. 'I didn't choose this violence, there was a miscalculation. I underestimated. I lost a good deal of money as a result.' Now that he was becoming composed, his words flowed more easily. 'What is the man capable of? That was the question I asked myself. The hardest question. What are any of us capable of? Would he push you down a long flight of stairs, like his father? Now we know that he would. Would he cut out your heart and eat it?'

He smiled genuinely now, pleased with this. 'I didn't choose violence,' he continued, 'but I have come to a more perfect understanding. He will continue gratefully to accept orders,

181

because he is incapable of anything else. I am in complete control. So you must stay here, because you're quite safe here.' He raised his eyebrows, as if he had made an irrefutable point. 'You'll talk to me. This is what I want to know. Personal reasons.' His raised hand shook a little as he pointed. The unsteady finger indicated Paul. 'Why are you less afraid?' And then Hazel. 'What did you have to do with it?'

She was still saying nothing.

He insisted: 'What's the secret of not being afraid?'

'I don't care what you want to know about,' Paul said abruptly, sounding, in his own ears, a little shrill. 'Do you understand?' He tried to control his voice but, attempting to sound reasonable, he only managed bafflement. 'Do you think it's right that you should dictate like this?'

Walsh tutted irritably. 'Of course,' he said. 'Everything I do is right. I have done nothing wrong in my entire life. It's in myself to choose what is right and wrong. If I decided to set another Staples on you, or to wind up my Foundation, or to have my treatment stopped, these would be acts of will. Right and wrong are not factors.'

Hazel moved a little in her chair, sitting forward. Walsh caught her eye, and then looked away, as Boyd had when faced by her camera.

She said, 'But you don't seem to have learnt much.'

He shrugged, the closest he had yet come to a defensive response. The padded shoulders of his jacket were a ghost of his former shape.

'I have been diverted. Diversion is valuable, in the face of what is approaching. I have got to know you both. In the normal run of things, one knows so few people. Isn't that so?'

'We're leaving,' Paul insisted, still not moving.

'Feather, you owe me a favour. I've changed you. Listen to me. Your neurotic behaviour. That anal obsession with tidiness. That irredeemably bourgeois approach. You were like Bea's tiresome parents, her squalid father. Hazel, it gave me pleasure to see their house invaded. It gave you pleasure too. Listen to me please. I want you to stay. We'll talk. You will eat well, I will gain some pleasure from watching you. And I will begin to understand better. Staples can be easily removed now, but I must talk to you both. Because of what has happened to me.'

Once Paul had visited Victoria, stayed with her for a while, and then discovered suddenly that he didn't want to be there, that he wanted to be back in his house, in its undemanding comfort. He had simply made excuses, overcoming her objections, and left. That had been their relationship in those days, departure contained in every meeting. A balance that he controlled: her wanting, his withholding. Something of that occasion, some physical sensation, now returned to Paul, sitting opposite this man whose power and influence he could only guess at, this man who had made a bet on whether or not Paul would be murdered. He asked, 'Are you alone here?'

Walsh squinted into the lowering sun, looked round at the house as if he expected someone to come out. He shaded his eyes with his hand. 'Alone?' he said. 'What makes you say that? No, I have a houseful of associates. As well as several unconventional ways of killing time.'

'Then enjoy them,' said Hazel. The movement of her hand included the garden and the house. 'This is what you've created with your choices. You've courted despair. Shall we leave now, Paul? Are you ready to leave?'

Walsh watched them stand, squinting more as he looked up at them. His breathing was uneven again.

'If you take this decision,' he said. 'No protection. He will find you. Because he is a determined man. And behind him is Boyd. I would be sad to lose you. So few pleasures.'

Paul looked down at the man who was leaning on the table, wheezing, holding his glass, spidery fingers wrapped around it. Then he left.

If he had wanted to call them back he would not have had the strength. He sat quite still for a while, still shielding his eyes, and then took a pad and pen from an inside pocket, and began making notes. He wrote quickly, in large, looping letters. It was one of his few pleasures to concoct rumours about himself which would be circulated in the media. He liked to think that others still spoke about him in the present tense. He paused for a moment and, with a wary glance at the house to see if he was watched, surreptitiously exchanged his empty glass for Paul's half-full one. He took a sip, relishing it, and then continued his work.

Twenty-One

When he woke up, she had gone.

(But he wasn't yet sure that he was awake.)

The room was unfamiliar. She had brought them to this hotel, saying a busy seaside town was a good place to be, in the circumstances. And the night had been disturbed. The night came back to him in fragments. Some of what he remembered hadn't happened, because some of it was a dream. Several dreams. But most of it undoubtedly had happened. His memory was reliable, because he had trained it. A conversation with his sister.

(Where was Hazel?)

Was he awake yet? What was confusing was that his dreams had been of the dozing kind, where you think you are in control, although really you are running behind them, or surfing on top of them, but never actually leading them. You think you are standing back, wry, detached observer, but you are more involved than you know. He had certainly been asleep. There had certainly been a conversation. Now he was awake.

(If he was awake now, then where was Hazel?)

He was thinking very slowly, cautiously, like someone stepping on slabs of ice floating on dark water.

'I'm thinking very slowly.'

This was the beginning of consciousness. The next thing was

becoming aware that it was light, and that he should be out of bed, working, or if not working then doing something. There is something that he is supposed to be doing. He closed his eyes again, allowing his trained memory, in its own time, to tell him what had happened.

He had tried to disrupt her system. Give her nothing to listen to, to evaluate, to reply to. Another flirtation with his old friend, silence.

She said to him, 'Tell me a memory of Mum.' It was towards the end of a slow monologue, riddled with pauses. 'After the accident, when that man attacked her, what did you feel? Did you feel anything?'

She said, 'It was ironic that I was just becoming close to her again, making a connection, when she had her second stroke, and couldn't speak any more.'

She said, 'I used to visit different worlds, when this one became too difficult. In childhood, of course, and then later as well. I had a favourite one at Malory, that I used to keep returning to. Shall I tell you?'

This was how the memory returned at first, stuttering, like messages on an answer-machine. It was as insistent as Boyd, intruding, not allowing him to be alone, reminding him that there was something that he was supposed to be doing.

She told him about this different world. There is an illness which wipes out half the men, and severely weakens the rest. Things change. There is no more violence. Women live together, with their daughters, sharing one man. Bea and Hazel and her mother. Boy children are taken away, to be brought up with proper regard to their health and prospects, trained in suitable accomplishments. The women go out to work and the man stays at home. His function is to keep house, cook, and, especially, try to provide babies with his impaired sperm. Things change. A good man is attractive, demure, and a father, that's what is meant by masculinity. Men and women essentially the same? No. A cranky notion. Violent men? Hardly. If there is any violence, it is against men. Women with grudges. All this occurs within a few generations. Some illness that appears and then disappears. 'And everyone,' Hazel said, 'would adapt. Because things change. They do, there's no law which says they don't. Things turn inside out. You agree, don't you?'

She waited several seconds for some response.

She said, 'Towards the end it was very difficult. She seemed to decide that it was time to die, she seemed to stop trying. That's what that man had done to her, he changed her personality. You must have been aware of that, even though you kept your distance. But although she was ready to die, she wouldn't go into hospital. I wanted her to, and felt bad of course for wanting her to.'

They could hear each other's breathing, and if they had looked, they would have seen each other, lying a few feet apart in the diluted darkness. It was very hot. He had turned the pillow over, because his sweat had made the pillowcase damp.

She said, 'I can forgive you. Have I told you I've forgiven you? For keeping your distance. We have our different ways of coping. But then for Walsh to expect me, or us, to hold his hand for him: that was too much.'

Paul saw him. 'Help,' he said, and paused to take a breath, looking at his dying garden.

Paul remembered it all.

Hazel spoke softly, and he listened. Twin beds.

He turned and saw the duvet, shoved back against the wall, revealing a big rectangle of rumpled sheet. Her absence admonished him.

He listened but didn't feel like answering. Turn the tables. Listen and evaluate. Only listening, giving himself time. Words were out of reach. (Talking is not something I do.) Until, during a pause, in a shifting moment, something happened.

His breathing changed, or hers. There was a small movement of his arm, a small movement that seemed laborious, because of the heat, because he was tired. In that moment, the quality of the silence changed, took on a texture, a weight. Now it contained words.

'It doesn't sound so bad, your different world.'

'Then you'd be no help to men's liberation.'

'No.'

'Which in any case would be a very distant concept.'

'A cranky notion.'

'Just so. Tell me a memory of Mum.'

He said, 'Cleaning windows.'

It was like word-association, it was what came into his head without premeditation. In this dark place, nothing but a hearing consciousness, he suddenly felt eloquent. He described her, sitting on the ledge, her legs inside but all the rest of her outside. She reaches up high to clean the top of the window, nothing keeping her in but her legs braced against the wall. She is leaning out, two floors up, and Paul is inside, watching her through the glass, sitting on his bed. Four years old? It is only when he starts to cry that she comes in, aware she is frightening him. 'But she was a woman who wasn't scared of ledges,' he said, eyes closed, seeing her. 'She wasn't scared of narrow places. Until the accident.'

Hazel picked up the theme of the past without comment, as if he had been answering her all night. It was another world she visited sometimes, a place where they were all different. Paul careless and her tentative, unsure of herself. 'Once I wrote down all the people who liked me. I pretended it was a Christmas card list, but it wasn't. I was just trying to convince myself I had connections in the world. It was reassuring to work on this list of names. Afterwards I phoned some people I hadn't talked to for a while, arranged meetings, trying to bump up the numbers a bit. I had this careful, planned gregariousness.'

She recreated one of the phone calls, both sides of the conversation. Hazel was good at telling stories, she played the parts, did the voices. Now she was telling Paul about a woman she knew who got into trouble when she hitched up her skirt in the street, down at the end of Pall Mall, pulled down her knickers, and urinated over a guardsman's boots. Asked in court why she did it she explained: 'He wouldn't talk to me.' 'What else do any of us want,' Hazel continued, 'but communication?'

In response to this, another silence. Paul remembered the past in lucid fragments, but didn't have the kind of access to it that Hazel seemed to enjoy. He found it difficult to bring to mind, as it is difficult sometimes to imagine one season when you are in the midst of another.

'Victoria likes you,' he said, seeking a safe subject. 'We're almost like a family, aren't we? So tell me about this man of yours. This Bernard. The man in your life.'

He was hoping for the luxury of more silence, but she didn't answer. It wasn't an ordinary conversation, question, answer, question, answer.

'Go on. You made me talk to you.' Petulant, like Walsh. 'Do you ask him to swap clothes with you?'

He glanced over at her, seeking a rare bit of eye-contact to stress his point, but she appeared to be asleep. Lying naked beside the duvet, she didn't seem to be oppressed by the heat. Unlike him, she spoke dreamily, without animation.

'Does that upset you? The clothes? Why does it? Tell me, why can men be in drag, but women can't? It seems to me that women have twice the choice. Is that fair?'

Hazel's verbal games, her probing. How had he answered her? 'I'm not playing any more of your games, Hazel.' Agressively. 'You have assumptions of your own that I don't go along with. Are you aware of that? I have my own method: the more you shut your mouth, I say, the more you know. You've said nothing to change my mind, so don't try to teach me. Pedagogue. Don't *tell* too much. We can just talk, talking is all right.'

She said, 'I am talking. Aren't I talking? There's nothing personal about this. I'm talking about things. Habits based on prehistoric assumptions. We're all fossils, shadows of prehistoric men. And I'm only talking about it because I think it's starting to change. Things do change. Evolution. There aren't so many cavemen any more, there's ear-rings instead, pony-tails, colourful shorts, baggy T-shirts, and all those timid men in suits hiding their flowery braces. Pushing at the limits of the acceptable. Suits haven't changed in 200 years. I'm only talking about growth, about men and women.'

Paul closed his eyes. 'I know you are. Suits. Memory, change,

189

growth. Couldn't be clearer. Men and women.'

'It isn't safe to be a stereotype,' she said mildly, not responding to his scorn. 'I investigate different ways to be. Are you going to sleep?'

Paul lay with his eyes closed.

(Where *was* Hazel? What was he supposed to be doing?)

What had all that been about? She liked, he knew, to provoke him. She didn't seem to mind if he didn't follow her. 'Does that upset you?' She liked to upset him. What was he supposed to make of it? He was supposed to avoid suits, that appeared to be the message. Because stereotypes weren't safe, they only had one way to be. He hadn't gone to sleep, not at that point. What had happened to his strategy? He was talking again, she was listening. She made him talk, it was one of the things she could do.

'Let me sum it up. A man killed his baby, because it cried during his favourite programme. I saw this, in a paragraph, in a newspaper. He picked up his baby and swung it against the wall, because he wanted to watch television. If I was writing the full report, and not just researching, if I was writing the book, that would be the introduction.'

She was on her back. He was lying on his side facing her now, his head propped on his hand. Sweat slid between. He was awake.

He said, 'It's not my job to explore his personal history. It's the wider view. Follow it through, what does it mean? The television is more important to him than his son? Or he lacks the imagination to see this little squally thing will soon grow into something he can love? Or he's lost the capacity to love? Why? Selfishness? Hardship? Has his soul been squeezed out of him, like toothpaste, or never been given a chance to grow in the first place? Is this the kind of man who attacked our mother?'

She put her hands over her head and burrowed them under the pillow, staring at the ceiling. 'Questions,' she said.

'This man who's after me, Staples, at least I can console myself that he's passionate about something more than a twice-weekly soap opera.'

'You work yourself up into a state,' she said.

'And is there nothing to get worked up about? Isn't it horrifying?'

But she looked so serene, lying there on her back, naked.

'*Horr*ifying,' she said. 'It means nothing. The only place to start, is not being afraid, because from there, you can go anywhere.' Horrifying. Slippery word, rollercoaster word with slippery stresses on it. There is a connection, if he can remember it, with another dream. 'You titillate yourself, the way you do with guilt. What did you feel, when you weren't coming to see Mum? What did you feel when you weren't coming to visit me? Guilt. And what did you do about it?'

His silence was her answer.

'You tease yourself.'

He said, 'It may be that I think too much. I observe things and I can extrapolate from them. Someone playing a radio too loud. It's easy to follow that frame of mind towards selfishness, a lack of concern for others, murder. It's easy.'

'What are you really afraid of, Paul?'

The curtain edges were framed in light, but they couldn't yet make out each other's faces distinctly.

'Everything.'

They listened to the silence.

'What about you?' he said. 'Superwoman. Be honest with me.'

'Young men with no morals. Old men with too much power.'

Question, answer, question, answer. Was it that simple? In the morning, Paul couldn't be sure. His well-trained memory wasn't accustomed to disclosure.

She said, 'There are different ways this could go now. Do you sense the balance?'

(All he sensed, in the night and in the morning, was lack of balance. Falling. There was a lot of death, and there was a lot of falling too.)

'Do you sense the balance? It's one of those times where you can see the different paths. He could still kill you. That could happen. You could kill him. You could do that, couldn't you? Walsh would bet on you being able to kill if you felt you had to.

191

Or you could become ill. You've been playing with that for a long time, haven't you, dreaming of serious illness, flirting with breakdown? That would be a kind of balance: as I become healthy, you subside. It's time for choice to play a part. You've abdicated it for a long time now, you've evaded it like a child stepping one place back in the queue for the injection, but the time has finally arrived. You knew that it would. You know what you have to do. You found me. Now you have to find Edmund.'

Here is the other dream, or a small part of it. A rope bridge, one of those flimsy things that crosses a chasm and sways in the wind. Through cracks in thin planks, the thread of a river is visible below. He is all right, though, he isn't on the bridge, he is standing on solid ground. It is strange to be standing on the earth and yet looking down so far. He is all right, until he realises that someone is behind him. Staples is behind him, with murder in his mind. Fretting, stepping forwards and backwards, he understands that his choice has been made for him. He steps on to the bridge and instantly – no dramatic tension here – something tears and then something snaps so that it rolls and he is tipped over and left hanging from a fraying rope, treading air, so high that it's hard to believe he wouldn't simply float if he were to let go. He can't conceive of being so high. After all, a moment ago, he was on the ground. Now he is weeping. He is going to be sick. Treading the yielding air. Nevertheless, he knows what he must do. He has to move hand over hand along the rope to the other side. Edmund won't be able to follow. He just has to put one hand in front of the other, and not look down or behind him, then he will be safe.

She said, 'We were writing the same report. We were writing a report on why our mother died. How not to be a killer, how not to be killed.' She said, 'Men and women. Couldn't be clearer. Memory, change, growth.'

Twenty-Two

His eyes opened wide and he sat up with an expulsion of breath that sounded like a whimper. Having suffered the same dream twice, Paul was now finally awake. He pulled aside the curtain and let the light fall on his face to convince himself of this. He was awake, and suffering from a hangover caused by too many words. But where was Hazel? She can't have gone out, he thought, she knows how dangerous it is.

Even as the thought formed, Paul knew it was untrue. It wasn't the kind of danger that would worry her. Edmund, his file suggested, was a deeply moral young man. And why had she said this resort was a good place to be? Because she wanted Edmund to find them there.

Morning, and Paul remembered it all, and began to understand. He lay back on the clammy sheet, with the light on his face. He had survived encounters with his would-be assassin on three occasions, only for his sister to virtually arrange an appointment with him. People appeared to have designs against him. He thought of Boyd, the fat man with the slow face, deliberate eyes. Boyd in his home, mocking him, 'Yours but to do or die', and on the balcony of his office, watching them leave. He thought of Walsh, still exerting his influence, under the careful eyes of his servants, dwindling. 'How naive are you?' And he thought of Victoria, and regretted her absence. If she was next to him now, she would give him strength. Together, they would be stronger than apart. Like Hazel, she would at least have words that might help him. Everyone seemed to have words to offer him, suggestions about how to improve himself. Even Tod, who never had much to say, had an air of competence that he lacked, probably harboured a few words of advice. Paul had been bombarded with words. How could this have happened, when he had been so careful, so scrupulous to protect himself? All these intrusions, eroding, cracking and then shattering the quiet, self-contained life he had arranged for himself.

And he thought of his mother, leaning carelessly out of the window, and he finally knew, although he didn't want to know, that he was going to find Edmund. With the knowledge, although it scared him, came relief. A decision. Perhaps he was becoming involved again in the management of his life.

The unfamiliar bed wasn't comfortable, and the air in the room was stale. His eyes were sticky and his throat dry. Had they drunk before going to bed? They had, at the hotel bar. ('It'll help you relax,' Hazel had said.) He sat up again and twitched the curtain aside, staring out on to the street as if waiting for something. His face was still with disappointment. The view was empty, and heat was gathering. He felt diminished. The night had left him weak and his hands trembled gently.

Breakfast, which was closer to lunch, was on a terrace where black wrought-iron chairs with comfortable seats waited stiffly at tables draped in pastel cloths. A striped awning protected guests from the sun. He looked out over the garden of the hotel in its hot summer green, parched in places to a pale, dry brown. He read a newspaper with close interest, propping it in front of him and seldom taking his eyes from it. The waiter looked at him over half-moon glasses, finding pleasure in his composed manner. A quality of reassurance.

'Is everything to your satisfaction, sir?'

'Thank you, everything is fine. Everything is excellent.'

He had corrected himself, feeling that 'fine' might sound grudging. Everything was excellent. The rolls fresh, the butter smooth, the jam thick with fruit and the coffee strong. He could have wished that breakfast lasted longer, that he might stay on the sheltered terrace, overlooking the garden, with the solicitous waiter hovering. Unlike Walsh, Paul happened upon perfection, rather than creating it. The waiter smiled, and retreated to inspect other tables.

Pushing his chair back, he left his folded newspaper and the remains of breakfast in a neat still-life on the table. That is what he thought when he looked back over his shoulder, that it looked like a simple, attractive picture. The newspaper no more than a black-and-white pattern, the background an uncomplicated wash of green. Complementary colours. And he was leaving it, re-entering the three-dimensional world. It seemed that anything peaceful in his life could be no more than a brief interlude.

In his room he went to the window, paused, and then returned to the door. His back to it, he looked around, assessing the characterless space. His half-empty suitcase was lying open by the bed. He took out a shirt and laid it on the mattress to cover another pause while he wondered what to do. He knew what he was going to do, but he allowed himself the luxury of pondering, as if he had several choices.

Alone again. It was some time since he had been alone, and he was no longer sure that he liked it.

('I get anxious,' said Vic, 'I get restless, I pace up and down.')

Paul felt slightly dizzy, as if after all he still hadn't entirely woken up.

Behind him there was abruptly a soft hiss and a fuzz of interference, sounds muttered out of the teeth of the radio. Two voices were arguing in loud yet muffled tones, as if the old-fashioned bulk of the thing was suffocating them. It was a big block of shiny black enamel, with ribs over its belly designed in sharp, interlocking triangles. Teeth. He put a finger inside one, traced its shape, and felt the slightly yielding, woven surface of the speaker behind it. The sounds conveyed effort, and suggested distress, but nothing intelligible was being said. This is the sound that anger makes. Just noise, but he didn't like noise, it made him wince, he needed silence. Recently he had been robbed of silence. Why had it come on? It continued to berate him while he tried several switches, but he couldn't seem to turn it off, or even affect the volume, so he followed the flex, down behind the table, along the floor on his hands and knees, thick, brown flex, half under and half over the carpet, intending to trace it to its source and unplug it, remembering the incident in the bath, the water that was live, crawling along the skirting, but when he found himself half lying, half kneeling on the sideboard, stretching his arm down behind it, trying to squeeze his arm into the narrow gap between it and the wall, he stopped suddenly, bent in this ungainly, almost indecent position, and rested his head in the crook of his elbow, breathing quickly and then slowly through his mouth. He heard his breathing and he heard his heart. He heard himself say something that Hazel had said to him:

'What has happened to you?'

That same regretful, accusing tone. She had said so much to him by this time, it seemed that she didn't even have to be there for the dialogue to continue. The radio barked its opinion, beginning to lose its patience, or its nerve, as he closed the door on it.

Summer had arrived late that year, and suddenly. It had been dry for months, and then, one day, heat.

Freak heat. Two weeks ago, strolling to the post office after an ordinary day's work, he had been considering weather in his usual, objective way, looking at its effects on patterns of behaviour. Since then conditions had changed, things had closed in on him, like a circle tightening around him. His large view had shrunk. The weather was implicated. It seemed inevitable that the day he was looking for Edmund should be the latest contender for the hottest day of the century.

He kept close to the shop-fronts, but the light reflected off the pavement and darted in now and then between canopies. Killing time, he stood and looked in windows and studied his reflection. The man in the cotton jacket, comfortably creased, sunglasses, a remarkably calm expression. As he walked and stopped and walked again, he was continuing his dialogue with himself. Someone glanced at him, only glanced, and he wondered for a moment whether his lips were moving.

He had given himself an idea, another delaying tactic.

The post office was across a daunting expanse of empty car park. Heat crept gently from the concrete, and the lines of paint shimmered. His thin shirt stuck to his body, heavy and constricting. Inside however, it was cool. Paul stood at a counter, Position Closed, with a pen on a chain poised over his card. What to say? If he had the right words for the card, perhaps they would also show him how to behave, what to feel. Sometimes, in writing the report, he found that he discovered his opinions and feelings only on writing them down. What to say? His continuing internal dialogue was no more than a series of disconnected phrases.

Watch me catch fire.

All I miss is . . .

I feel as if someone is dogging my steps, likely to trip over my heels.

What do I miss?

Dear Victoria . . .

The heat is sinking into my skin and travelling through my veins. I feel the blood in my face. Watch me catch fire.

The radio came on and it sounded like a message meant for me. Does this mean? I didn't have my breakdown when I should have had it. Is it due now?

Dear Victoria, he wrote, and he wrote down a brief apology, said that he was all right and hoped to be home soon, and he bought a stamp and posted the card, irritated with himself, his lack of words, this unsatisfactory consummation. The blotter was left covered with different versions of what he felt.

Wrong to delay, now is not the time to delay.

In all the wide car park there was hardly any air. The concrete was expanding in the heat, it was stretching further away as he waded across it, and the air was fried away, wriggling like steam. A car park like an airstrip. He thought it was unlikely that he would make it to the other side; he became fully conscious of his breathing; he took deep breaths and tried to swing his legs to a rhythm that might build its own momentum.

If he was right, then the three of them, himself, Hazel and

Edmund, were moving around the small town, looking for each other. It felt like the end of the world.

He couldn't remember how he had got there.

First he stopped for a while, for a drink because he was dehydrated, and then he found that too much time had passed. Then there was heat, and there were more questions asked of himself, and there were people walking past him. There was an alleyway which, when he looked up, seemed to be curving in above his head. After that there were several steps and a heavy door, and for the first time since the breakfast on the terrace, things began to become clearer.

He became aware of his tension. He could feel the tightness in his back, his taut muscles threatening to seize up and not allow him to move. There was no glare here, and he was able to open his eyes wide, breathe in cool air. He sat gratefully in a pew, and bent his head. In the dialogue, continuing in his head, words and questions were beginning to resolve themselves into what seemed like sense.

He had been trying not to think about several things. His mother, Hazel's breakdown, his report, Boyd's malice, Walsh's influence, Edmund. Unwelcome things had spread into his life, carried like a virus with the information he had gathered, thin lines of disease entering a healthy body. Wasn't it possible, then, that he had good, objective reasons for his actions? He was trying to make himself healthy. His fat report, stuffed like a doctor's textbook with all the unwelcome things he could think of, was an instrument towards that end. And now, finally, it had its conclusions, its connections, its gratifying sequence of cause and effect: Jerome, Staples, Boyd, Walsh. Conspiracy.

For this he could be grateful. Not many people could explain all their most dubious actions and their most outlandish fears so objectively, so reasonably, as if they were functions of the weather. He had an alibi: it wasn't my fault if I behaved weakly, shabbily, or even oddly, no conclusions about me should be drawn. Responsibility lies with the conspiracy.

Sweat was drying coldly on Paul's bent back. He felt the grain of the wood of the pew, and he smelt the dust which he knew was hovering in the light of the window. There was nothing to hear. He sat up, and then stood up, and he walked back down the aisle, out of the church. His mistake was simply that he had been avoiding confrontation for too long, with too much success. All he really needed to do was communicate his discovery to Staples: it's not my fault, it's a conspiracy, it's Walsh that you want. Not me. Perhaps Hazel had already found him and told him. In which case, his problem was solved. If he wouldn't listen, then the police would deal with him. This man has been following me. You'll find his fingerprints in the Standish house. Yes, of course I wish to press charges. I have an alibi, this man, among others, is to blame. I am innocent.

The sun was lower, at that awkward angle where it seems to be always glaring, penetrating your skull. At the top of the steps the change in temperature, from the cool quietness of the church to the lingering heat of the street, brought on a sneeze that bent him double – ha-tschu! – and for several seconds he remained bowed over at the top of the steps, clutching his stomach, as if the weight of his recent revelation had crippled him. He was still not feeling himself. Diminished, as if whittled by words, the familiar chipped away, removed, leaving new, sensitive surfaces. The shape exists in the block of stone, it is only a question of releasing it.

He straightened shakily, swaying a little at the top of the steps, looking down. He had almost fallen, his unreliable body playing tricks again. And his mind was playing tricks too, he was having trouble remembering the conclusion he had just reached. He needed to be vigilant with himself. He stood at the edge of the top step, and looked around, as he did on tube platforms.

Diminished. The sea, washing at driftwood, making of it something new. Hazel, ('There's nothing personal about this'), talking, talking, talking, working on the new, exposed surfaces. Shaping, sculpting, releasing. He seemed to feel Edmund's helping hand on his back, but he shook it off impatiently and stood poised at the edge of the top step, toes instinctively curling inside his shoes, as if he was on a high diving-board. He stepped out, and then jumped. In the jump, in mid-air, Paul found himself not exhilarated or afraid, but watchful, as if while making this reckless leap he was holding something precious, a tray of crystal glasses, say, lucid, light-scattering and unbearably fragile.

Twenty-Three

Tod had shown Hazel his photograph of himself with Clint Eastwood. 'Clint thought my outfit was terrific.' She showed an interest, not like her brother. The thing about Paul was that beneath his politeness you sensed his indifference, the slightest flavour of scorn. Since being introduced to Hazel, Tod had felt less respectful towards him, and may have shown it the last time they had met. Hiding his amusement, Tod had given him a kind of semi-salute for a good-bye, three fingers touching his temple, and then coming down to point at his chest. 'Be seeing you, Mr Feather. You take care now.' He had made a friendly clucking sound with his tongue as Paul left the shop, and only then had he laughed. His mother appeared.

'Seems to me somethin's eating him,' he said, nodding at Paul's retreating back. 'Kinda strange thing to ask for, wouldn't you say? He's not exactly what you'd call Gary Cooper.'

She said, 'Can I leave you in charge, Philip?'

'Mu-um,' he said, 'it's Tod.'

'Can I leave you in charge?'

He smiled lazily. 'Sure thing, ma.'

He sat behind the counter, beneath the big clock he had found in a junk shop in Swaffham. It had Roman numerals, and a pendulum that swung back and forth as regular as a metronome. Its ticking got on his parents' nerves, but he wouldn't

201

allow it to be moved. When Tod looked up at it, he was always reminded of the constantly repeated shot in his favourite film: the camera angle ensuring that the clockface dominates the screen, the hands approaching noon. He gazed at it, and he was no longer in the cramped grocery.

He is riding through Monument Valley. His horse gleams damply, and snorts as it scuffs the sand. He sits in his comfortable Western saddle, all but leaning back into its gentle curve. It's necessary to get the image right, and the image at the moment is restful. Laconic. Tod's response, perhaps, to Paul's tension. The reins lie loosely in crooked fingers. The horse accepts that he is an accomplished rider, and is guided by the smallest movements and sounds. The tongue against the roof of the mouth. The sun is hot, but the handkerchief at his neck soaks up sweat, and his Stetson shields his eyes. He narrows them anyway, as he looks at the way ahead. In the future Tod envisaged, the near future, the future within reach, the way ahead was clear. He can barely make out the horizon. It shimmers like a dream. Behind his counter, he was whistling softly, eyes unfocused, a wistful smile on his lips. Do not forsake me.

Paul had asked, 'What is it about this man? Have you an idea that there's an affinity between you? That's crazy. He's like no one you know.'

How had she answered? It didn't matter. In Hazel's view, most people had reasons for the things they did. It was a question of understanding. Paul, Hazel thought, saves time and bother by knowing the answers to all of his questions. That way he knows where he is. And where is he? In a secluded house with a camera trained on the step outside the door. Only the right people can come in. No crazy people, no one who scares him, no one who isn't like him. She looked at Edmund, who was sitting opposite her. An odd figure, certainly. The sun wasn't as strong as it had been, but, cross-legged in the sand, he was red-faced, bleeding sweat in his dark suit. His lips lurched from left to right, as he chewed different morsels of his cheek. His fist, full of sand, clenched and unclenched.

She had eventually found him in an amusement arcade, where she watched him for a while, walking around uncertainly, moving among the flashing lights, avoiding the drifts of people, flinching slightly at the occasional cry of excitement or rattle of gunfire.

Mid-afternoon, and the beach was becoming less crowded.

'Take your jacket off, Edmund,' she said.

He looked up from his hands to her, quizzical, as if translating her words. He studied her face for several seconds, looked at her loose white shirt, her frayed denim shorts and her bare feet, and then slowly complied. As he folded the jacket in the air between them, it swung lop-sidedly. He put it down in front of him, and rested his gaze on it.

'I'm pleased to have found you,' said Hazel. 'May I?'

As she spoke she reached inside the jacket and took out a gun. It looked absurdly large in her small hand. She laid it on the sand between them.

'Do you know what we look like?' she said. 'Father and daughter. You in your suit. But there's only a few years between us, because you're almost a contemporary of Paul. You must know that. I think you're very alike.'

His gaze had shifted to the gun. Now he looked up again, put a hand through his hair, smearing sweat from his forehead over his scalp. 'No.'

His first response. Paul might have recognised the small smile that arrived on Hazel's face. 'Tell me what's been happening,' she said. 'I'd like the whole story explained to me. I bet you're dying to tell.'

He landed clumsily, jarring several parts of his body that were still healing, but he didn't stop, because he could feel that it was important not to pause now. His search through the crowded streets quickly became irritable. He wasn't good at this, not practised at seeking people out. His discovery of Hazel had been a fluke, he was much better at avoiding people than finding them. Families encumbered by rubber rings, balls, towels and lilos seemed to take pleasure in getting in his way. He wanted to choose his own pace, but it wasn't possible to move without adapting to that of others. It was a small town, however, and he was running out of places to look. In spite of his inefficiency, it couldn't be long before he found them. He tried not to think about what he would do then. Paul headed towards the beach.

Edmund was talking to her.

'A big old dusty hall. Can you imagine it? Big as a barn, and dust hanging in the air, turning over in the sunlight. I entered, first one there, and felt at home. I sat in the middle of the front row and, while others arrived, scraping chairs, talking, I sat quietly and didn't look around. I was expecting nothing. I had read a leaflet, that's all. And I felt a certain approval when I entered the hall, which was a good sign, but not something to trust.'

He spoke in short, halting sentences, his eyes mostly on his hands or his jacket. Hazel had to concentrate, because he was speaking quietly, meditatively, as if he was alone.

'I talked to him once, to Jerome, I actually talked to him face to face. He liked me. He looked me straight in the eye, and I could see right away that he liked me. He must have taken an interest, because he told me some things about myself, what he thought I could be if I wanted, *who* he thought I could be. He made me feel good. So naturally, when the stories about him came out, I began to hate him. If he was a fraud, then what he had told me meant nothing. But the stories went away after a while, quite quickly, and I was left just with his words.'

Paul had approached from behind him, silent on the soft sand. He stood like an awkward guest at a party, not sure how to enter the conversation. He listened.

'It was a confused time. I didn't know what to think, and I didn't know what was going to happen next. It was one of the times when I thought about killing myself. And then Mr Walsh sent me the pamphlet your brother wrote. It wasn't really about Jerome, was it? It was about me, and people like me, people who believed in him. How could he say those things? I started to hate him instead. Easy for him to mock. Jerome had talked about becoming another person, becoming a whole person. *Becoming*, was what attracted me. I am attracted to the idea of growth, the idea of being one thing and becoming another. You understand: I don't like myself. I hoped to find a place, a way of being in this world. It's difficult to find a place. I know that not everybody finds it so, but I do. My father couldn't, couldn't live as he said that we should. That's why he was a drunk, that's why he was glad that I killed him.' He paused, and then used a phrase that Dinah had once used, and that he had remembered. 'It's hard for me to find a way to live.'

And then at last Edmund looked up. 'You understand that.'

This last comment wasn't a question, more like an insight. He looked at Hazel, and she nodded easily. His eyes shifted from her to the sea behind her, the incoming tide. It seemed to Paul that he knew much less than he had known before. He couldn't bring to mind a single fact that he had gathered in the course of his work. He still couldn't even bring to mind his most recent train of thought, the one which had briefly convinced him he was a blameless victim of events. Perhaps, if his memory was working better, he would be acting differently. Sitting down, he took out the gun he had acquired, and put it next to Edmund's. It was like joining a poker game, putting your stake on the table. Perhaps, if his memory was working better, he wouldn't see the comical element in this, the three adults sitting on the beach, all broadly in agreement that it was hard to find a way to live. Like Edmund, he was over-dressed, and he took off his jacket, laid it discreetly over the two guns. Although there was a nervous, half smile on his face, he dug his fingers into the sand, as if to anchor himself in place, in case of any sudden failure of nerve.

Edmund's reaction to his arrival made his tentative fingers clench the sand frantically. He felt grains digging beneath his nails. Edmund was pointing his gun at him, staring at him. He said, 'I have waited for this moment. I have dreamt about it.'

Paul was staring at the slightly-wavering barrel, which was aiming at his chest. It looked unwieldy to him, but Edmund was clearly comfortable with the heft of it, obviously competent. He was aware of Hazel, tense at his side, her lips moving silently, and he was aware even of pleasure, that finally something had surprised her, shocked her out of her complacency. He stared at the barrel and, when seconds had passed and nothing had happened, he raised his head, slowly, so that he could meet Edmund's gaze. He couldn't remember ever having achieved anything more difficult than raising his head at that moment.

Certainly, speaking to him was a much simpler thing.

'I'm sorry,' he said. 'I'm to blame. I'm sorry for the pain I've caused you.'

The two men looked at each other for an unmeasurable time, a pool of silence. Something passed between them, something more than had been said. They sat in the cooling sand, and the only sounds were the harsh noise of a radio, disappearing as it was carried away, and the sea's whispering background, a soothing interference. Far away, a hot-air balloon floated over the sea, a bulbous stroke above a square dot. Exclamation.

Edmund lowered his gun, letting it point into the sand between them.

Paul felt that his breath matched the movement of the sea, as it very slowly approached, retreating and then coming a little closer, trailing tongues of water towards them. He began to describe his report, his misanthropist's handbook. He found himself telling Edmund about the woman washing her car, paintwork gleaming in the sun, how he had wanted to swap places with her, because her job was more manageable than his, and less lonely. He told Edmund how he had discovered that something had happened to him that made him unable even to speak to her.

Continuing, as if the subject was exactly the same, he apologised again, shaking his head as he spoke, as if the actions he was describing belonged to some other person, whose motivations would have to remain obscure. 'I made an unforgiveable mistake,' Paul finished. Once again, Edmund looked as if he was carefully, deliberately, translating what he was hearing, delaying any reaction until the words went through this essential process, while the sand in his free hand escaped in slow trickles from between his fingers.

Hazel asked, 'What do you want?' and he replied, 'I hope to no longer be troubled by fantasies. I hope to live my life competently.' He slid the gun back beneath the jackets, but he lowered his head as he spoke, and stared at his empty hand. 'What shall I believe in?' he said, and they didn't answer him.

He began to describe the church his family used to attend. Its sole decoration was an eagle carved into the pulpit. He used to watch it. It was a beautiful piece of work, like a live bird somehow caught and frozen. He used to watch it and imagine it freeing itself, shaking off the clinging, dead wood, perching on the edge of the pulpit, huge and scary, and then escaping, flying out through the doors of the church, stretching its full wing-span and climbing away into the sky. It had been his fantasy for Sundays. Heaven was distance and space.

There was a breeze now, drying their sweat and moving clouds towards the sun. Time to move. The sea had already surrounded an elaborate sandcastle nearby, and was melting the fortifications. Some children with a patient father seemed to be trying to trample the tide into submission. He was talking into a portable phone, while watching them. They weren't succeeding. Now the castle was an uneven lump of sand, now it was smooth, now it was indistinguishable from the rest of the long, flat expanse of the beach.

Hazel noticed the balloon first. It was much closer to them, and she could see the garish red, pleated material, hear the throaty blowing of the propane gas burner. Edmund and Paul followed her eyes. Four men in the basket below it, one of them very thin, grey haired. It began to descend.

'This is Walsh,' she told Edmund. 'I thought we might hear from him again.'

The father who had been watching over his children came and helped as the basket hit the ground. Ballast and hot air were balanced to keep the balloon barely earthbound, while two men lifted Walsh out of the basket, as if he was as light as an air mattress. He gave the father an approving nod and then, on two sticks, approached the unmoving group of three which was watching him.

He was breathing heavily when he reached them. 'I told you I had unconventional ways of killing time,' he said. His mood was almost childishly enthusiastic, though painfully filtered through his effortful words. 'This is my latest decision. To ignore my doctors. The only difficult parts are taking off and landing. Once you're underway, it's a dream. One becomes a part of the wind, one surrenders to it. I wasn't previously aware, that there was pleasure in surrender. Although you see,' he raised his arms, like a magician accepting applause, 'even the wind has obeyed me.'

He sat down carefully, lowering himself, and drawing his knees up to his chest. The process gave the impression of a garden chair being folded.

'I'm intending to come down to earth as little as possible. Cultivating an image. I see myself as one of those American Presidents, playing golf in the midst of the crisis. Unfazed by devastating illness, I give casual quotes from the green. Interesting, that it's only now, that I discover absence of responsibility. Will you put that in your notes, Paul?'

Edmund, unspeaking, was staring at him.

In his pleasure at his new hobby, Walsh had shed his regal bearing. His sunken cheeks creased deeply as he smiled. He wore a short-sleeved shirt which revealed long, pale arms, liver-spotted, thin and hairy. There was a brittle quality in his unnatural good humour.

Hazel looked past him, at the man returning to his children. 'Is he working for you?'

Walsh looked over his shoulder, slightly vague. 'Naturally I have been keeping track of your movements.' He looked back, smiling as if greatly pleased. 'Delighted to have been proved wrong,' he said. 'It's a new experience for me. You've really both surpassed expectations. And this is Edmund.' He held out his hand. 'So pleased that we can meet at last.'

There was an effort involved in stretching out his arm. It trembled, and after a few seconds in which Edmund didn't move, his smile began to tremble too. It was at this moment, when Paul and Hazel were becoming embarrassed, that Edmund took the hand. He didn't shake it, he took it carefully in his own, like a delicate thing of paper and air. He held it, and then let it go. A brief, graceful movement.

The pause had been enough to alter Walsh's mood. His good-humour had vanished. 'They don't want me to eat, or to move much,' he said, as if complaining to people who might be able to change his treatment. 'I sit quietly in the garden or the house, highly conscious of my breathing. I feel like a colonial officer staying on after the Raj, with a fading villa and a few reluctant servants. My Empire vanished. I look at things, and I think a lot. It is a monkish life, one to which I am not suited. Hence . . .' He waved a hand at the balloon swaying slightly behind him. The sea was lapping at its basket. His smile returned, less plausible than before: 'I still have whims.'

Edmund, still staring intently, seemed unable to speak. Paul and Hazel seemed unwilling.

'I came to speak to you again.' Walsh sounded reluctant to come to the point. 'To see if you would come with me. I can offer you all appropriate rewards, I may not have made this clear, places within the Foundation. Security. Won't you join me? It's perfectly safe.'

'The tide,' said Paul, looking beyond him.

Walsh gave it an irritated look, then turned back to them.

'I thought not. I had hopes, but I thought not. Nothing remains then.' He tried to carry it off casually, but the process of standing took longer than that of sitting. Hazel helped. A steadying hand under his arm. 'It's too bad,' he said, leaning on her slightly as he organised his two walking sticks. 'Perhaps the balloon put you off? Not everyone relishes it.' Hazel shook her head. 'You must admit,' he continued, 'I still have the capacity to surprise.' She smiled and nodded. 'I'm not quite played out. I have in mind a monument, so as not to disappear altogether. An eighth wonder, something visible from space. Do you think that might be an acceptable way to spend time?' Hazel, with the smallest movement of her shoulders, indicated that she wasn't qualified to say. Solicitous, she delivered him into the supporting arms of his companions.

They watched him leave, the glorious red balloon rising with a brief roar, like a creature returning to its element, and then floating up and out, over the sea, the figure in the basket, still enjoying the unfamiliar taste of powerlessness, becoming less and less distinct. It was probably because they were watching that Paul and Hazel didn't see Edmund take a gun out from under the jackets. When they looked round it was resting on his knee again, aiming at the ground in the centre of their triangle, its barrel pointing, like a long finger, towards Paul. It seemed, judging from his expression, his short, shallow breaths, that he had now, at last, reached an understanding of all that he had heard, and seen.

It was a short period of time, five or six seconds, but things seemed to happen very slowly.

'My mistake was the greater,' he said. 'I misbelieved.'

'Oh, put it down,' said Hazel, with the first hint of anger Paul had heard. 'You know better.'

He smiled. 'You misunderstand.'

The balloon was still visible behind him, receding effortlessly, at the pace of the distant, fragmenting clouds, as he pushed the barrel of the gun up into his chin. Clasping it firmly in both hands, as if praying, (obviously competent), he pulled the trigger.

Twenty-Four

What happened to Walsh? He died, of course. But before that, he came back to Earth, having discovered another whim, one which might invest him with sufficient energy to see him to its conclusion. It was, in its way, the monument he dreamt of. He began, first of all, because he was a methodical man, to compile his notes, to examine the mass of information that had been gathered, to consider new ways of ordering it. What did he have? Material. Enough to produce something, a piece of work. Access to all the key players. He was looking forward to interviewing Edmund, hearing his story. He had piles of paper. Photos and films. Tapes and transcriptions. He had a collection of voices.

'I will spend my time poring over papers. I have plans. Plans are the privilege of the living. I will be Lord and Master of this world of people and events and places, they will speak on the cues that I give them, and I will approach the yearning heart of their dreams. There is pleasure to be found in reconstructions, they aren't the same as reality, they exist alongside it, but they have an attraction of their own. It is this: they are more clear and more logical than reality. More perfect.'

There would be a piece of work, and he would be its author.

The Assistant was a recent graduate with a first-class honours degree. He was on an accelerated stream which was ostensibly intended to lead him quickly to the post of Department Head. His duties however, were those of a secretary, and his superior always reminded him of a particularly short-tempered teacher he had once had, who used to rage at boys whose ties weren't knotted in quite the regulation fashion.

'You will keep your desk tidy if you wish to work here,' said Boyd, distastefully pushing papers to one side.

'Yes sir,' said the Assistant.

Boyd walked on slowly, eyes picking up every detail, through the rows of desks and into his office, where he found Victoria waiting for him. This was a surprise. His trajectory had been taking him to his balcony, the place he always liked to start his day, grasping the railing, looking out over his view. A hundred thousand offices, a caravan of cars, a hundred thousand people. Above them all, Boyd, conductor at the podium, Captain on the prow of his ship. She was sitting in one of the comfortable chairs at the low table where he had talked to Paul and Hazel. Her feet in fact were on the table, black court shoes, Boyd noticed, and she was examining her nails. She looked up as he came in. Surprise was something that Boyd tried, usually successfully, to avoid.

'Miss . . . Tucker?' he said.

'That's right,' said Victoria. 'Executive Assistant in Forward Planning, with responsibility for identifying and analysing areas of potential interest to the Foundation and its clients, according to my job description. Only that's not why I was appointed, is it? It's more to do with my connection with Paul, isn't it? Did you hope that, in time, I'd tell you all about him? And our relationship? Is that what you thought?' She took her feet off the table and sat up. 'You've used me, and I'm afraid I've made a promise to myself not to be used. I'm handing in my notice, and suing I should think, for breach of contract, or whatever is appropriate.'

Boyd, recovering himself quickly, sat down opposite her. 'Miss Tucker, I'm afraid I don't know what you're talking about, but if you wish to leave the Foundation you are of course at liberty to do so. We should be sorry, however, to lose you.'

212

It wasn't what Boyd would have been able to call a typical day. Outside his office, three people were approaching through the demure ranks of his Assistants and secretaries. It was an exceptional day for everyone involved. Edmund, who had recently been dressed as a policeman, a chef, a station porter and a security guard, now wore the same dark suit he had worn on the beach. With Hazel and Paul walking on either side of him, he didn't feel as vulnerable as he had expected. He admired the way they ignored the occasional objections raised. He had been surprised by how much he had found to talk about with them as they drove through Suffolk lanes, through roads sheltered by trees in their dying colours, and down the motorway towards the city. Uniforms had only been a beginning. Fantasies, communication and silence, God, and people who thought they were God, suicides, London and its Underground. They had been amused to find a certain symmetry, if that is possible among three people, in some of their views. For Edmund, in particular, it was an exceptional day. Everything, since the afternoon on the beach, had been exceptional. God-given days. His hand, reaching blindly beneath Paul's jacket, had found Tod's replica Colt .45. It was the sign he had been hoping for. Fear is the way to freedom, Jerome had told him, overcome it, and you become larger, capable of anything. Free to choose your own way.

Paul at this moment was feeling a little awkward. The way he had been living his life hadn't prepared him for this meeting. It had prepared him in fact for none of his recent experiences. He had no idea how to go about being assertive, let alone, and this is what he really thought was appropriate, insulting. He admired Victoria, for wanting to go in first, to confront the man. This had been the way of it recently: he kept finding things to admire in other people, and only deficiencies in himself. He felt he still lacked, among many things, decisiveness. But here he was, pushing open the door, it was heavier than he expected and he couldn't manage it dramatically, pushing it laboriously open however, and entering Boyd's office.

As they entered, Boyd swivelled round in his chair, surprised a second time, to watch them. Hazel, without much hesitation,

213

took the seat behind his desk.

'Well,' said Boyd, 'a quorum.' He poured himself a glass of water, taking his time. 'How pleasing,' he continued, eventually, 'to see all the players in one room. You've come to the end of your travels. Well done.'

Something about him, his weight, his sense of himself, some aura that surrounded him, made it difficult to imagine him ever being really thrown off balance. Hazel however, who had disconcerted him once before, was in the position of power, across the expanse of the desk.

'We thought,' said Hazel, 'that we'd bring Edmund to meet you.'

'I wanted,' said Edmund, 'to see you.' He gave Boyd the same attention he had given to Walsh. He began to tug at his lip with his teeth. Even now, it seemed, he would have been pleased to have his faith renewed. If Boyd had turned the carafe of water into wine, Edmund might have been no less pleased than surprised.

'Delighted,' said Boyd. 'I was just saying to Victoria – may I call you Victoria? – the Foundation has plenty of room for talented personnel like yourselves. It would make it a much more interesting place to be. This is a boom time for reports, of course.'

'Why?' said Paul. 'Because of the violence?'

'No,' said Boyd.

'Because of the blurring of sexual roles and identities,' said Hazel.

'No.' He looked expectantly at Edmund, his smile growing.

'The growth in religious belief.'

'No, no, no,' said Boyd, becoming quite jovial. He was beginning to enjoy himself, feel himself back in control, in the role of Master of Ceremonies. 'Because of the *space*. There's so much more of it than there used to be, now that everything's inside computers. Because of the ease of it. Information Technology. Technology brought to bear on the gathering, storing and disseminating, occasionally, of information. It's all there, literally at your fingertips.' He mimed touching a keyboard. 'So you'll join us? This is a good day for the Walsh Foundation.'

'Your information is compromised,' said Paul.

'Your system is sick,' said Victoria, 'it's caught a bug.'

'Look what happens,' said Hazel, beaming like a child with a new toy. She tapped Boyd's terminal, and then turned the screen to face him. It was snowing. Words were dropping out of sentences, leaving unsightly holes, letters were dropping out of words, making new meanings, cryptic new languages, until the remaining letters went too, gathering in a drift at the bottom of the screen, like remnants thrown aside in the making of a dictionary.

Boyd got up and hurried to his door. The Assistant opened it just before he did. 'Sir,' he said, 'something's happening to the computers.' Boyd closed the door on him and turned back to Victoria.

She shrugged. 'I'd guess some disgruntled employee did it,' she said. 'I imagine it's fixable. Eventually.'

'Try,' said Hazel, as the last letter floated down the screen, 'to relish the sensation of powerlessness. Before very long, when illness or old age catch up, you'll have no choice.'

'Edmund,' said Boyd, trying valiantly to rise above it all, 'I hope *you'll* work for us?'

'I will not.'

'Oh, you must reconsider.'

'I will not.'

'Leave him alone.'

'Victoria, if you'll just kindly allow me . . .'

'Don't take that tone. I don't work for you any more, if you remember.'

'Edmund, I'm sure you'll be conscious, if you'll think for a minute, of the debt you owe, if you'll just listen, Edmund . . .'

'Just listen to me for a minute,' her finger jabbing towards his chest now, 'big man . . .'

An argument developed.

Paul, on his hard straight-backed chair, caught Hazel's eye, and smiled. It was the first smile of complicity that they had shared. He turned away, and in turning, saw the view from the window. He walked out on to Boyd's balcony, confident that she would follow. He didn't look down, or around. (Cars, offices, people.) He looked up. He didn't understand his mood. He saw no grounds for his optimism. He said something as Hazel came up beside him. 'Everything is still in the future,' he said, his tone non-committal. She answered, whispered a few positive words, and he felt like an actor receiving encouragement from a colleague, just before the curtain rises. After a few moments, maybe longer, they had lost track of time, the furious argument behind them subsided, nothing resolved, and first Victoria, then Edmund, joined them. Boyd stood alone in his office. There were still things that he wanted to say. He had envisaged forging somehow a connection with these people. It was just a fantasy, he now understood. He had thought of booking a table in his regular restaurant. Something convivial. Everything was still in the future, and Boyd, understanding this, felt a small ache, like the first sign of a mortal disease. This wasn't something that he had predicted, these backs presented to him, his balcony, prow of the ship, crowded with Captains.

Victoria had retrieved a fat file from a little-used room on the third floor. She divided it into three and handed the sections to Paul, and Hazel, and Edmund. Without any prompting they began to tear up the papers into small pieces, letting them fall to the floor of the balcony. When they had finished, Paul looked slowly from face to face. 'Well,' he began, with more than an edge of doubt in his voice.

Edmund looked at him and then, as the pause began to lengthen, looked beyond him, during the uncertain silence that developed, studying the view. Clouds, fragmenting again. Distance, and space. As the four of them stood there, a gust of wind brushed through them and swept up the shards of paper so that they flew off the balcony, squirming and twisting on the wind, spreading and dispersing, like ticker-tape greeting travellers returned after some extraordinary endeavour. They leaned against the rail and watched the fragments scatter, and each of them wondered what in the world they could do next.

A Note on the Author

Mark Illis was born in 1963, and was educated at University College London and the University of East Anglia. His short stories have been published in the *London Review of Books*, *London Magazine*, *Fiction Magazine*, *Critical Quarterly* and several anthologies. His previous novels are *A Chinese Summer* and *The Alchemist*. Mark Illis teaches, reviews and has been a Literature Development Worker. He is working on a collection of short stories.